IN

She licked her full lips and pressed her mouth to mine, tongue protruding after a moment's pressure. Then she broke away, saying, 'What we are doing is very naughty, you know.'

'I'll never tell,' I vowed. 'I love you.'

'How sweet,' she cried, taking my face in her hands and covering my mouth with her open lips. In turn I reached to cup the smooth firm orbs of her heavy tits so enticingly hanging before me. I fondled, squeezed, scratched the hardening nipples, until she straightened her back and began undoing the buttons from the high neck down to her waist. As the blouse opened it revealed startlingly big mammaries that nestled together, such was their fullness and size. She had come wearing nothing to impede sight and touch of the glorious objects. She pulled my head down and fed a nipple into my eager mouth . . .

Also available from Headline

Cremorne Gardens
The Temptations of Cremorne
The Lusts of the Borgias
Love Italian Style
Ecstasy Italian Style
Body and Soul
Sweet Sensations
Amorous Liaisons
Hidden Rapture
Learning Curves
My Duty, My Desire
Love in the Saddle
Bare Necessities
The Story of Honey O
Saucy Habits
Night Moves
Eroticon Dreams
Eroticon Desires
Intimate Positions
Play Time
Carnal Days
Carnal Nights
Hot Type
The Sensual Mirror
French Frolics
Claudine
Wild Abandon
Fondle in Flagrante
After Hours
French Thrills

In the Mood

Lesley Asquith

HEADLINE

Copyright © 1992 Lesley Asquith

The right of Lesley Asquith to be identified as the Author of the Work has been asserted by her in accordance with the Copyright, Designs and Patents Act 1988.

First published in 1992
by HEADLINE BOOK PUBLISHING PLC

10 9 8 7 6 5 4 3

All rights reserved. No part of this publication may be reproduced, stored in a retrieval system, or transmitted in any form or by any means without the prior written permission of the publisher, nor be otherwise circulated in any form of binding or cover other than that in which it is published and without a similar condition being imposed on the subsequent purchaser.

All characters in this publication are fictitious and any resemblance to real persons, living or dead, is purely coincidental.

ISBN 0 7472 3934 7

Phototypeset by Intype, London
Printed and bound in Great Britain by
HarperCollins Manufacturing, Glasgow

HEADLINE BOOK PUBLISHING PLC
Headline House
79 Great Titchfield Street
London W1P 7FN

In the Mood

PART ONE

Chapter One

I remember brother Rodney's wedding with good reason. It was a modest affair, due rather to the forced situation of the marriage than to the economies and shortages of wartime. The reception was held in the family drawing-room and the guests, mainly army officer colleagues and their wives, waved off the newlyweds as they left on honeymoon, a forty-eight-hour pass Rodney had been granted by his commanding officer.

His wife was a well-built girl, older than he by several years and considered a poor match in our circle with her rather plain face and lack of style. Exactly right, however, for the wife of a village parson, which was what Rodney intended becoming after the war. Grace was the daughter of a local shopkeeper, in trade as they said – another minus according to our mother. She did not approve of the match at all, and made it obvious by not being her usual charming self when entertaining guests.

Grace had stood embarrassed throughout, with a permanent blush on her healthy cheeks, clutching her new husband's hand for moral support. She wore a flowing going-away gown of blue silk and looked as ever wholesomely attractive if you like buxom wenches, which I did, but the carefully chosen loose dress could not disguise the fact she was well and truly in the family way, four months on and blooming as country girls do.

In The Mood

The pair had been childhood sweethearts and engaged for two years. I didn't know if old Rodders had been up her or was marrying her to do the decent thing – saving Grace from disgrace – typical of the fine upstanding idiot he was. I had the feeling she had cajoled him into bed on an earlier leave; as I had suggested to her she must as it was better for all concerned in the circumstances.

He was still getting the best of the bargain. Say what they would about his apparently dull wife, underneath her quiet exterior raged a storm. Grace was all woman with the big breasts and hungry cunt of a voracious sexual animal, when brought to the right pitch. Such sexuality would be wasted on my gentle brother, I knew, but then I had been the one who had awakened and aroused her true amorous and wanton nature. I was also the father of the child within her belly.

The reception was therefore a hurried and almost furtive affair, not the sort of ceremony my parents would have wished for their eldest son. The wedding feast such as it was consisted of daintily cut sandwiches, bridal cake, port and sherry taken around on silver trays by three village women brought in for the event and suitably dressed as waitresses. All had worked for mother before. Looking around the spacious room my chest swelled with youthful pride. Molly Dewhurst, a cuddlesome widow, circulated with the sandwich salver and I had had the pleasure of seducing her. The drinks were offered around by Charlotte Plummer, whom I had shafted vigorously on occasion. Mary Pullen collected the empty glasses and plates. She too had allowed me to fuck her firm slim body. And finally of course there was the bride herself with whom, sexual experimenter that I was, I had attempted just about everything one could do with a willing and compliant female roused to heat. Four conquests under one ceiling.

In The Mood

Apart from mother and the bridegroom I was the only other representative of the family present, the only young male not in uniform as just past my seventeenth birthday I awaited call-up, having volunteered for air-crew training. I couldn't wait to get away. Out in the wider world and in uniform there would be plenty more female sport for me to enjoy, I anticipated with relish. I had been pressed into being 'best man', perhaps the right description of the term in my case. As ever I was randy in the company of scented women, especially older married ones for whom I had a special lech. There is an added piquancy when mature ladies surrender their all to a supposedly inexperienced youth, a ploy I had successfully used in the past. But the women present were with partners and I was the proverbial spare prick at the wedding. For once I envied Rodney. Did my diffident brother but know it, he could have the night of his life with his bride. I feared he'd disappoint her.

'Thank goodness father wasn't here to witness that fiasco,' mother said to me as the bride and groom departed. She was referring to the absence of her husband, who was well out of the scene serving as a major with the gallant Royal Army Pay Corps in India, far from the conflict in Europe. Brother Edwin was missing too, actually missing, shot down over occupied France and hopefully a prisoner-of-war in Germany. I had the feeling Eddie would make it; we were two of a kind. Mother was on the point of weeping and no doubt would have but for the fear of ruining her immaculate make-up. She was noted as somewhat of a local beauty and did everything to warrant the label.

She had never liked Grace and the thought of being a grandmother did not thrill her either. She had drowned her sorrow pretty well at the reception, unusual for her, taking either port or sherry as the trays passed by. In this she was encouraged by having to accept the sympathy of Aunt Margaret, who was

In The Mood

not really family but us boys had always called her so. She was mother's closest friend and another county beauty. It was a love-hate relationship as the pair of them vied to be the best hostess and, according to father, the most expensively dressed in the district. Mother usually led by a short head but I had to admit Margaret looked particularly attractive, with the pretty painted face of a former actress who had married well and the fine mature body of a forty-odd-year-old female who kept in trim riding with the local hunt or dancing until dawn in the more exclusive night clubs of London.

They said the Prince of Wales had fancied her and she never denied it. Her fat fool of a husband was guffawing at one of his own jokes across the room and she glared at him in annoyance. 'I think your mother should go upstairs now and lie down,' Margaret said to me, a malicious edge to her voice. 'She's been an absolute darling over this wedding but it's all been a bit too much for her, poor dear.' Of course, it was a triumph for her, Rodney's marriage to a local yokel. Her own son was as good as engaged to an Honourable Miss Somebody, daughter of minor nobility. This was one up on Grace, whose father was the village ironmonger and whose mother had ran off with the farm manager of Margaret's landowner husband, a huge brute of a man, whose womanising had been the talk of the district. There was even speculation that Margaret herself had not been immune. Whatever he had, Grace's mother had liked it enough to bolt with him. No doubt it was from her that Grace had inherited a secret dissolute nature.

'Rodney married, poor Edwin missing and father overseas,' my mother complained, no doubt listing the tragedies in order of precedence. She looked at me. 'Soon you'll be leaving me too. I don't know what I'll do by myself in this big empty house. Go mad, I expect – '

In The Mood

'There, there, Olivia,' soothed Margaret, enjoying every moment of mother's misery. 'Why, Grace will need a place to live while Rodney's away in the army. And there'll be a baby before you know it. You'll have lots of company.'

Mother was not so low in spirit that she couldn't direct a look of loathing at her friend. Then she allowed herself to be led off upstairs. I watched them go, admiring Margaret's plump buttock cheeks, two lovely rounded globes that bounced seductively under her silk sheath of a dress as she mounted each step. As ever, John Thomas stirred in my trousers. Riding, the horsey kind, certainly gave country women splendid backsides. I pondered how Margaret would be when she was the mounted one.

It was to be my good fortune to find out, one of those marvellously unexpected treats a woman has the power to bestow on a man when so inclined. They don't do it often enough and would be more highly thought of if they did. Still dressed in my best suit, that evening I went to the village hall where a War Savings Dance was taking place. Every week seemed designated for something in those days: 'Dig for Victory', 'Warship Week', 'Save for a Spitfire', even 'Knit for a Soldier'. My intent had nothing to do with anything remotely patriotic. I was on the hunt for cunt, hoping to get off with a receptive partner who would allow me to have my horny way with her after the usual preliminaries: chatting up and a bit of 'gum-sucking' as smooching was then known. The dance floor was packed, the local band sweating as they ground out the popular numbers of early 1940. A glance around showed the wall seats filled with powdered and painted factory and shop girls hoping to dance the evening away and meet a boyfriend. The competition was strong, the hall packed with servicemen. In my civvie suit I stuck out like a sore thumb and about as welcome, surrounded by army khaki from

In The Mood

the nearby camp. I was already taller and stronger than most men present, not a few of whom sarcastically suggested I should be in uniform.

I walked home alone. The dances I'd had with girls considered most likely, their closeness and scent of feminine body sweat and cheap perfume, only served to increase my frustration. I was boiling in my loins, fit to burst, randy as a bucket of frogs — as only a deprived seventeen-year-old knows. I hadn't had a fuck for weeks; the local certainties I'd cultivated, the sure things, had deserted me for more reliable boyfriends, courting strong as the saying went. So it was off to bed, looking into the ornate drawing-room on the way. It was as if Rodney's wedding had never happened; all was swept, dusted and back in place. I shivered under the bedcovers for the winter was claimed to be the coldest since records were kept. I thought of Grace and her warm cushiony pliant body, and being allowed to do as I wished with it. Now *there* was a submissive and consenting partner. What we had got up to under my imaginative direction had been excesses of erotic lust, to our mutual pleasure. The memory of it made my prick rise full-cock demandingly. Something had to be done for it and I naturally clasped the upright shaft. I was thus engaged in the five-finger exercise when a light tap sounded at my bedroom door.

To my great surprise it was 'Aunt' Margaret who entered wearing one of mother's dressing gowns and smoking a cigarette. 'I've got your mother settled down,' she said. 'She was far too upset to leave alone, so Hubert and I are in the guest room for the night.'

I nodded, wishing she would go so that I could continue tossing-off. Instead she approached and sat on the bed, smiling as if greatly amused by some secret thought. 'God, but it's chilly in here,' she said. 'You should have something in your bed. A hot-water bottle anyway. Here, take a puff of this. It will warm you up — '

In The Mood

If she noticed me trembling it was the combined effect of my aroused state and her scented nearness. She held out the cigarette and I drew on the lipsticked end. 'They say that's as good as a kiss,' she teased. 'Do you think so?' As she leaned towards me her breath was warm and aromatic. No doubt she had continued drinking and was giggly, tipsy. Randy too, I dared hope. She was certainly flirtatious.

'I would rather have the kiss, wouldn't you?' she said innocently. Her perfume was cloying and heady. The open neck of the dressing gown allowed a glimpse of the tight cleavage of full rounded breasts. She put her hand on the bed. Either deliberately or by chance it rested on my engorged prick. She curled her fingers about it, testing its girth. I sat still, bolt upright, praying she would continue what I had left off. Margaret then gave it a definite squeeze and laughed softly.

'I've heard about you,' she said. 'Your mother told me she caught you with Dewhurst, when the woman was maid here. Playing mummies and daddies, were you? I believe you're a naughty boy. Come on, own up –'

'Slip in beside me and I'll show you,' I said hoarsely, daring a rebuke. They say faint heart never won fair lady and it's true. Margaret looked seriously at me as if considering, then laughed softly again and rose from the bed, giving my rigid prick a pat.

'I really believe you would,' she smiled. 'Goodnight.' So saying she pressed a quick peck to my forehead and turned off the bedside lamp. In the deep dark, for there were blackout curtains at my window, I agonised over further frustration. But minutes later the door was reopened and closed silently. I sensed her presence joyously and sat up to welcome her return.

'Sssshh,' she whispered, putting a cool slender hand over my lips. 'Your mother is asleep and Hubert's snoring his head off. Move over –' I heard the dressing gown fall to the floor and the rustle of silk as she

In The Mood

drew off her nightdress. She slipped into my arms deliciously naked, her mouth and tongue seeking mine hungrily, her hand going down to clasp my throbbing cock. As I turned towards her she shuffled to get below me, opening her thighs. 'Don't hurry,' she whispered. 'My husband goes out like a light with drink. Take your time, darling, love me nicely. Do I have to show you?'

We kissed and I stroked her cunt, its velvet feel turning moist. I fondled her tits, sucked the nipples. Soon she sighed and pulled me across her, guiding my knob into her slit. 'Oh, my dear,' she moaned as I penetrated her to the balls. 'I'd almost forgotten what a young man's prick does to a woman. So very hard, I can feel its shape inside me. Fuck me, fuck me – ' Her cunt lips clenched my stalk, she lifted against me, pushing for depth, arms and legs pulling me tight to her undulating body. 'God, it's good ... so good ... ohhh.' I felt her movements quicken, our stomachs slapped. Her whimpers changed to a harsh order. 'Fuck me hard now, I tell you,' she rapped out. 'Shove it up my cunt, you whoremaster. Oh, you dirty sod, what are you doing to me!' And she thrashed below me, almost unseating me in the strength of her climax. Truly the governor's lady and Rosie O'Grady are sisters under the skin!

It was almost dawn before she slipped away from my arms. The thought of fat Hubert snoring along the corridor from where we lusted increased both our ardour. It was Rodney's wedding night but no honeymoon was more energetic and pleasurable than that romp spent with Margaret. She eagerly participated in all my requests, sucked me rampant between bouts, took up the positions I desired to have her in, and climaxed gloriously with groans and utterances, jerking as if taking a fit in her spasms. When she departed she tucked me in, planting a kiss on my cheek.

In The Mood

'You're expecting to be called up soon, I believe,' she said.

'Any day. I'm in no hurry now though –'

I could almost sense her smile in the darkness. 'Come and see me when you are on leave,' she invited. 'You know I'm on the Comforts for the Armed Forces committee. There might be something you want –' Wicked chuckle.

She kissed me again full on the lips, lingeringly, with the delicious wicked point of her tongue in my mouth. I reached out for her breasts but she stepped back. 'Young man,' she taunted. 'Enough is enough! I'm your mother's oldest and best friend. She'd never forgive me for this. Now go to sleep, I'm sure you must need it. I know I won't be up until mid-afternoon. Sleep tight.'

So she left to return to her room, leaving me to stretch and yawn in the sumptuous afterglow of sated lust. Margaret had proved every whit as sexually adventurous as myself, an insatiable bed-mate. Of course, I was well aware that apart from indulging herself with me she also enjoyed the thought of having one up on mother by sleeping with her son. Her ploy suited my own ends very well if she wanted me that way for her lover. It was yet one more episode in the deliberately rude lewd life I had determined for myself. Where better to begin that story than at the beginning?

Chapter Two

It was the first day of a new year, an appropriate time for the start of what was to be the abiding passion of my life. My parents had celebrated with friends until the early hours; my two brothers were in London for the day, separately, for they were different as chalk and cheese. I breakfasted alone with the maidservant piling my plate. A growing lad needs filling, Molly always declared. Then I went out on one of those clear crisp January mornings that turn each breath into an icy vaporous cloud.

Along the road I met a local youth going to Nine Acre Wood. Motorways and huge roundabouts were decades away from dissecting the countryside and the whole area was a safe playground for youngsters. 'Come to the common,' I urged the boy. 'There's usually a football game on in the holidays.' I was keenly interested in all forms of sport. Now a chance encounter was to alter my whole outlook. The boy laughed at me, someone I'd always considered an insignificant weed.

'Kiss-chase is more fun,' he said. 'The village girls play in the wood. Catch one and you get a kiss at least.'

'And they let you?' I asked naively.

'They like it,' I was assured. 'Why d'you think they go there? Didn't you know that, stupid?'

Normally I would have twisted his arm behind him for his cheek but I was intrigued. 'You mean they *want* boys to kiss them?'

In The Mood

'Some of them want more 'n that, if you're in a quiet spot,' said my informant, enjoying his superiority. 'Alison Barber lets us pull down her knickers and look at her quim. She's got hairs there.'

'You're boasting. You made that up,' I accused. Of course I knew what a quim was. A girl's 'thing', her secret place. I'd never seen one.

'I did not make it up,' he indignantly denied. 'I've seen it and felt it. Find out for yourself if you don't believe – '

My boyhood had been spent in the village, which was near the coast in Sussex, a fine place to be brought up with both unspoiled countryside and sea to enjoy. For the hard depressed years of the 1920s and 30s my life was secure and happy with father, mother and two brothers. Having no sisters and attending an all-boys' private school meant little contact with girls. Not that I wasn't intrigued by their mystery, but most of my time and energy had been spent in sporting activities. There was a glass case full of cups and shields to prove it.

Father was a city accountant, on the board of directors of several large and well-known companies. Mother was a handsome and statuesque woman in the very prime, whose great love was entertaining guests and giving parties. When these took place my brothers and I were packed off upstairs. I remember hearing the shrieks of fun and games going on below. All men flattered and made a fuss of my good-looking mother. Father seemed most pleased to have her admired by his friends. We resided in a large rambling house with a gardener to attend to the grounds, which had a tennis court and a field used to stage village fetes and cricket matches. There were servants too, including the stout, middle-aged Molly. She lived 'in', which was a sloping roofed room in the attic, where she consoled her widowed state with the gin bottle. This failing was

In The Mood

excused. She had been with us so long and was rarely too tipsy to attend to her duties diligently.

Life wasn't all luxury. In the days before central heating was commonplace, coal fires provided the warmth and kettles and copper boilers were used for the entire hot water supply. Rising early of a wintry morning would have tested an eskimo. Comfort was not the necessity it is nowadays. Often I had to break the ice inside the water jug in my unheated bedroom to wash before breakfast. It was considered good for the spirit. I then cycled five miles to school; freezing classrooms where six of the best across the hand or bottom were statutory and accepted. For all that I grew up sturdy and strong, a picture of rude health, bounding with energy.

My brothers went to boarding schools, returning each end of term for the holidays. The elder, Rodney, was quiet and serious, deciding between following father into business or preferably taking holy orders as a minister of the church. Edwin was a spirited and clever youth, lazy but successful in school exams and destined for a flying career in the Royal Air Force. Even though younger I had outgrown them both. On bath nights, when we shared the hot water, it was with pride I noted who was most splendidly gifted in what we called the 'waterworks department'. My penis was much longer and thicker than Eddie's, who was a year older. Roddie was nineteen and his puny thing could hardly be seen among the bush of hair around his balls. I had become aware of the pleasure to be had manipulating my splendid endowment. Boys at school joked rather shamefacedly about the habit, which had many names that were almost terms of endearment for a universal and popular practice. 'Pulling the pud', 'Bashing the bishop', 'Beating the meat' and 'Stroking the eel' were but a few. We had been warned of the dangers at school of self-abuse; onanism could cause blindness, lethargy and even death. Despite this I sus-

In The Mood

pected we all did it. It was my secret vice as well. Fresh air and cold showers didn't work. When I awoke each morning in the privacy of my bedroom the size and iron-hardness of my prick delighted me. I'd pose before the wardrobe mirror with it thrusting out menacingly, admiring its cockiness. Rubbing it brought about the most curious and delicious sensation. If I continued so I convulsed in ecstasy, shooting thick creamy fluid in spurts. If I felt guilty at all it was temporary. The following morning I was compelled to repeat the performance.

I can't explain the strange mixture of excitement and anticipation I felt accompanying the boy to Nine Acre Wood. Among the bare trees he quickly caught and chased a girl who made little attempt to evade him. Then he held her for me.

'Go on then,' he urged. 'You try her – '

It was a simple kiss on the mouth but the girl's sweet breath on mine, the softness of her face and lips, the closeness of her pliant body left me faint. This was for me, I at once decided, and kissed her again. Off went the boy in search of other fair game, leaving me with her. I knew her by sight as a village girl, Charlotte Plummer. She was about sixteen, employed as a maid in the vicar's house and enjoying a rare day off. At her age she had filled out splendidly. On a cold morning, wearing a buttoned-up overcoat, the curved mounds of her big breasts was evident of advanced development.

'D'you want to play this kid's game or go for a walk?' she asked. I must have shown disappointment. Caught in the spirit of the game I fancied hunting about for more sweet kisses.

'Why chase about if you want to kiss me?' she reasoned, as if knowing my mind. 'Come on. I know a place by the marsh where no one will see us. Fancy me, do you?'

In The Mood

I replied that kissing her was very nice. She laughed at my polite innocence and led me off by the hand. The way was well-trodden and we reached a little dell overgrown by dead brambles and hidden by a thicket of bushes. I noticed a space had been trodden flat by use. 'Good! Nobody here,' the girl exclaimed. 'You're called Tyler. Funny name. I knows your brother Eddie –'

'And you're Charlotte,' I said. 'I remember you at Sunday School.' I could recall the sturdy girl who could hold her own in tussles with boys. She had changed into burgeoning young womanhood with the apple cheeks and round face of the local country stock. I stared at the swell of her breasts bulging inside the thick overcoat and she regarded me with interest.

'What you looking at so hard, dirty devil?' she chided me. 'Never seen a girl's tits before? Here, your brother Eddie isn't half one for the village lasses. Can't leave 'em alone.'

This was a revelation to me. It showed how little I knew of someone I thought close to me. And common local girls! We sons of a city businessman and County Councillor were supposed to be above having such friends. Evidently not, and looking at the enticing girl before me I understood why.

'Eddie's a lad all right,' she went on. 'You call me Lottie like he does. He's different from your brother Rodney. Such a goody-goody. I sees him when he visits the vicarage with Miss Pettinger, the ironmonger's daughter. What are you then?'

'Same as Eddie,' I was quick to assure her.

'Never seen you at kiss-chase before, or heard you bothered the girls.'

I stood silent. Lottie put her hands on my shoulders and kissed me full on the mouth. 'Don't know much about it, do you?' she teased. 'Proper little innocent, I'd say. Don't you open your mouth?'

'What for?' I asked dully.

In The Mood

'For this, silly,' she replied, putting her arms around me and kissing me again, this time with wet open lips, pushing her warm tongue into my mouth. She rolled her lips around mine, thrusting her body hard against me. I discovered the thrill of reciprocating. Tingling to my toes, penis surging with lust inside my trousers, novice that I was I kissed her hard in return, tonguing back in the way she had showed me, pulling her closer and moving my hips against hers.

'That's better,' she complimented as we drew apart for breath. 'You're a quick learner –' She giggled as I drew her back to me, my mouth opening for more kissing. 'Getting a good bone on you too! I can feel it against me –'

With more lewd kisses and embraces by the naughty willing girl my prick stiffened gloriously like never before, so hard it was painful. I pressed it against her as if the most natural thing in the world, eager to continue the delightful new experience which heated and set my body trembling. We kissed long and lustfully with the unbounded sexual energy of youth. Our wet tongues probed, our bodies worked in a rhythm, thrust against thrust. We gasped and grunted. We overbalanced and fell to the ground.

'Phew! That was good,' Lottie said, sitting up. 'You're a strong boy and good-looking too. How come you haven't got a regular girl? I never heard you were courting. How old are you?'

I ignored her questions, reaching for her to resume the sweet kissing and cuddling. 'It's much better lying down,' Lottie said at our next pause for air. 'Ground's dry too.' She unbuttoned her coat and took one of my hands, placing it over a cushiony young breast. 'Don't you want to go inside and really feel them?' she asked. 'Your brother isn't slow like you. He's always getting them out and playing with them.' Cupping and squeezing her nice big tits had excited a great desire in me to kiss and suck them. Girls were the most delightful

In The Mood

things, I was finding out. My hand trembled as I fumbled to unbutton her dress, all fingers and thumbs with anticipation.

'Hurry up and go inside then,' Lottie complained. 'Do I have to do everything for you?' She pushed aside my hand and undid the front of her dress quickly. My fingers went down her woollen vest to sample smooth ample flesh. Her breasts were as big as a mature woman's. I pinched each hardening nipple and she trembled. 'Boys like to kiss and suck on them,' said the aroused girl. 'If it wasn't so cold I'd let you see my titties. Here, look down my vest –'

She held out the neck so that I looked down on two creamy hillocks, nestled together and tipped with rosy nipples jutting out like finger tips. My hand went inside again and I fondled and cupped each tit in turn. 'I'd like to see them out. I'd love to see you with *all* your clothes off,' I told her.

'You make me go all funny, saying that,' Lottie said. 'Now let me see yours. Come on –'

I realised what she meant when she gave the front of my trousers a hard squeeze over my rampant prick. Without a shred of shyness now, in fact proud to show off what I considered a fine specimen, I opened my fly and she immediately delved in her hand and drew it out, clasping the shaft and jiggling it. I fell back to give her full play at me.

'Oh, it's a big one,' she praised me. 'Fancy hiding that whopper all this time. Your Eddie hasn't got one like this.'

'You've done this to him?'

She threw back her head and laughed. 'Many's the time. In the pictures mostly.' She stroked and rubbed me deliciously. 'He hasn't got one like you,' she said again. 'It's as stiff as a poker. Come on then,' she ordered. 'You touch me up too –'

She lolled back, opening her legs and clutching up her dress with her free hand to reveal woollen

In The Mood

knickers. 'They come down if you pull 'em,' she said, almost resignedly. 'You are a slow-coach.' I did as bid, revealing a white belly and a plump mound with a sparse covering of downy hair around the split lips of her cunt. The inside glistened pink. With my prick still in her grasp she urged me to feel her.

'It won't bite you,' said the forward girl, so I penetrated the pouting lips, going up to my second knuckle in a moist channel. Lottie sighed and gave a little moan, moving back and forth on my finger and pumping my shaft vigorously. To my utter amazement she shuddered and shook just like I did when playing with myself. She jerked and cried out, heaving her bottom off the ground. I gasped my all too, the hot emission spurting over her hand and wrist, spotting the sleeve of her coat.

'Don't you worry about that,' she laughed as I anxiously wiped it off with my handkerchief. 'My ma will think I've wiped my nose there!' She pealed with laughter, still clutching my diminishing cock in her hand. I decided I had never met such a person. Were all girls, whom I'd considered soppy and shy creatures, like her? I sincerely hoped so.

Lottie then pulled me flat on top of her and pushed her bare thighs against me, her mouth glued to mine. In that position, astride and between her legs, I thrust against her crotch. My limp prick nestled nicely on her mound and began to stir. I could smell the sweat of her body, pungently arousing, cradled between her warm thighs as she crossed her legs behind mine and levered me into her. My erection returned, the knob seeking the opening of her cunt. She pushed me urgently with the palms of her hands against my shoulders until I was raised, looking down at her face wonderingly.

'You can't put it in,' she said. 'Not without a rubber. You'd give me a baby for certain, the load you come.

In The Mood

You can't fuck me but I'll let you push it against me. A dry rub is the next best thing.'

I got my prick in place against her mound and thrust until she called out for me to work faster, her body lifting to match my heaves. 'I'm coming. Oh dear, I'm coming off,' she cried, her legs going straight out and quivering to the toes. 'Oh, oh, goodness – ' I drained myself over her at almost the same moment. When we drew apart her belly-button was filled to overflowing with my unction, the thick grey surplus running down towards the triangle of wispy hair between her legs. I mopped it up with my now-sodden handkerchief.

'You've got a fine one on you,' she said, watching me tucking my now flaccid prick back into my trousers. She straightened her dress and tidied her hair, considering me. 'That will please a lot of girls when you get better at it. I wouldn't mind trying it myself.'

Try it one day soon she would, I vowed. And I *would* get better at it. Not that I didn't think I was quite good already. But if there was more to it, I was certainly going to find out all I needed to know.

Chapter Three

Exhilarated by my experience with Lottie I wanted to share my wonderful discovery with someone; the great pleasure a female body can bestow. Girls were marvellously designed by nature to tempt and delight. Such sweet lips, soft skin, pliant breasts, flaring hips and rounded buttocks. And most certainly not least the plump mound with its wisps of hair and moist split lips nestling between cushiony thighs created for man's ultimate delectation. I was a confirmed addict already.

Brother Edwin was the obvious choice to confide in. On his return from London that evening I found him in his bedroom, puffing a cigarette beside an open window to prevent detection. So he smoked as well as dallied with local girls – Eddie was a much deeper character than I'd ever imagined. When I related my sexual adventure he nodded agreement.

'You've finally got around to the pleasures of the flesh, and not before time,' he told me. 'A good start too. You were lucky with the girl. Charlotte the harlot, I call her. Lottie's one of the best sports, as randy a piece as you'll meet. Some bits let you do things to please you, which is well enough in its way. Lottie does it all because she can't help herself. She's always on heat, a real baggage.'

'I thought perhaps all girls were like that.'

My brother laughed at me. 'Not enough of 'em. The world would be a better place if they were. Of course, they can have kids letting us have our way and that's the worst possible disgrace in a village, so they have to make out they're not that sort. But with the right approach you'll get what you're after. Remember they are all liable to get as horny as us if truth were told –'

How to get my way with the delicious creatures was what I most wanted to learn. I listened enthralled. My dreamy expression did not go unnoticed. 'You've only found out how good it can be kissing and feeling them,' he went on, 'but there's lots more and better. You didn't fuck her.'

'We frigged each other. Then had what she called a dry rub. She wouldn't do it without a thing called a rubber.'

'A frenchie, sheath or condom,' nodded the wordly-wise Eddie. He brought a little packet from his bedside drawer and showed me a fine rubber object. 'You roll it over your chopper when you've a good hard-on. Sometimes the girl will do it for you. When you come the spunk is caught in this little knob on the end. Saves giving babies to the willing darlings.'

'Wherever did you get that?' I asked amazed.

'Any chemist shop sells them. I get my supply from older village fellows. Sam the carter goes to Brighton every day. He'll get you all you want for a sixpence tip.'

'Have you fucked Lottie?' I asked incredulously.

'As many times as you've had hot dinners, dear brother,' Eddie grinned. 'You will too in time and find that fucking is the greatest thing ever invented. Everybody's at it, even the stuffiest of stuffshirts and the most respectable. It's better than all your cricket, football and sailing put together. Did Lottie show you her great big tits? She's proud of them.'

'It was too cold,' I said sadly. 'But I did feel and squeeze them.'

'A pair of beauties. Be sure to suck her nipples next time. She goes all weak then. I had every stitch off her in the woods last summer –'

In The Mood

'You've seen her naked?' It seemed my brother had already done all I wanted to do, lucky bounder.

'Much more than her,' he replied, lighting another cigarette. 'A fair few in fact. Alison Barber – '

'She's got hairs on her quim,' I said to show my knowledge.

'They all have at her age. A nice pouting hairy cunt is a splendid sight; much better, I'm certain, than the Bay of Naples at dawn or the Taj Mahal by moonlight.'

'I know what I'd rather see,' I agreed. 'Go on, who else have you seen without their clothes –?'

'I've had Pearl Calvert stripped off in her house. Her parents were out at work. She pretended to protest but I got her dress and knickers off. Don't let them stop you if you are certain they like it. Most of 'em do.'

I determined to remember his advice. 'The lady doth protest too much,' I misquoted, from Shakespeare I supposed.

'That's the idea,' Eddie agreed, warming to the subject. 'I've had snooty Nancy Todd in the bare buff too. Her tits are pointed and pear-shaped, and her cunt sticks out on a lovely hairy bulge so plump it keeps the tops of her legs apart. It's the best kind of cunt to fuck, I tell you, a natural mound to hump against. She's seventeen going on eighteen. The older they get the better the tits and quim. Firmer. Same for a woman's arse and hips. Older women have better bodies. Riper – '

Getting working-class village girls naked in his romps was one thing; they now seemed fair game to me, but mature women? I couldn't believe they would allow it, even for the persistent Edwin. 'Who have you seen that's older?' I scoffed.

'All right,' he said, taking up the challenge. 'Today I visited a certain house in London. The lady is in her thirties and sells her favours. She's worth it. You should see her body. Lush. But I've viewed a few older ones around here too – '

In The Mood

'Who?' I demanded, eager to know.

'Ma, for one,' he said calmly, watching my reaction.

'Mother?' I gasped.

'Many times. At the beach hut for a start, when we go swimming –'

The family's wooden hut had stood for years at our local beach. We used it to store deckchairs and change into swimwear. 'How could you see her there?' I said disbelievingly.

'Made a slit at the back of it,' said my crafty brother. 'Used my trusty scout knife to prise out a splinter where the boards join low down. Then I'd pretend to sunbathe behind the hut or read a book. When ma went in I'd fix an eye to it. Saw her all last summer I tell you.'

The fact that Edwin had ogled mother while naked should have disgusted me. Instead, I regarded him with increased admiration. The very illicitness of the secretive act made my prick stir in my trousers. He saw the growing bulge as I lolled on his bed, making a grab for it and squeezing the hard stalk.

'That made you horny,' he chuckled, 'the thought of me watching ma stripped off. You'd like to see that yourself. Well, she's the best I've seen, I'll tell you that, especially when she comes out of the sea to dry herself. You get a good long look from all angles.'

As I have mentioned, mother was a handsome and statuesque woman in the prime of her early forties whose large uplifted bust, flaring hips and shapely legs made for a splendid figure. In the thin cotton bathing-costumes of that era, which clung moulded to the body when wet, I had myself stolen many admiring and fascinated looks at her coming out from a swim. She had what Edwin had described as a sticking-out cunt mound which positively bulged between her thighs, and the split of her quim showed plainly under the clinging costume as if drawn in by suction. Her big breasts were perfectly round globes, firm and high on

In The Mood

her chest with large prominent nipples. The splendid moons of her buttocks were sculpted by the sodden bathing suit, leaving little to a fevered young imagination. And Edwin had seen more! He encouraged my arousal by retaining his grip on my prick and gave it several frigs to urge it on, not that it needed encouragement in its heightened state.

'She has a marvellous backside,' he went on salaciously, knowing me to be completely under the spell of his lewd talk. 'A real grown-up mature woman's arse. Two solid cheeky buttocks of rounded flesh, firm and smooth as marble. Rubenesque, if you know what that is. No wonder father likes to cane it. I should love to do so myself – '

'I don't believe you,' I said. This was going too far.

'Please yourself. I've seen him do it – '

'But why?'

'Because he enjoys it, you idiot,' Edwin said scathingly. 'Don't you know anything? What a fine big target it presents.'

I had to think about this. Father was a mild man, I truly considered, if successful in his profession. Mother was by far the stronger of the two. He never punished us boys. He was a shadowy figure who disappeared off to London every morning in the week on the eight-fifty train and arrived home for dinner.

'And mother allows that?' I enquired dully. I was an innocent in worldly things to be sure, unaware of anything that went on under my nose. 'She lets him cane her bottom?'

'Her absolutely bare bottom. She loves it, I can tell. Her cheeks go a bright pink and she wriggles and writhes. You can almost feel it tingle. I've seen the old man increase his strokes to make her jump. I tell you, bending over, her cunt sticks out between her bum cheeks like a large split peach, all hairy as far back as her arse-hole. Then the old man mounts her while she's still quivering bent over the chair. He shafts her

In The Mood

right vigorously doggy-fashion and the pair of them go at it like knives.'

Doggy-fashion? This again was a new expression to me, yet I could imagine it vividly in my racing mind. I even hoped it was all true, not a figment of Eddie's fertile imagination or a fantasy he enjoyed. I had to know. 'Where did you see all this, if it happened?' I demanded. 'Surely not at the beach hut –?'

'Of course not. Right here, in the house. It was after some of their parties when the guests have left. I've no doubt they're tipsy with wine. I sneak down the stairway for a look; if you crouch on the landing you can see into a good part of the drawing-room, especially where an armchair is placed before the fireplace. They always use the same chair for their game. I've even moved it slightly so that the view was unimpeded.'

It was true. On going downstairs one could see into the large room kept for special dinners, musical evenings, parties and such. Above the wide oak door was a panel of leaded plain glass. 'Why didn't you tell me of this, rotten bugger?' I complained. 'And about the beach hut –'

'I thought you more concerned with healthy sporting activities,' Edwin grinned. 'Besides, too many cooks spoil the broth. The beach hut peephole is no more anyway. Religious Rodney caught me spying and threatened to tell. He sealed the slit with putty, damn him.'

'That's Rodney,' I commiserated. My brother was still lightly stroking my engorged tool and I had to warn him. 'Much more of that,' I said, enjoying his slow expert massaging of my prick, 'and I'll be shooting off in my trousers.'

'Bring it out then,' he ordered. 'All this horny talk has got me worked up as well.' I did as bid and he looked over my upstanding member with much interest. 'You always did have a whopper, lucky boun-

28

In The Mood

der,' he complimented me grudgingly. 'Let's measure it – '

To comply, and made conceited by his obvious envy, I lay back with my cock proudly stiff and bolt upright. Edwin brought a wooden ruler from his desk.

'Almost seven inches from balls to knob.' He gave my shaft a few more vigorous rubs and it reared in his hand. 'It's a good one; bigger than the best any sixth-former can flash at my school. I've seen them all. Have you ever wondered why your prick's so much bigger than old Rodney's and mine? Why you're already much taller and don't even look like us?'

I had noticed the difference in us brothers but gave it little thought except to be glad I was the handsomest and biggest. Edwin changed the subject quickly. 'Have to do something about this magnificent hard-on,' he said. 'Stand-by with your handkerchief unless you want rice pudding on your belly – '

He manipulated my prick most enjoyably and I gasped and writhed in helpless pleasure, uncaring who was providing the source. 'The senior boys at school do this to each other all the time,' he informed me. 'Some of them would love to suck this fine cock for you – ' A few more rapid movements of his wrist and I convulsed my hips, polluting a great load into the readied hankie, my third come that day.

'I can see I'll have to take you in hand in more ways than that, young Ty,' Edwin reflected, as I lay before him weakened but gloriously relaxed. 'Now that I know you have a truly lecherous nature it's up to me to point you in the right direction. So you'd like to eyeball a real grown-up woman bare naked, would you?'

I nodded eagerly.

'Then I'll show you one tomorrow for certain,' promised my confident brother. 'Two even, if the other female is available. What do you say to that?'

What could I say? I was filled with admiration for

In The Mood

my clever mentor. I didn't know how he could do it, but I had no doubt in my mind that Edwin would be as good as his word.

Chapter Four

The following day, a long Sunday, proved an agony of suspense awaiting Edwin's fulfilment of his promise. He said no more about it, smiling secretively when I reminded him of his boast. After supper I thought the chance over and found it hard to conceal my bitter disappointment.

'Patience,' he advised. The house settled to its Sunday evening routine. In the drawing-room mother and father entertained guests. The sound of the piano filtered up to Edwin's bedroom, where we waited. Rodney had borrowed father's Austin Seven car to drive to the village to see his first-ever girlfriend, Grace Pettinger, about whom we teased him, she being to us an old-fashioned spinster some years older. We joked she lied about her age as twenty-one; more like thirty-one Edwin and I taunted Rodney. The pair would be going to their usual Band of Hope meeting where magic lantern slides of missionary work in the South Seas would be shown, then on to the vicarage in a jolly group for cocoa and biscuits.

Edwin himself sat with ear cocked as if listening for some special sound. To keep me amused and my impatience at bay he allowed me to view the store of pornography secreted in his wardrobe. There were postcard-sized photographs bought only the day before on his trip to London, half-a-dozen black and white prints of naked men and women indulging in wanton sucking and fucking in a variety of positions. How I envied the men and wished I were included in their posing. I also avidly read Edwin's store of tattered handwritten dirty stories, the pages almost falling apart at the folds with usage. I still remember the titles: 'Janet the Gym Mistress', relating lurid lesbian goings-on at a school for young ladies; and 'Auntie and Nephew on a Train Journey', which dealt with seduction by an older woman in the most lewd details. I knew I should enjoy participating in all the sensual and dissolute acts described and vowed one day I would. In the meantime I knew real frustration. As for seeing two real naked females, I sadly contented myself that even Eddie couldn't work miracles.

At last my brother bounded off his bed. 'That's it,' he declared. 'Come and give a hand – ' Mystified, I followed him to the kitchen, where our maid was filling buckets of hot water from the copper boiler.'

'We'll help you, Molly,' he offered grandly. 'Ty and I will carry the water to your room,' So saying, he and I took a full bucket each up the two flights of stairs to her quarters. In the cosy attic, which contained her brass bed, table and chairs, sideboard and other furniture, a long tin bathtub was set out on the carpet before a blazing fire. We tipped in the steaming water, adding to the amount already there.

'Molly's bath night,' Edwin said, winking. 'I was waiting to hear her plodding upstairs with her buckets.'

It was a sound I knew well but had thought nothing of it. Molly bathed every Sunday evening after her week's work. On other nights, she had told me herself, she 'topped and tailed', meaning a wash up and down. Eddie grinned and dived his hand under her heaped feather pillows, bringing out a half-empty bottle of gin.

'Moll likes a tipple. Sits up in bed after her bath knocking back the gin to keep her spirits up – ' I knew her as a clean, kindly soul who wore her brown hair up in a bun and was buxom and cuddlesome, many

In The Mood

years in my parents' employ and a sturdy, healthy woman. She was about the same age as mother, widowed as a young wife in the first world war, the Great War as it was then known.

We made several trips upstairs, emptying the buckets into the tin tub, and finally met Molly on her way to her room. 'Good boys,' she thanked us. 'Saved my legs a journey or two.' She then went in and Edwin and I bounded downstairs like a herd of elephants, only to tip-toe noiselessly up to her door again.

'Deadly quiet now,' Edwin advised. 'Take a peek – '

I bent to the old keyhole, a large brass one big enough to poke a fat finger inside and ideal for spying. It had a brass cover too, fashioned like a miniature bunch of grapes which Molly kept polished like gold. I tilted it carefully aside and glued an eager eye to the hole. There, not more than a yard or two away, Molly stood in her cotton petticoat, the rest of her clothes strewn around her bare feet on the carpet. Her legs were strong and shapely. She added a kettle of boiling water to the bath. Replacing the kettle in the hearth she drew the shift over her head, revealing to my eyes a fine mature female body. It was indeed a sight to behold for the randy and inquisitive boy I had become.

First the shapeless garment was hoisted to reveal strapping thighs, between which was the hairiest cuntmount I ever hoped to see, a veritable forest of dark brown growth from her lower belly down to between comfortable thighs. The petticoat then travelled up and over a plumpish ivory-white belly with its deep navel, and on gloriously upward uncovering an enormous pair of breasts. I had to suppress a gasp of admiration. They were long and pendulous, heavy and full, shaped indeed like fat vegetable marrows plump with flesh. They were not the least droopy but firm and supportive for their size. On the end of each great teat were rubbery brown nipples, shrivelled now but big as thimbles. Oh that I could have rushed in and sucked

In The Mood

them! Molly put a tentative toe in the water and sat down in the tub, her back to the fire.

I turned to glance at Edwin, who was delighted my face expressed such lust. 'Big-built, eh? A fine specimen,' he whispered. 'Wouldn't I love to have her across that big brass bed and give her what for! You could lose your balls fucking her great cunt. Go on, keep looking. I've seen her dozens of times. You wait until she stands up to wash her lovely big bum – '

I put my eager eye back to the keyhole. Molly rose up to lather her legs and thighs, opening wide to soap her splendid cunt, which had lips like a purse. She lingered there a little longer than necessary, I thought. Did she too frig herself to obtain relief and pleasure? She then paid attention to her huge tits, lifting and washing each one in turn in her cupped hand. Finally she rubbed the soap between her rounded backside, facing the fire and going between the cheeks thoroughly, allowing a perfect view. The soap slipped from her grasp and skidded in the tiled hearth, making her bend over to retrieve it. I saw for myself what Edwin had described as a mature cunt seen from the rear of a bending woman.

It thrust out between her cleft bottom as large as a big duck egg, the brown and crinkled outer lips peeping through a growth of hair. I could see her arsehole too, a puckered star-shaped indentation which she soaped meticulously in its turn, almost too scrupulously, with a finger up the tight entrance. She dried her top half while still upright in the tub, her tits wobbling deliciously as she drew the towel across her back in short sharp movements. Then she stepped out upon the clothes discarded for washing and dried her feet while sat upon a stool. This position too afforded a fine view of her cunt. Then she put on her long nightdress and the show was over.

Edwin and I tiptoed downstairs to the kitchen, where he carved himself a thick slice of cold beef from the

In The Mood

remains of the Sunday roast in the larder. 'Didn't I tell you,' he said. 'Trust old Eddie to deliver the goods. Now for naked woman number two, but I don't see why I should do all this for no reward. This will cost you. Got any money in your box? I know you're a saver.'

'About three pounds,' I lied. I wasn't saying what I had.

'Well, this will cost you two of them if the bird in question is available. I had an expensive day in London yesterday. Go get your scarf and overcoat, your cycle clips too. We, dear horny brother, are going visiting.'

Mystified as ever with Edwin's schemes I did as I was told. On returning to the kitchen I found him wrapped up in muffler and overcoat, slipping a bottle of cooking sherry into a deep pocket. 'It's the stuff Molly uses for trifles, all I could pinch with the booze cabinet in the drawing-room,' he explained. 'It will do well enough. Quiet now as we leave the house – '

In the cold air our bicycle lamps glowed frostily in the deep dark of the country lanes along which we rode. There was no other traffic. I asked no questions but felt an air of intrigue and excitement. After all, Eddie had proved himself already that night. At last, before a lonely cottage a mile or so away, he signalled we should leave our machines against a hedge. We went through a gate and up a well-trodden path, our shoes crunching on frosted gravel.

'This is where Mary Pullen lives,' I said.

'Clever boy,' he commented. 'I'll do the talking if she invites us in, which she will if there's no other visitors. Mary likes company.' He knocked lightly, so as not to awaken sleeping children I learned later. The door opened allowing a shaft of light and warmth to escape, with a woman silhouetted there.

'What are you young devils wanting at this time of night?' she chided, but not angrily or unkindly. 'I was just off to bed.'

35

In The Mood

'An excellent idea,' said the cheeky Eddie. 'I'll keep you company.'

'You!' she laughed, in a broad country accent. 'You wouldn't be much use. What do you want?'

'We were passing,' Edwin said. 'Thought we'd say hello. It's pretty lonely out here for you, miles from anywhere. I've brought some cake and sherry. Cigarettes too – '

'Come in then,' Mary allowed, suspicion in her voice. 'It's freezing out here – ' I followed my brother into a room as warm and cosy as an animal's den, with a blazing log fire and old stuffed armchairs, home-made rag carpets on the planked wooden floor but all as neat and clean as a new pin. We made straight for the fire to warm our hands while Mary regarded me.

'Well, young man,' she said. 'I hope you haven't let that brother of yours give you ideas?'

'Not a bit of it,' Edwin assured her, lying artfully. 'It's his birthday. Thought we'd have a little party.' He dug into his overcoat pockets. Out came the bottle of sherry, slices of the cake Molly had baked that morning, and a flat box of cigarettes which were kept for guests at home. 'Mother's having one of her musical evenings,' he said. 'No fun at home tonight, so here we are – '

Mary brought three old glasses from a shelf and placed them on the table. I well knew her reputation in the district; three children by different fathers and still unmarried. I'd always found her a cheerful and friendly woman, but apart from being shunned by respectable people she was considered too far gone to be a source of scandal any more. Mary herself obviously didn't care what people thought. She earned what money she made the hard way, working in the fields at harvest time, lifting potatoes and turnips, picking fruit; or scrubbing and ironing for those who needed a low-paid willing worker. She had helped Molly at our house during spring cleaning or washing

In The Mood

up the masses of dishes when mother gave one of her larger dinner parties. Her kids were clean and rosy-cheeked, well fed and looked after better than many village children with both parents. Who could blame her if she sought a little pleasure in her life?

'We can play cards,' she suggested. 'I love a game.'

'Right-ho,' Edwin agreed readily. 'See, I've even brought a pack with me – ' and he produced cards from his jacket, ones I knew were conjurer's cards with marked backs.

'I'm glad you boys came,' Mary said, settling herself at the table. 'I was off to bed 'cos there was nothing to do.' I could see no wireless set, wind-up gramophone or books anywhere. She was indeed a simple country-woman without guile, in her early thirties and with a broad Hampshire accent. It looked as if she had cut her hair herself, which was neatly done and likely if money was hard to come by. It shone dark and clean, fringed and framing a smiling face free of blemishes or make-up. She was slim but well-proportioned with firm pointed breasts bulging the front of the darned knitted cardigan she wore. Her hips flared from a narrow waist and below her skirt her legs were strong and shapely. Edwin poured sherry into our glasses and shuffled the cards like a card-sharp.

'What do we play?' I asked, thinking a game of cards pretty tame stuff to what I had hoped for.

'Strip Jack Naked,' Edwin announced without consultation, dealing the cards expertly around the table-cloth, a rough brown blanket.

Mary protested. 'Oh, no we don't, randy sod. Not with him here. You've had your eyeful before and will make do with it. He's not like you, I hope.'

'He's worse,' Edwin swore. 'Besides, it's his birthday and deserved a treat. Who says you'll lose anyway?'

'I always do, playing with you.' Mary nevertheless picked up her hand and studied it. Edwin winked broadly at me, pouring more sherry into Mary's glass.

In The Mood

I was first to lose and both laughed and clapped shouting, 'Off, off!' I removed my jacket, glad to do so as the room was warm and stuffy. The game had possibilities, I decided.

It was a fun evening that proceeded with much banter and jokes, Edwin sharing his cigarettes with Mary and frequently topping up her glass. Before long I was down to my shirt and trousers. Mary lost more frequently and discarded her slippers and both woollen stockings. Her cardigan was next to go, leaving her in a vest. As she wore no brassiere it did little to hide the outline of breasts and protruding nipples. Edwin had merely lost a shoe and his tie. He was in complete control of the game, dealing winning or losing hands at will, a skill he had learned at boarding school, I was sure. Mary grew flushed and merry and Edwin unmercifully dealt her bad hands in rapid succession. Most of the sherry had gone into her glass and it was with a shrug of compliance that she shed more clothes. She drew off her knickers, drawing them down while still wearing her skirt. One more losing hand and she drew her vest over her head, shaking her hair back into place and setting her now bared tits wobbling nicely.

'Go on,' she admonished me, sitting directly across from her and gawping at her milkers. 'Don't stare so. You're looking at them like a starving baby. Here, you never seen any before?'

They were well worth a good look, lily-white and sharp pointed with uptilted nipples. 'Never mind him,' Edwin chipped in, dealing a new hand to her. 'Play your cards. Maybe your luck will change – '

Hers didn't, but ours did. With anticipation I watched her lose and she rose, giggling, to step away from the table and drop her skirt, stepping out of it and standing before us bare naked. 'There,' she said, tipsy with mother's cooking sherry. 'That's what you wanted, wasn't it? Horny young devils that you are.

In The Mood

Well, take a good look. It's the same as every other woman's got and that's a fact.'

Her strong thighs were no doubt the result of much bending in the fields and walking far to work around the area. Even the village shops were two miles away. Between her crotch was a thatch of dark silky hair covering a neat little cunt split by thin lips. Hard to think the gossip was she had been shafted by so many men, with that tight little quim like a young girl's. It had produced babies too. Molly, our maid, had prominent lips and quite a slack mouth on her cunt, yet had borne no children and been with no man since her widowhood so far as I knew. It only went to show. Cunts could be very different; all of them delightful things. Looking at Mary's firm uplifted tits I was reminded too of Molly's pendulous bubbies. I had certainly learned a few things since the day before and was already a confirmed comparer of the nude female body.

'That's it, show's over,' Mary said firmly as Edwin and I goggled her. She picked up her discarded clothes and went to the fireplace. 'You lads have had your fun. Time you was home. I've kids to get up and feed in the morn, and work to go to.'

For all that she stood enjoying the heat of the fire on her body, unconcerned by our presence. I noted how her long back narrowed into a violin curve as her hips and buttocks flared out into two firm round cheeks. Edwin moved to put his hand there but she slapped his outstretched wrist playfully.

'Come back in a few years' time,' she giggled. 'Maybe you'd be fit for me then. Takes a man, not his breakfast.'

Chapter Five

As we pedalled home Edwin said boastfully, 'Didn't I promise you two naked women? That's well worth the couple of quid you've got on you –'

On a strong impulse I stopped and told him I was going back. I said Mary deserved the money more. He didn't argue, but he called back as he rode off into the darkness. 'You're wasting your time. She'll strip off but won't let you screw her. I've tried. You're cunt-struck –'

Cunt-struck I was and admitted it freely, and I wasn't giving up a chance so easily. Edwin was not the only one to scheme. The fact was I considered myself a far better candidate than he to get a ride from Mary or any other female. I was better equipped in all ways: size, looks and endowment. Oh, I'd soon leave Eddie behind despite his successes of the past. Back at her cottage Mary opened the door dressed in an old army greatcoat, her dressing gown no doubt.

She eyed me with surprise. 'Did you forget something, lad?'

I walked into her house uninvited. She had put out the two oil lamps after our departure and the room was cosily lit by the glow of the fire. I poked the embers with my shoe, coaxing flame. 'I thought you could make use of these,' I said, craftily humble, turning to press the two pound-notes into her hand. 'It's my own money that I've saved. I'd rather you have it.'

In The Mood

'What are you wanting for this?' she asked suspiciously.

'Nothing. I enjoyed this evening. It's a present – '

'Then bless you,' Mary said. In the glow as she regarded me I saw her doe eyes soften and fill. 'That's real kind. It's more'n I earn in a week. I haven't two pennies in the house at this minute. This is a Godsend to me – '

The overwrought woman took my face in her hands on impulse and gave me a smacking kiss on the lips. I immediately returned the favour, trying the tongue in mouth technique that Lottie had taught me. To my delight after a moment's hesitation Mary opened her mouth and our warm tongues touched. We continued hugging and kissing fervently. Taking full advantage of the situation I began pushing my thighs hard against hers. My prick rose stiff as iron and I pressed it into her. For several delightful seconds she allowed it, her crotch rising against me, meeting thrust with thrust. Then, breathing heavily, she held me off at arms' length.

'Here,' she panted, puffed by our exertions. 'Should we be doing this? You're a bit young for it, I reckon. Not that you haven't worked me up, saucy devil – '

I stood silent but no doubt with appeal in my eyes, so obvious that she laughed at me. 'Well, men are all the same, I suppose, even if they's still boys,' she said. 'You're a nice lad. Is it truly your birthday?'

'Yes,' I lied. 'Like Edwin told you.' I reached for her and she came into my arms, allowing a quick kiss, followed by a second longer one. Her body felt firm and strong against mine and my prick surged as she pressed it to her.

'I'd better give you a present then, hadn't I?' she said. 'Is that what you want – ?'

'Yes, oh yes,' I replied hoarsely. 'Oh, please.'

'I can't take you to bed, lad. There's two of my little 'uns in it. You'll have to make do with the fireplace – '

In The Mood

'Anywhere, anywhere,' I vowed.

Off came the greatcoat, which she laid out on the rag carpet before the hearth. Next to be divested was her long flannellette nightdress, which she carefully placed before the fire to warm for later. I stood again like a hypnotised rabbit staring at her smooth naked body. The pear-shaped breasts seemed swollen, ripe and mellow in the fire's glow, her pert nipples stiff with arousal. I had brought that about! I was eager and rampant as never before as the woman laid herself down in the fireside light, legs parted and displaying her neat cunt. She looked up at me and laughed at my hesitation.

'Changed your mind, lad?' she teased.

'No, no!' I hastened to assure her.

'Then are you just going to stand and stare at it?' she complained. 'Come on, it was you who got me all lathered up. Now do something about it. Take off your clothes; let's see what you've got in there – '

There was nothing more in the world I wanted to do, but I was still hesitant and naive. A thought had struck me. 'I haven't one of those rubber things, a sheath,' I admitted, cursing myself for not arming myself with one of Eddie's. I'd never be without again, I vowed. Mary was laid back expectantly, one hand touching her breasts and nipples, the other engaged in stroking the lips of her cunt, which seemed to have parted in her aroused state and were peeping through the fine wreath of hair around them.

'It doesn't matter,' she said. 'I'm already in the club, you see. Near three months. Come on, love – '

She was telling me she was with child! That made it safe to do as I liked, shoot my load with impunity. I began to throw off my clothes, and when I cast off the last item to my delight she pursed her lips and gave a whistle.

'You're a big lad all over right enough, ain't you? Proper giant, you'll be,' she said in admiration. 'Not a

In The Mood

skinny runt like your brother –' My tool reared thick and straining, almost level with my stomach it was so taut, pulsating for relief. 'Such a fine big cock on you for a boy. That will please a lot of women in its day –' The girl in Nine-Acre wood had said almost the same words. Full of the confidence and inexperience of youth I threw myself down between Mary's thighs, intending to ram her.

'Not so fast,' she complained as my knob pressed against her cunt, seeking entrance. 'Take your time about it and we'll both enjoy it. That's the trouble with young lads. Poke it up and finish, it's all you knows –'

Lying between her strong legs, belly to belly, her sharp nipples and firm breasts against my chest, I was impatient to mount and ride. My prick was pressed to her cunt lips and, like a dam bursting, they parted and I penetrated deeply first go. I was overwhelmed by the pleasure of my rammer being embedded in a warm and juicy cunt channel. I ignored her pleas. In no time at all I ejaculated strongly inside her, coming off with sighs and groans, my body convulsing. Mary waited below me until I was still.

'Were you a virgin?' she asked kindly. 'Did you never have it up a woman before – ?'

'Of course,' I told her. 'Many a time –' This was where I was completely wrong. Better by far for the novice to place himself completely in the hands of an older woman, should he be fortunate enough to find one willing to instruct him. Mary was not fooled. She shook her head. 'Wasn't it good for you?' I asked. 'Didn't I make you come off?' I must have thought a big hard prick was all that was necessary.

Mary smiled up at me. 'Never had time to, did I? Not with you going at it like a battering ram. I wanted to get some fun out of it too, you know. Women ain't made of stone. Take your time and it lasts longer. I told you that. You've a fine big cock, big as any man's already, but you don't know how to use it. There's no

In The Mood

loving in just banging away. Gently does it, kissing and touching like, till the woman gets so worked up she'll beg for it. *Then* you'll know what a good fuck can be – '

'I thought it was great. It was lovely,' I told her.

'For you. But there's two of us here. It's blessed marvellous when done proper, lad. I likes it too much then – '

I was keenly disappointed she had not responded wantonly as did the females in Edwin's tattered pornography. But I could see her point well enough; there had been little opportunity for her to perform like that. Sensing my awareness that I had not pleasured her she touched my cheek gently, smiling up at me. 'It don't matter that time so much,' she said kindly. 'I could tell right away you was new. Nothing to be ashamed of there, just as long as you learned something from it.' She pulled my head down and kissed my mouth long and slowly, her tongue probing, rolling her lips around mine. I kissed her determinedly in return and she began to undulate the fork of her open thighs against my limp prick. Her pliant tits and erected nipples rubbed on my bare chest.

'Come on, son, don't fret yourself about what's past,' she soothed me. 'Get on with pushing against my cunt. We'll soon have that fine big chap rearing again. Young lads gets another stiff prick quickly. Then we'll do it right. Here, you kiss my tits. Suck on them hard – '

I did exactly as ordered, delighted to get a second chance. Her hand slipped down between us and massaged my prick lightly. She cupped my balls, exerting a pleasant pressure. I sucked each nipple then returned to her soft mouth, tonguing her. She gripped me tightly before pulling her mouth away.

'Talk to me,' she whispered as if ashamed but unable to resist the request. ''Twas you that got me all worked up for a fucking. Say you'll ride me till I begs for

In The Mood

mercy. Tell me you're going to shag my cunt rigid. Go on, a woman likes to hear those things. I does, anyway. Dirty talk makes me right horny. Go on – '

Such talk had its effect on me as well. My prick had already nearly fully stiffened in her hand. Now it reared and she guided it to her upthrust cunt. It slid inside easily and for a long moment I left it at that as if in soak, unmoving over her until she heaved her buttocks off the floor as if desperate to receive my full length. 'Ride me now, love,' she pleaded. 'I'm right on heat. Shove it up to your bollocks. Fuck me, fuck me do – '

Looking down upon her I saw a face twisted in the utmost look of pleasure I had ever beheld. Her eyes rolled back, her mouth gaped, she grunted and gasped and locked her legs behind mine in a vice-like grip, thrusting and heaving below me like a demented creature. That I had aroused her so, delighted me more than the act of fucking her. This time I determined there would be no mad gallop on my part. I hardly moved above her except to match her upward motions and kept my prick firmly embedded up her cunt. I kept my eyes open, watching her goatishly, thrilling to every lewd cry and gasp forced from her throat. She mumbled the whole time, encouraging me to fuck harder.

'Darlin', oh my darlin', it's so lovely,' she uttered in her throes. 'Keep it up and make it last. Don't you dare come – ' But we had run our course. She shivered, shook, and was lost in that glorious surge of feeling that has no equal, sobbing out her pleasure. In return I quickened my pace and thrust mightily. Moments later we lay side by side, sated and exhausted in the most luxurious enervation.

"Twas a lovely fuck, lad,' she said at last, almost dreamily, staring up at the ceiling. 'You brought me off better than many a man who's been at it for years. Better dress now and get off home, your ma may be wondering – '

In The Mood

'I'll come and see you again if I may,' I volunteered. In my savings box was more than enough for several visits. I couldn't think of a better use to make of it and help Mary at the same time. To think I had amassed it to buy a new cricket bat when the season started!

What I had enjoyed was beginner's luck, of course, although I didn't know it. Success wouldn't always come so quickly and easily. It had to be worked at, cultivated. However, for the next few weeks my good fortune continued. I made secretive calls at night several times to Mary's cottage, taking care Edwin was unaware of my visits. I didn't want him demanding a share. The money in my box dwindled, payment for her services really but also to ensure my lust got full rein. The more I had the more I wanted. I anticipated each visit with mounting pleasure. I grew fond of Mary too, a woman whose natural honesty about the enjoyment she got from making love was a rare trait. She needed the money I brought and accepted it gratefully, but welcomed my arrival each time with loving hugs and kisses, truly happy to see me. Every few days, she confessed, she craved a good fucking.

Always we took our pleasure before the fire, but now she laid blankets and cushions there to make a cosy bed. Then, without further preliminaries she would strip off to the skin and lie down with open arms to receive her boy lover. I joined her with the added pleasure of not having to hurry our session with several hours before us to indulge ourselves. Outside the wind and rain rattled the windows, making our domain all the more snug as the fire roared. She was every bit as keen as I to get satisfaction and took me in hand to ensure her own needs were catered for. She instructed, directed, took the initiative. Through her I learned the secret of finding the clitoris when fondling her cunt, and the effect it had. She calmed me in heat to prolong my orgasm for our mutual benefit. Yet looking back, good apprenticeship that it was, Mary was no sophisticate. It was always straight fucking with me on top and she below, enjoying a good shafting. I don't think she considered any other way or any different position. Neither did she ever suck me or indicate she would enjoy her cunt being licked by me. It was all so good with her, bringing her to absolute ecstasy with my probing shaft, then relaxing with fondling and kissing until the next bout ensued, that I never questioned there could be much more.

'Here, lad,' she'd say. 'I'm getting too almighty fond of your visits and they'll have me for cradle-snatching – ' But our times together came to an abrupt end. The fellow who had made her pregnant decided he would do the decent thing by her. I was tearfully informed that early in February she would be a married woman at last and was moving to his farmworkers' cottage a few miles away.

I had not forgotten Charlotte of the kiss-chase game. Armed with french letters obtained through Sam the carter, I hung around the vicarage until one afternoon as darkness was falling she appeared in the garden to unpeg the washing. I called to her from behind the stone wall where I hid and, curious, she came over to see me crouched furtively awaiting her. Later she joined me in the graveyard nearby, where with a pale moon appearing and disappearing behind low clouds, we kissed and cuddled behind a tall stone angel. Edwin had been right about her; she could not help herself once aroused. I put down my overcoat on the grass and helped myself to her plump breasts and lubricating fanny, finding her clitoris to induce her to such a state of arousal that she welcomed all advances. When I suggested we fuck she herself rolled the sheath over my prick and laid back eagerly with legs apart to receive my all. Remembering Mary's good advice I took my time and shafted her slowly to start, up to the hilt

In The Mood

and withdrawn to the knob, bringing her to lift us both bodily off the ground in her urgency. When she came, with convulsions and sighs, she declared it the best fuck she had ever experienced. Suspiciously, she asked me what I'd been up to. I wanted a second bout and made to get on her again. 'Come here tomorrow after tea when it's dark,' she said. 'I've got to go or the cook will give me what-for, leaving the sink –' But she kissed me before hurriedly straightening her clothes and bolting into the night.

I relished several such trysts but then found that another consideration precluded further meetings. Charlotte advised me to call no more on her services. She had begun recently to be courted by a steady boyfriend. They had been 'walking out' for several weeks, even while we had been meeting secretly in the graveyard. He had been to her house for Sunday tea, always a sure sign of the seriousness of the friendship. He worked for himself and had intentions of settling down. When I learned her boy was none other than Sam the carter, who had obtained the very french letters I'd used on his girl, it was with wry amusement I promised the minx I would not try to contact her further. All the same it left a void in my sexual activity difficult to fill in mid-winter.

I really was at a loose end, my run of luck over, back to consoling myself by jacking off frequently with the images of my recent successes in mind. There was Molly to spy on too when she took her Sunday evening bath, but this merely added further frustration. The outlook was bleak. Rodney was at university, Edwin at school and the weather set in blustery and wet over the whole of February and March. I merely came home from school to several hours of homework and if I ventured to the village found it deserted of people in the rain-swept night. Thus it was in desperation, seated in the kitchen one evening after tea, noting Molly washing dishes at the sink, idly considering the

In The Mood

roundness of her firm buttocks and feeling that the world was passing me by, I made the decision that perhaps what I sought was available under my own roof. She was after all but a year or two older than Mary Pullen, who had found me more than satisfactory as a lover. Her plush body would be a delight to fondle and fuck, as I well knew from viewing her. It was worth a try; wheedling my way into her affections and perhaps winning her over. I'd always been her favourite, and now with some attention and a little flattery who knows what might result? She was a lonely woman and, as a widow, had been bedded before. There was no other choice available anyway. Slim chance that it was, Molly had been elected for seduction.

There was no time like the present to start. I rose and stood beside her, picking up a drying cloth, and commenced wiping the plates stacked on the draining board. In surprise she turned and stared. 'You don't need to do that, Master Ty,' she said. 'Not that I'm ungrateful for your kindness. You get back to your homework – '

'All done,' I assured her. 'You've had a long day, Molly. I'm sure you're looking forward to getting up to your room and getting your feet up. I'll finish these dishes then clear the table for you.'

'You always were a good boy,' she praised me. 'When you were little you used to come to my room at night and pop into bed beside me, especially if you'd had a bad dream or there was thunder. Never went to your mother. We used to hug and cuddle down, then you'd toddle back to your own room in the morning before anyone knew – '

'Dear Molly,' I said, and kissed her lips. For a moment she allowed it, even kissing me back, her plump breasts pressed into my chest. Then she reddened and held me off. 'What's up, Molly?' I asked. 'I just wanted to kiss you – '

'Well, I don't know if it's right,' she said, embarrassed. 'You're a big boy now. Get on with you –'

She hung up her apron behind the door and went upstairs. A start had been made, I considered. Not a bad start.

Chapter Six

With my seduction scheme in mind, it was to my great advantage that mother decided to spend a week in London at this time. I was therefore left alone in the house with Molly, not an unusual situation. My parents often stayed at their flat in town. Now I could give my full and undivided attention to the task in hand. I'd already made full use of the past few days: praising her cooking, making a fuss of her and helping with little chores that saved her work. She thought I had turned over a new leaf and suspected nothing.

With the house to ourselves I hurried the operation. To save work I took my meals in the kitchen, the warmest place anyway, and together we grew cosy and chummy. She enjoyed the company, receiving me home from school always with a favourite meal, and afterwards we would sit before the range and toast muffins or crumpets before she went off to her room. As if in fun I began tickling her at the sink. She would giggle and scream as if in a fit, but my hands often came in contact with her huge firm bosom and she'd go strangely silent, pulling away from but obviously disturbed in a curious way, arousal at having her tits felt I was certain. She'd upbraid me, but allow more tickling, which led to me holding her and pressing against her warm body during the supposed foolery. She would blush and warn me again to keep my hands to myself but most obviously enjoyed the contact.

I insisted on kissing her too. At first she merely

In The Mood

offered her cheek but, during one of our games, holding her close face-to-face with her breasts in my chest and the beginning of a hard growing in my trousers, I placed my mouth squarely upon hers and kissed her passionately. 'Oh,' she sighed, 'you mustn't do that, boy. No, no – ' but I silenced further protests by kissing her soft lips again and again until she regained the strength to hold me off. 'I don't know what came over me, letting you do that,' she said breathlessly, having to sit down to regain her calm. 'Goodness gracious, I ought to know better. Why, I'm the same age as your ma. I'm a silly woman – '

I wasn't going to allow the situation to pass. She was still shaking from the onslaught, so I crouched before her chair and took her hand. 'There, there, dear Molly,' I said. 'I love kissing you because it's nice, because you're nice. Tell me you liked it too. Go on – '

'I'll do no such thing,' she vowed. 'It's wicked.'

'How can it be, when it's so sweet? Didn't you like it a little bit?' How well I remember buttering poor comely Molly up for my own ends, my prick surging with lust for her body. 'Come on, own up. It would be our secret.'

I saw her look down at me with tear-filled eyes. 'You shouldn't tease a lonely woman so,' she complained, sniffing. 'It was very wrong. You're just a boy. Such thoughts shouldn't enter your head, or mine. I'm going to my room.'

She went off leaving me well pleased with myself. Nor did I intend to let matters rest there. I had that week made a point of taking up her scuttle filled with coal and a few logs of wood. I gave her an hour to 'top and tail' herself, her nightly wash, then tiptoed up to her keyhole. She was wearing her nightdress, her bun untied so that her hair fell down her back, sitting contemplating the fire with a glass in her hand, her nightly gin pick-me-up. I brought the filled scuttle up to the landing, got into my pyjamas as if ready for bed,

In The Mood

then went up the next flight of stairs and tapped at her door.

I had to control my own feelings, I realised. My throat felt dry, my body shook and my prick thrust out the front of my pyjama trousers. 'What do you want?' Molly asked. 'I'm in my nightie –'

'I remembered your scuttle of coal,' I said through the door. 'It's such a cold night I'm sure you'll need it.' With that she opened up and I resisted her attempt to take it from my hand, carrying it to the hearth. The long white cotton nightdress bulged at her breasts and hips voluptuously, her nipples projected invitingly. They were definitely raised. 'Oh, Molly,' I cried, 'I do love you so,' and threw myself into her arms, holding her, throwing myself upon her mercy.

It was exactly the right strategem to employ. I was at once the pitiful creature, needing consoling. I knew she had a good heart and played on it. Also, I had aroused her during our kissing session and she had had time to ponder it, plus no doubt having a gin or two to relax the inhibitions.

'There, there,' it was now her turn to say comfortingly, patting my back as she held me, her ample breasts nicely against my chest. 'Don't take on. I knows how boys get at your age. It's all my fault, allowing you what I did . . . oh, oh,' she added, now aware that my fully stiffened prick nestled comfortably against her mound. 'We mustn't, we mustn't,' she repeated, but with little strength in her voice.

I began to move against her slowly, working my upright cock where the cloth of her nightdress bulged between her thighs. I held her tight so that there might be no escape from my arms. My mouth sought hers and she sighed, hesitated, then gave me her soft lips, allowing my tongue to probe hers. I felt her shudder, then increase her grip, moving her crotch in reply to my thrusts. I had to be careful not to come there and then. What I desired as much as my own pleasure was

In The Mood

to bring her to such heights as Mary Pullen had reached with me. That would surely lead to repeat performances without further seduction. Allowing the hot surge in my lower belly to subside somewhat, I kept up the sweet kissing and murmuring, repeating 'Dear Molly, how I love you,' over and over until she was saying 'Dear boy, oh dear boy,' and kissing me all the time as if she couldn't get enough of me.

It was time to make the next move. I guided her to the big brass bed and she fell back upon it, her legs over the side with me standing between them. When I lifted the hem of her nightie she made one last attempt to save herself. Her hand gripped my wrist, holding it. 'No, Molly, no,' I said, as masterfully as I could. 'Let go. I want to see you. I'm going to fuck you – ' Her eyes widened but she did as I ordered. I raised the nightdress up over her strong thighs, uncovering the mass of hair over her mound and cunt. Then I lifted it more, tugging until she raised her buttocks and lifted her arms. The garment went over her head and she was laid out before me gloriously naked.

It was indeed a sight to thrill, her ample flesh displayed for my pleasure. Her great tits had fallen apart; below, the wrinkled brown lips of her quim seemed parted and pink soft inner lips peeped from the hairy bower, a tighter entrance that I vowed in its turn I would penetrate. Meanwhile there was so much to see, to touch. Molly lay back looking at me as if mesmerized. I lifted both heavy teats in my hands, squeezed them, kissed them, then sucked both thimble-sized nipples making her sigh and pull my head to her breast. I then moved down, putting the tip of my tongue into her belly-button, and on until I was at eye-level with her cunt. She did not move but remained with legs parted and over the edge of the bed, her crotch thrust forward. I examined it, fingered its moistness which I knew was the sure sign of arousal. I found her clitoris and under my touch it erected like a stiff fingertip. I saw it plainly and on an impulse went forward to touch it with my tongue. It brought forth the utmost groan of pleasure from her lips. Encouraged, hardly aware of what I was doing, but impelled by an urge that made me want to do it, I covered her quim with my mouth and sucked, lapped and licked. Her moistness tasted like nectar to me.

It had the effect of making Molly react like the most wanton creature in Edwin's dirty stories. She gripped my head, raised her buttocks, thrust her cunt into my mouth and began to grind herself against my face. There was no escape. She let out loud cries, grunting helplessly until at last she fell back from me, her body twitching. 'Oh, God help me,' she said. 'It was heaven, heaven. Oh, dear boy, it was such a relief to me, you'll never know. I feel I'm eternally damned but I don't care. It was so good –'

She had no shame now and I swelled with pride at the sight of the relaxed woman before me. In the strenuous heaving she had performed while being licked out, my pyjama trousers had fallen to my ankles. I stood and kicked them aside, throwing off the jacket too, standing naked before her. She looked intently at my rampant cock, eyes widening. As if the most natural thing in the world her thighs opened for me, making an inviting cradle. I fell across her and she gripped my tool, guiding it to her orifice. 'His turn now,' she whispered.

I still intended to give her a fucking to remember for all that I was bursting with balls tight with agitated sperm, plus the fact that she had already spent strenuously. Once deeply embedded up her juicy channel I commenced the slow beginning movement which was always to be my technique. I had already recognised that my greatest pleasure was in bringing the women I fucked to heights where all modesty was cast to the winds and they performed as the most wanton

In The Mood

sluts. With Molly my system worked beautifully moments after I had sunk in her up to the balls. She crossed her legs behind my knees, lifted and thrust, whimpering and even whinnying like an excited horse. She too couldn't resist giving orders, as women do when roused enough. 'Fuck that big prick up me faster, do,' she urged. 'Shove it far up. Fuck, fuck, boy – '

When we had run full course we lay side by side on the bed. 'My Tom used to love a good rump,' she said, almost dreamily, thinking back no doubt to the young soldier dead for twenty years. 'We were both a couple of randy things on the leaves he spent. Couldn't lay off it, but then he was going back to the trenches. He enjoyed his naughties, as he called what he liked to do – '

'And did you, Molly?' I asked.

'So I did,' she said. 'But then we was both youngsters.'

I reached across to fondle her tits, overflowing in my cupped hand. 'What did he want that was so naughty?' I enquired.

'That would be telling,' Molly giggled. 'Goodness, what I let you do is naughty enough. I should be ashamed of myself – '

'But you're not, are you?' I insisted. 'Because it was so nice and we both wanted it. No harm in that – '

'Plenty if they got to know of it in the village,' Molly warned. 'Why, I'd be tarred and feathered. I used to put your nappies on you when you were a babe. And now – now – '

'Now we've fucked,' I said, putting the words in her mouth. I kissed her lingeringly, my hand going down to her well-lubricated cunt. 'And we will again before long. Let me stay the night.'

Stay that night I did after sweet talk, cajoling and fondling that wore down her resistance. And so I did for the next four nights. It was marvellous to have her nakedness to cuddle against, breasts beside my face to

In The Mood

play with and nipples to suck upon until I drowsed into sleep. Molly proved a surprise in many ways once she had given up her guilt about our association. After a good fucking, when she cuddled down with me in the friendly darkness, she loved to reminisce. Oh, she had courted a few chaps before Tom married her. Lusty fellows by all accounts. Then there had been her first employment, maid to a tenant farmer whose wife was crabbed, an ill-tempered woman. Well, he had to get a bit of pleasure, didn't he? That, Molly shyly confessed, was how her virginity went at the age of sixteen. Proper good at it, he was, she giggled. 'Made me too keen on it – and it seems I still am,' she admitted, kissing me fondly. As for husband Tom's 'naughties', I wheedled that out of her too. She had nothing further to hide from me. Tom, it seemed, had dearly loved her plump bottom. He made her kneel with her bare buttocks raised for close inspection, when he would fondle it, kiss it, part her cheeks to finger her, give it friendly slaps – and do worse than that, she hinted darkly, giggling at the memory.

I determined to enjoy the same and the following evening before we got into bed she agreed to my request. There was no doubt that, decent woman though she was and despite her long abstinence, she was more sexually skilled than Mary Pullen, with three illegitimate children to show for her lapses. Molly it was who introduced me to varying positions. She loved to squat over me impaled on my prick and marrow-like tits dangling over my face to suck upon. Another first – I awoke one morning with a start, fancying I was dreaming of fucking, to find her with the bedclothes drawn back and busily sucking upon my shaft. Shyly she told me she had done so often with Tom, but did not like to mention it to me at my tender age. I told her to proceed and she gobbled away until I heaved and shot my seed deep into her throat. Once I had her do this to me in the kitchen, on my arrival

In The Mood

home from school, when after some cuddles and kisses and a passionate plea, she unbuttoned me and got down upon her knees to suck avidly until I fetched her a mouthful.

So it was as we were naked and about to get into bed that she got on all fours on the counterpane, displaying her broad buttocks in all their splendid glory. Perhaps she did it for me, or in memory of the long-lost Tom, or just because she liked to do so for her own pleasure. Suffice to say the two big firm fleshy moons before me were a delight for a young lecher to touch, smooth, tickle and kiss. I parted the cheeks, gazing long at her arse-hole before looking down the cleft to between her thighs, where nestled a fat juicy cunt, slightly parted as if readied for penetration. My prick stood out as never before, a mere inch or so from her opening. 'Oh, Molly,' I cried, and thrust my hips forward, taking her from the rear and sinking inches into her channel first go.

She reared with a groan, then went back on her elbows, pushing her buttocks hard into my groin, taking my all. Still embedded in her, I hunched over her waist, my hands going beneath her to grab her hanging tits and grip them for purchase while I fucked away lustily. This time there was no slow movement on my part. Utterly lost in the lustful feel of her buttocks against me, I thrust away on tip-toe to get deeper. My balls slapped against her cheeks. She reared again, crying out, 'Oh, oh, oh, what you are doing to me, young fucker. Ram it in. Split my arse. Take it out and shove it up my bumhole –'

I had no doubt then that is what the buxom widow had enjoyed with her late husband. The idea intrigued me too, but I was too far gone. My body heaved involuntarily and I ejaculated what seemed a non-stop jet of come into her. She practically galloped in her own spasms, matched perfectly with my own jerkings and shudders. As my limp dick withdrew from her cunt

In The Mood

some second sight made me turn toward the door. It was ajar slightly and there stood my mother with a glazed expression on her face. To my great relief she closed the door quickly and silently, and was gone.

What to do at that precise moment needed careful thought. Molly was still crouched before me, bottom raised, recovering from her fucking, shoulders heaving as she gasped for breath. No doubt during our excitement I had not heard my parents' car approach on the gravelled driveway. My mother had seen us in the last stages of our fuck at least, but had departed stiff-lipped, no doubt too shocked to raise the roof at that moment. I decided Molly would remain ignorant of the fact we had been observed, hoping mother would ignore what she had seen or at the worst put the entire blame on me. After all, I was in Molly's room and must have gone there of my own volition. I'd take what was to come and consider it worth the experiences of that week. So I shook the still crouched Molly and informed her I had heard a car in the drive.

She sat up like a scalded cat, reaching for her nightdress. I put on my pyjamas and went to my room. I heard my parents coming upstairs, go their way past my door to the main bedroom, and then all was quiet in the house. In my bed I stifled a laugh at the thought of Molly and I being caught in the dog-fuck position, evidently according to Edwin one that my mother enjoyed herself. I fell asleep shortly, pleasantly exhausted by my earlier exertions. In the morning when I arose I found Molly in the kitchen as normal, making breakfast. I cycled off to school hopeful that nothing would come of the matter.

Chapter Seven

Perhaps my mother was too embarrassed to make an issue of what she had observed in Molly's room, or maybe she had no intention of losing the services of a good servant. Molly went about happily unaware we had been caught in the act, but I was not to escape lightly. A few evenings later I was called into the lounge, where my parents were having a cocktail before proceeding to the dining-room. Father looked unusually serious and informed me it had been decided I should leave at once for boarding school, miles out of the way in another county. All that was necessary had been bought and packed in a trunk. The next morning I was on my way to start as a new boy in Rossall Abbey, renowned for discipline and the healthy outlook it imparted to its pupils. The subject of my being seen fucking Molly was not mentioned, but I knew well enough the reason for my sudden exile.

My form at Rossall Abbey, I discovered, was a hotbed of randy boys, aged sixteen and deprived of the sight of girls just when the opposite sex and their mysteries was the uppermost thing in mind. Consequently the dormitories after 'lights out' became veritable masturbation factories, both solitary and mutual. Despite the warnings of the awful effects of self-abuse, 'Wankers Doom' as it was cheerfully known, tossing-off oneself or doing it to a friend was the only vice available. Gallons of sperm must have been shed, coaxed by hand each night. Sheets and pyjamas were

In The Mood

stiff with dried spunk. 'Oh, sir, it was the dream I had,' went the excuse.

I made friends with a large cheerful youth called Dinky Pettifer. His sexual exploits matched my own, I discovered on comparing notes. During various hols he had fucked both his cousins, one of whom was nineteen, and a kitchen maid at his uncle's house. Some village girls too, and a black whore in a fashionable house of prostitution during a visit to Paris. There was more, he hinted darkly, and not a million miles away, but he had been sworn to secrecy.

He had been named Dinky because his prick was the largest in the school, as proved in competition. I was glad to note in the showers after games that I more than matched him. He had an admirer, a girl-faced boy known as Dolly-darling, who was to be his undoing. A few weeks after my arrival they were caught in bed together. Despite claiming that they had done so because of the cold night and had huddled together for warmth, Dinky was expelled. Darling, that was his actual surname, escaped with a caution. He swore Dinky had forced him to share his bed, which all the boys knew was farthest from the truth. His powerful father was also a patron of the school, which no doubt helped his plea.

With Dinky gone, Darling turned his attention to me. Waking one night I realised a hand was below my blankets, lightly massaging my tumescent tool. It was too pleasant to stop. I groaned as if in disturbed sleep and the hand rubbed harder, expertly. Soon I came off with a shudder, polluting myself in a torrent. As the shadowy figure slipped away I saw it was young Darling. The treatment was repeated over several nights until, with growing confidence, the kneeling figure beside my bed drew back the sheet and covered my rampant cock with his lips. His mouth was warm and wet, the sucking motion drew me in deeper until his face was almost against my stomach. At least, I

In The Mood

thought, I won't be making a mess with my come. He sucked avidly and I let it continue until the surge came up from my testicles and I gripped a handful of hair and held him to me, filling his mouth. I heard him swallow, then pad off into the gloom. The next day in class I was passed a note from him, read by a dozen boys en route who giggled loudly, attracting the teacher's notice.

'Bring that to me,' he intoned. 'Don't try to hide it, boy.' My heart sank as I went forward to his desk. To be expelled after leaving home under a cloud was the last thing I wanted. 'What does this mean?' the master said, thrusting the note under my nose. It said simply: 'Did you like what we did last night? Do please be my special friend. Love D.' I was hauled off to the headmaster's study for interrogation.

I denied anything improper had taken place between myself and Darling, swearing that no more had happened than he had approached me to be his friend. We had talked and told jokes. The note was his way of reminding me he had asked to be my chum. Knowing of the recent incident with Pettifer I had decided against it. Reluctantly, the wizened headmaster released me from his study and I breathed a sigh of relief. But that evening I was told to report to his study again. This time his wife was there, a dried-up old crone with a slit of a mouth who had taken it upon herself to guard the morals of her husband's pupils. A boy had seen Darling beside my bed, had reported it sneakily, and I was branded a liar. There and then I was told to bend over the arm of his study chair, with trousers down to my ankles, and given six hard thwacks with the cane across my bare buttocks. Even the thought of the old witch watching with eyes gleaming gave my prick a stirring. Added to the heat of the strokes across my buttocks it reared healthily. When I stood to pull up my trousers it stuck out in all its glory, a fine specimen.

In The Mood

'Disgusting boy,' spat out the head's wife, nevertheless looking her fill. 'Get out of here. He's lucky not to be expelled, isn't he, Godfrey?'

'Very,' agreed her husband. 'There had better be no more nonsense. As it is I shall place him under restriction to the school grounds and ensure he has extra duties.'

So I escaped expulsion. But if the head's wife had regarded my rampant cock with apparent horror, she had been impressed enough by its girth and length to describe it to others among the teachers's wives, I suspect. I was given work to do, as a punishment, sweeping the paths for instance. Whenever one of the wives went by I noted I was under close scrutiny, whereas boys were usually ignored as lesser mortals. One teacher in class even dared a reference to my claim to fame. The word 'gargantuan' came up and he smirked and made me stand to give the explanation, adding I should know very well what it meant. The class of boys understood his sly tribute and much hilarity ensued. For my part I stuck out my chest, pleased to receive the accolade. In truth my prick was a giant, and still growing.

One cold dry afternoon near the end of March I played football and after the game the other boys went off to shower. I was under probation and as part of my punishment had to return the goal nets and corner flags to the games' store in a handcart. This was a former stable next to the cottage occupied by Mr Cave and his aloof wife, Stephanie. Cave was the classics master, a tall cadaverous man with staring eyes and a perpetually blue chin, well named 'The Skull' by his pupils. He was at least fifteen years older than his wife, who was perhaps not yet thirty.

She taught first-year French to the younger boys, a smart tall woman who wore the largest and roundest spectacles I'd ever seen, making her face somewhat owl-like. She was attractive, all the same, with thick

In The Mood

black hair which she wore drawn back from a centre parting in severe Victorian style. Her lips were full and slightly parted, moist and made for kissing. Like everyone else at the school she had a nickname from the pupils, who were well aware of her femininity in a desert of females. 'Iron Drawers' she was called for her severe manner. In class she was a tyrant that made small boys cower and wet themselves in terror. Her best assets to my lecherous eyes were her big bosom and fine rounded buttock cheeks so nicely prominent under the tight tweed skirts she favoured. She also invariably dressed in loose silk blouses of bright colours which could not disguise the size of her breasts. They thrust out before her like magnificent domes and such was their fullness they bulged sideways to her arms as well. When she was taking her class I looked in through the window to admire her splendid figure whenever passing.

I was locking the games' store when she drew up outside her cottage in her box-like Austin car. She got out, looking smart in a wide brimmed hat with veil and fur-collared black coat. Her stockings were of fine black silk too, the colour of mystery. I could imagine the smooth white flesh where her stockings reached and silken knickers began. Of course such a woman would wear the finest undergarments. She noted my interest and demanded to know what I was doing there.

'Putting away sports' gear,' I explained curtly. I was cold and fed up being the dogsbody. Who was she to regard me so imperiously?

'You will address me as ma'am, or Mrs Cave,' she replied sharply, 'and not in that tone of voice.' Her eyes narrowed. 'You're the Wight boy, aren't you?' It sounded like an accusation.

'Yes, ma'am.'

'Well, bring my packages into the cottage for me.'

She went inside and I was left to carry several par-

In The Mood

cels and a basket of shopping into the hallway. I was still in my soccer gear including studded boots, and I waited to be dismissed beside a potted fern on a tall stand. When she reappeared she had taken off her hat and coat, revealing a purple blouse bulging as ever with magnificent thrusting tits that bobbed as she walked.

'Take off those boots and take the packages through to the kitchen,' she ordered. I did as bid, noting a kettle sitting on the lighted gas ring. 'Will you take tea?' she said to my surprise. Without waiting for a reply she added, 'Go through to the parlour.'

In the parlour I stood waiting, with dirty knees and socks fallen to my ankles. I heard the kettle whistle. It was a chintzy room with comfortable covered sofa and armchairs, vases of early flowers, a piano and shelves of books. A banked fire glowed in the fireplace behind a wired guard. Mrs Cave came in with a tiered plate-holder. She had brought small neatly cut triangled sandwiches, biscuits and cakes, which she placed on a low coffee table before the sofa.

'Sit,' she commanded.

I sat, while she poked the fire, adding one or two lumps of coal, placing them precisely after removing the fireguard. While she was bent over the hearth accomplishing this I watched furtively. Her back to me and kneeling, I could see the heavy droop of a breast under her arm, such was its mass. The tweed skirt was stretched tightly across her glorious backside, letting me view flaring hips and the ripeness of her bum cheeks. She was, without doubt, the most fuckable of creatures within miles. I pictured her naked, bending over the fire, with me going behind her to put my hand under her cleft to draw a finger slowly along her liquid lips.

'There,' she said, turning and rising. The smallest movement made her tits move beneath the blouse like live things. 'It's still wintry and dark early – ' She

In The Mood

drew the curtains after switching on a tall brass lamp. The comfortable room seemed at once much cosier.

'Eat, boy,' she again commanded, leaving the room.

I was tucking into the potted meat sandwiches when she returned with a second tray bearing a silver teapot, cups, milk and sugar. She poured tea for me and one for herself, regarding me over the rim of her cup as she sat directly opposite in an armchair, long silken legs crossed and the tight skirt risen to above her knees. I was under close scrutiny.

At last she said, almost to herself, 'You *are* a big fellow for your age,' as if she had doubted before. 'You were good friends with Pettifer, I believe? Where is he now?'

'Switzerland, ma'am. At another school – '

'He writes to you?'

'Only once. He's not much at writing, I think.'

'Did he ... did he mention me?' She was watching my face intently as if to detect any lie. The atmosphere was what authors called 'electric'.

'Why, no, Mrs Cave.' My surprise was evident.

She nodded, apparently satisfied, even relieved. 'No reason why he should, of course,' she said, almost too nonchalantly. 'Except my husband recommended his expulsion. A bad influence that boy.'

I said nothing, but nodded as if in agreement. She pursed her cupid-bow lips almost sardonically, the witch.

'Well,' she continued, still with almost an undisguised smirk on her face. 'I know you yourself were most fortunate not follow him in expulsion. It couldn't be proved, I know, but you were seen in the night with that creature Darling at your beside – '

'That was all,' I pleaded. 'I told him to get away from me.'

'Did you now? Well, well,' she said, exactly like a spider with a fly. 'Look at me when I'm talking to you.

In The Mood

Nothing that girl-boy Darling gets up to surprises me. No doubt he seduced you.'

Her eyes narrowed, as if daring me to deny it. I squirmed under her stare. For this cool creature to be saying such things, obviously salaciously curious, had the effect of making my prick stir inside my shorts. I could only think she was arousing herself and doing so to me in the process.

'Don't be too ashamed about it,' she advised. 'Adolescent boys do these things, I'm well aware, seeking excitement and relief. No doubt he did tempt you, but you must put that sort of boyish thing from your mind. You're too manly for that.'

'Yes, Mrs Cave,' I said obediently, all I could think of.

'Then he did seduce you,' she said, almost triumphantly. I saw her move in the deep armchair, as if rubbing her thighs. 'What exactly did you two do? Come on, you can tell me. It will go no further. Confession is good for the soul.'

Whether it is or not I have always doubted. I did know her presence, leaning forward slightly with heavy spherical breasts bulging her blouse, heady perfume reeking in my nostrils and her intimate questions, all had my ever-ready prick rearing. Or rather, it would have reared had it not been imprisoned in my football shorts in a sitting position. There was only one way it could grow and that was outwards. I actually feared its plum head would project through a leg of the shorts. Mrs Cave's gaze lowered, well aware of what was taking place, appraising the enlarging tumescence with her usual calm. I wondered if inside she was as cold and calculating, or would her cunt be lubricating? She squeezed her knees and shifted.

'Tell me what that boy did to you,' she ordered.

'He . . . rubbed me, ma'am,' I whispered, burning.

'No doubt. Was that all?'

'Yes.'

In The Mood

'I don't believe you – '

'That was all.'

'Did you sodomise him? You know what I mean, I'm sure. Buggery. Pettifer did, on many occasions.'

I didn't know that and wondered how she did. 'Nothing like that happened,' I swore.

'Did he want you to? He would have – '

'I don't know,' I said. 'I hardly spoke to him.' Of course there were his nightly visits, the quick hand-jobs and that one delightful gobble he gave me. I wasn't admitting to that.

'He just rubbed you,' she shrugged, 'nothing else. Tell the truth. Did he suck your penis?'

'No, Mrs Cave. Truly. Only rubbed me.'

She nodded resignedly, almost disappointed I imagined. 'And you liked that? Did you ejaculate?'

'Yes. He made me. But I didn't know what he was doing – '

'Whatever do you mean?'

'I was asleep. When I awoke . . . he was rubbing me.'

'Hmmm. You didn't stop him. So you enjoyed it – '

'I suppose so.'

'No suppose about it. You let him do it often after that.'

I remained silent and she said, 'He did it to you many times, I'm sure. I know what boys are like. You don't have to tell me.'

Again I squirmed under her gaze. I put my hands on my lap, hoping to cover my embarrassing hardness. Had I been but sure of her intentions I would have let it show proud. I could not risk expulsion and considered her a torturer.

'Can I go now, please?' I begged. 'I've got to shower before dinner and prayers. The water will be cold if I don't go – '

'You can shower here,' she said abruptly. 'There's plenty of hot water. Come.'

She stood waiting until I rose from the sofa. My

shorts were erected like a bell tent. 'Boys!' she uttered. 'If your brains were down there, teaching would be less trouble. What has made it so?'

She knew very well and so did I, yet I mumbled that I did not know. I followed her to a tiled and chromed bathroom such as I had never seen yet in old country houses. No wonder my mother often wished, or claimed to wish, to live in one of the smart new modern bungalows just appearing. There was a long bath with marble boxed sides, a wash-hand basin on a pedestal, a low toilet and that French importation the bidet, all in pastel pink. Around the bath was a railed curtain in waterproof material, and a shower spray head affixed to the tiled wall.

Mrs Cave turned on the water, adjusted the control, and held long slim fingers under the spray. 'About right,' she assessed. 'Take off your things and get in – '

Chapter Eight

I hesitated to strip as Mrs Cave made no attempt to leave. Another thought worried me too. 'Mr Cave,' I asked, 'won't he mind me using his shower?'

'Why should he? He's in London, giving an illustrated lecture on Ancient Greece this evening. Now get on –'

I pulled my striped jersey over my head. Mrs Cave, I observed, regarded my bare shoulders and chest. Her hand hovered over my shoulder, brushed at a fleck of mud. 'You'll need a fresh towel,' she said. 'I'll get one. Don't forget to draw the shower curtain or you'll flood the place.'

Under the warm spray I soaped myself luxuriously, pondering my situation, aroused and intrigued. How far was she wanting to go with the charade? It was a question I was often to ask myself, and women in such a situation could help greatly by letting one know. How many chances have been missed by the randy male being unsure with a willing female who would not reveal that willingness? Mrs Cave, I was certain, was to say the least 'curious' about me. Did she wish to 'play' with me, as she had wormed out of me what Darling had done? I hoped so. The thought made my still turgid prick rear. I soaped it and it responded as ever, growing thicker and longer under my administrations, hard as an iron bar and straining. A few quick strokes would see it off, and it would be lascivious to send my spunk flying where the voluptuous Stephanie

In The Mood

must have been naked. The thought excited me tremendously and I was cock in hand giving it the old one-two when the curtain rattled back on its rings and she stood before me holding a large fluffy towel.

'What *are* you doing?' she said coldly.

'Soaping myself,' I replied feebly. I took my hand off my prick reluctantly, and it reared red and angry.

Her eyes remained fixed on my rampantness as she handed me the towel. 'Dry yourself off, young man. Why is *that* in a state of excitement?' She reached across to turn off the spray.

'Because of you, and your questions. It made me want to do this to myself – ' I heard my voice saying. I gave her a feeble smile of excuse, and perhaps for her to pity me.

'I'll dry you,' she announced, enveloping my shoulders in the towel. For the first time I hopefully suspected a catch in her cool tone. She sounded huskier, edgy. Her hands rubbed my shoulders, arms and back through the towel, which hung from my shoulders like a cloak. Then her right hand moved below the towel, resting lightly on my buttocks. For a moment she actually caressed the smooth skin, drawing her palm across both cheeks as she took her hand away. I heard her draw in breath.

'Oh, Mrs Cave,' I sighed. John Thomas stood straight up from my balls, erect as a soldier.

'Is your erection painful?' she enquired. 'It looks so very inflamed.'

'It's so stiff it hurts me,' I whined. 'I can't help it – '

'Very well. You can relieve yourself.'

'You do it,' I said boldly. 'It's nicer. I mean when someone else – '

Her eyes narrowed at me. 'I know what you mean. All right, just this once. To get it over with – '

She took my prick in her left hand, standing outside the bath, the other hand cupping my buttocks as if to steady me. Slowly at first she rubbed, uncapping the

In The Mood

head, moving her wrist, her slender fingers grasped about my stalk. It was so delicious with the woman doing it so gently that I writhed in ecstasy and she ordered me sharply to stand still. I crouched slightly, then stood erect; all the time the soft rub-rub went on tormentingly. She was exceedingly good at it, now moving faster, now slowing to a regular stroke, my cock throbbing in her hand. 'Oh, ahh,' I groaned. 'Lovely, lovely. Don't stop, don't stop. Oh, Mrs Cave –'

Her free hand slid between my buttock cleft as my knees buckled, her fingers stroking my balls, touching my anus with pointed nails, even venturing to enter teasingly. 'So heavy, so full,' she said, her voice almost a whisper as she cupped my bollocks, weighing them. I let out a final groan, straightened up and convulsed, shooting several gouts of thick come the length of the bath. I shook, gasped, gave a final shudder and the deed was done. Several large gobbets of spunk stuck to the slope at the far end of the bath and I saw a tap drip my slime like a snotty nose.

'Better?' she asked. 'Don't worry. I'll clean the bath. You too. Stand there.'

She rinsed a face flannel in warm water at the washbasin and meticulously sponged off my steaming prick, stroking and wiping, all the time holding it in her hand. She took her time, sponging my balls and pubic hair until the inevitable occurred and it stirred in her grasp. Still she continued, uncapping the head and dabbing at the tender pink glans. She seemed engrossed by the task. Soon my prick stiffened noticeably in her hand, stretching out and increasing its girth.

'Surely not,' she said admonishingly, the one to blame for my condition. 'Not so soon. Whatever is up with it?'

'It's so nice. It's you, Mrs Cave.'

'You can't need relief again already –'

'I believe I could,' I dared. 'If you rub it for me again.'

In The Mood

'Get dressed,' she ordered. She went to the washbasin and sluiced her fingers. 'Put on your things and leave. It will soon be time for prayers –'

I was in the hall on my way to the door when she appeared out of the lounge. 'Not a word of this,' she warned, 'or you will certainly not be invited here again.' The threat was more than enough, and the implication was obvious that other 'relief' sessions might take place. 'This has been strictly between you and I –'

Words of warning from older women to young men they have dallied with must have echoed down the centuries. 'Of course, Mrs Cave,' I promised. 'Strictly between you and I. Always.'

'Then remember that. You would like to visit again?'

'Oh yes, very much,' I assured her. 'More than anything –'

'Good,' she said nodding. 'Then no more foolishness with young Darling. Avoid him.'

So saying, she looked at me steadily behind her large round spectacles as if considering something. Then she took my face in her long slender fingers and advanced her lips to mine. They were soft and yielding. They parted and a long warm wet tongue went in over mine, its tip flicking the roof of my mouth. There in the hallway our bodies pressed together, her breasts squashing against my chest. Of course I responded immediately in time-honoured fashion, holding her and moving forward with rhythmic pelvic movements, belly to belly and hard against the junction of her thighs. She allowed this for a long moment and my own tongue probed deep into her mouth. Then she held me away.

'We don't want you getting another of your painful erections, do we?' she said, lips compressed in sly humour. 'Go now or you'll be late.'

Of course she knew very well she had given me a throbbing hard-on, but I left her house in the highest

In The Mood

of spirits. What luck, and a fine young married woman too! I looked forward eagerly to the opportunity of fucking her, having those lovely tits bared and fondling and kissing them, sucking her nipples until they grew taut. Mrs Cave, I felt, was going to make my stay at Rossall Abbey a memorable event in my life.

My mind was filled with nothing but the delectable Stephanie over the following days but I saw little of her, occasionally passing each other around the school premises. She never gave me so much as a glance, aloof as ever she was. The anti-climax was hard to bear but I consoled myself she was being careful not to show in any manner that something special had happened between us. She was also, I suspect, hanging fire to judge whether I had kept my word and not boasted of what had taken place in the cottage. All went very normally for all but me.

I had hoped for a secret smile in passing, a nod of the head, or a note slipped in my hand. To give her such a chance I loitered wherever I might meet her. Almost a week went by and I was reluctantly coming to the conclusion that the lovely Mrs Cave of the ever-bobbing breasts had toyed with me for her own amusement, and having played had satisfied her whim. Then I saw her as I was leaving a class with shoving and skylarking boys surrounding me on a flight of stone steps. I hesitated, looking longingly as she went by, then was pushed and fell awkwardly down the steps to land at her feet with a badly sprained ankle.

'Stand back and give him air,' she ordered my classmates as they crowded around. They fell back under her sharp voice. Then she kneeled and raised my trouser leg, gently as possible, her fingers cool and soft as she examined my injury. Already it had swollen until my ankle was twice its size and turning a splendid purple. 'Can you stand?' she asked. 'Some of you boys help him to his feet – '

In The Mood

So it was without further words from her that I was half-carried to the school's infirmary, the only patient. My ankle was strapped and I was confined to bed in pyjamas, my school books brought to me, and the only company the aged matron who brought me meals considered fit for an invalid, mainly gruel and steamed fish. I cursed my luck. From my bed all I could see were the bare branches of trees beyond the window. Time hung heavy and, worst of all, there was no possibility of getting a secret invite to the enchanted cottage. I did not even dare have a wank to relieve my feelings, as matron insisted I use a bottle or bedpan and remain off my feet, precluding visits to the privacy of the toilet.

On my third evening I heard voices outside the door and who should enter beside the matron but *my* Mrs Cave! She wore a belted camel's hair overcoat and her dark hair was covered by a silk scarf. In her hand was a paper bag with grapes. My heart leapt and my loins stirred at the sight of her but I was cunning enough to hide my feelings. She chatted to matron, ignoring me completely as if I were part of the furnishings. They discussed the wild winds and rain we had been having, how it was still indeed quite unseasonably cold for what was officially springtime, and where they intended to spend the forthcoming Easter holidays. I huffed and grimaced as if in mortal agony but neither took the slightest notice until the matron remarked that I was a difficult patient; so restless, she added, like a caged animal. I saw the ghost of a smile pass across Stephanie Cave's attractive face.

'I'll stay with him a while,' she said, glancing at her wristwatch. 'I want to see if he's completed the studying my husband set him. It's your hour off, isn't it? Don't you have dinner at this time?'

As an interested party I listened avidly and my hopes rose at the thought of being alone with the cool woman who spoke so ingenuously to the unsuspecting

In The Mood

matron, who thanked her kindly. 'I'll be glad to see the back of him,' matron said as the two women walked to the door. 'Such an *agitated* boy. All that energy, I suppose, and forced to lie in bed. If he'd been a junior I'd have smacked his bottom for him – '

Mrs Cave smiled sweetly as she closed the door behind the matron. 'Take your time,' were her parting words. Looking at her tall curvaceous figure as she slipped off her overcoat I noted her breasts hung loosely under her blouse. She took off her headscarf, placing it with her coat on an empty bed, coming towards me swaying her hips insolently. I had no doubt she was a highly sexed adventuress, given to games of seduction, and I was by no means the first of her husband's pupils chosen to amuse her. The thought made my prick rear, raising the sheet. I would play along with her, but was already considering a time when, after sampling the kind of fucking I intended to give her, it would not be such a one-sided arrangement.

'Would you have liked that?' she said teasingly. 'Matron taking your pyjama trousers down to smack your bare bottom? It may well have relieved your . . . agitation. Has it been so very hard for you?'

I felt every one of her words were carefully chosen to titillate, herself as well as I. She drew up a chair beside my bed and leaned forward, her heavy breasts filling the front of her blouse. 'Thank you for coming to see me,' I said, quite soppily like a stricken swain, which was how I imagined she wanted her slaves to act over her. I touched her hand, which rested on the bedcover. 'I've thought of you all the time – '

'Silly schoolboy crush,' she said severely, 'and when you are better you must stop trying to catch my eye. I was well aware of you hanging around where I'd be between classes. That must stop, silly boy.'

'I'm sorry. I didn't mean any harm,' I pleaded.

'It was rather sweet, I suppose, but no more of it. Did you want to see me so badly –?'

In The Mood

'Yes, oh yes – '

She nodded, smiling, satisfied and pleased she had an ardent worshipper. 'May I kiss you, please?' I dared ask. Time was wasting. 'I want to, very much – '

'Well. Just once then,' she conceded.

She licked her full lips and pressed her mouth to mine, tongue protruding after a moment's pressure. One slender hand held the back of my neck, pulling me close. Then she broke away, removing her spectacles. 'What we are doing is very naughty, you must know. Dangerous too, if discovered – '

'I'd never tell. Never,' I vowed. 'I love you – '

'Come now,' she smiled. 'You only think that.'

'It's true!'

'Puppy love, but sweet, sweet,' she consoled me, taking my face in her hands and kissing my eyes, nose and cheeks in turn. Then she gave an audible sigh, almost a groan, and covered my mouth with her open lips, circling mine in an 'O' with her warm tongue probing. Again the free hand sought the back of my neck to pull me closer. In turn I reached to cup the smooth firm orbs of her heavy tits so enticingly hanging before me. I fondled, squeezed, scratched the hardening nipples, until she straightened her back and began undoing the buttons from the high neck down to her waist. As the blouse opened it revealed startlingly big mammaries that nestled together, such was their fullness and size. She had come wearing nothing to impede sight and touch of the glorious objects. My head was brought forward as she lifted one with nipple aimed and it was fed to my eager mouth.

I sucked both in turn, drawing as much of her breasts into my maw as I could. She smoothed my hair, cuddled me, sighed and caressed me, moving as if finding her seat uncomfortable she so shifted her bottom. Then she lifted my chin and kissed me deeply again while my hand went back to fondle her raw wet breasts. We had not spoken but now she said, 'Are

In The Mood

they nice? Do you like them –? See, my nipples are quite erect and tender through you.'

Remembering the advice Mary Pullen had given me about women in the throes liking lewd talk, I told her they were marvellous tits, made for sucking, that I wished there was milk there for me to draw from her big nipples. She drew back in momentary surprise, as if suspecting I was not the complete innocent.

'Why did you say that? It was rather crude –'

'That is how I felt. They are marvellous, beautiful. I love to suck and play with them. Let me suck them again –'

'No, they are sore enough. You may look at them.' She sat back in the chair with the blouse wide open, thrusting her breasts forward. The nipples were indeed deep red from my administrations. My saliva glistened on them. She in turn watched my face. Her hand on the bedcover lifted until two fingers stood like legs and walked forward to the mound my engorged prick had raised under the sheet. She drew the two fingers along each side of the shaft, making its shape mould the covers. 'I suppose it's painful again,' she suggested teasingly. 'In need of relief –'

I sat up with my elbows on the pillows as she peeled back the sheet. My pyjama front gaped open and my rod stood up like a truncheon, hard as wood. Below it my balls nestled in their nest of thick hair and it was to them her attention was first attracted. She cupped and squeezed them as I had to her tits, but I reached forward and placed her cool fingers around my hot rammer. I wanted to order her to wank it, but again she looked at me with surprise at my forwardness. Nevertheless she began the slow rub-rub movement she was so expert at, uncapping the head as it grew even more rigid under her stroke. I lolled back and groaned, my hips lifting.

'No,' she warned. 'There'll be a mess –'

'I'll clean it up,' I gritted. 'Finish it!'

In The Mood

'It will show. Traces. Matron – '

'Fuck matron,' I swore. 'I'll do it myself.' Such was my state I took her hand and worked it up and down.

'You're quite masterful in your way,' she said, not in a reproachful manner, but rather grudgingly, accepting I had a will of my own. She looked down at the rearing prick in her hand as if deciding. 'There is a method,' she admitted. 'I mean to save any mess after . . . after ejaculation. Has it ever been sucked?'

'No,' I lied, 'but I think it would be a great idea!'

Her head dipped and her lips brushed my uncovered knob. She kissed it lingeringly, then licked around the shaft, holding it firmly upright in her hand. 'Don't come yet,' she said in her old strict voice. She wanted to make it last! I controlled my urge and she bent further over, roving her nipple tips around the glistening fiery red plum. She encompassed my whole shaft within the cleavage of her creamy breasts, moving up and down with it trapped between while she clasped them together. The urgency returned within me. I writhed and twisted. Quickly she released my prick and covered it with her soft lips, sucking avidly until I was drawn deep in. I grasped her head, heaving my thighs into her face.

'Suck, suck,' I ordered. 'Suck my balls dry – '

'Yes,' she mumbled, my cock throbbing in her mouth. 'Tell me! Say what you like. Talk to me – ' I saw her hips writhe in helpless arousal, her knees rubbing together to give friction to her cunt. She half-rose from the chair, excited now and sucking harder, her tongue working and making slurping gobbly sounds. I was delighted by her complete wantonness in the throes of an orgasm. That it was before my very eyes while sucking my prick meant nothing to her at that moment. Uncaring, and helpless to be otherwise, she drew my sperm up from my balls by suction.

'Take it down the throat, swallow it,' I shouted in my intense excitement. 'Cocksucking bitch, eat it – '

In The Mood

Her head bobbing over my prick she swallowed and cried, 'Fuck my mouth. Fuck it for me – ' In answer I increased my hip movements and felt the molten flow of spunk leap from my cock in jets, drenching her tonsils I am certain. She shook and convulsed, swallowing hard, then as I collapsed back utterly drained she seized me and kissed my mouth fervently with the taste of my come on her lips.

I watched then as she crossed to the washbasin to rinse her hands and straighten her hair. She buttoned the blouse, looked in the mirror to brush something from the corner of her mouth, then put on the coat and scarf she had placed on the empty bed. It was not a moment too soon. A tentative tap sounded at the door and matron looked in.

'You weren't long,' Stephanie Cave said, unruffled and calm as ever. 'Has it been an hour?'

'No. It was rissoles for dinner. I didn't fancy any. I thought I'd come back and have some steamed haddock when I make the boy's supper. Was your visit satisfactory?'

'Very. He's progressing. We had a nice French lesson, didn't we?' she said, turning to me. She left the room with the matron and I heard them chatting normally beyond the door. I sank back in a stupor, gloriously sated. She, the cool Cave, was a horny cow. I wouldn't rest until I had fucked the pouting silky black-haired cunt between her splendid thighs.

Chapter Nine

Released from the infirmary, my period of extra work punishment and restriction to the school premises ended. I could now join other boys on the once-a-month Saturday afternoon outing to a nearby market town. It was our only chance to buy sweets, banned magazines, cigarettes and other contraband, or pick up with a local girl. Besotted with my sweet-smelling older married woman, I intended to buy her a present. I'd then wait for an appropriate moment to surprise her, hopefully during another visit to her school quarters.

I was leaving a class bearing an armful of books when the desirable one approached on her way to take a class. A throng of boys in the corridor parted for her, respectfully making a passage. Stephanie halted, eyed me sternly, then called me to her. If I appeared nervous at her singling me out, I was not the only boy to be so. She had that effect on all the pupils.

'Do I detect forbidden reading matter, Wight?' she demanded, inspecting my books wherein, like the other boys, I often secreted comics. I was handed them back silently and she went on her imperious way. To a man the boys stood admiring the full and shapely cheeks of her arse moving under her tailored skirt. One heard the expelling of breath, wistful sighs all around, an exclaimed 'Gaw!' I noted the edge of a paper projecting from one of the books like a bookmark. It had not been there before.

I bolted myself in a toilet for privacy and read with

In The Mood

my hands trembling. The message bore no address or signature, was written in capital letters to disguise the handwriting. It began 'DESTROY,' then in the fewest words instructed, 'TWO O'CLOCK OUTSIDE MOORE'S CHEMIST SHOP, ARCHERY ROAD, SATURDAY OUTING.' Obedient to the letter, I flushed the note down the toilet. I saw no more of Mrs Cave that week and the days dragged interminably.

It was before two when the school bus dropped us in town and in a side street I found the chemist shop. I entered and bought a small bottle of scent, the brand my mother used, which would ensure it would be acceptable. The smiling girl assistant, no doubt guessing it was a present from a youth to his girl, used pink striped paper to wrap the little box and tied it with silver tape. Through the shop window I saw the Caves' Austin car parked outside.

I hurried out to greet my loved one, impatient as a bridegroom. Instead I was halted by the sight of the sullen Mr Cave, the blue jowled Skull himself behind the wheel. 'In, boy,' he ordered, the passenger side door held open for me. We drove in moody silence to a cottage on the edge of town. My great fear was that he'd discovered his wife and I played games and an inquest was about to be held.

But Stephanie awaited with a beaming smile as I was shown into a cosy parlour. She patted the couch on which she sat to indicate that I join her. The husband sat across from us in an armchair, watching balefully, his presence hardly conducive to putting me at ease or getting what I'd hoped for from his wife. Perhaps she had not reckoned on his being there and would act as if I'd just been invited for an innocent visit. If so, I would go along. The small package was still in my hand and she asked what it was.

'It's for you,' I said awkwardly, my eye on the reaction of the vulture-like figure perched on the arm of the chair opposite. He frowned disapprovingly, rose

In The Mood

and paced the room as if much agitated. His wife did not seem to notice, taking the gift and opening it. 'Silly boy, spending your pocket money,' she said, 'but how thoughtful. Isn't it thoughtful, Arthur?' Her husband scowled, going to a window, staring out with his back to us and hands in his trouser pockets.

'I trust you are not taking one of your moods,' she told him sharply. 'Tyler was being thoughtful and it's a very good perfume. I must thank him.' Arthur Cave turned his head and his wife drew my face to hers, giving me a kiss. It was no peck of gratitude but one that went on and on lingeringly, drawing me closer, her succulent open lips moving in circular motions over mine, the tip of her tongue probing my mouth. Her left hand was behind my neck keeping me close; her right hand flopped negligently into my lap, falling across my crotch. Already at half-cock, my prick reared and lifted her hand. She gave the engorged shaft a promising squeeze.

Cave said sarcastically, 'No doubt you'll entertain him now with our holiday photographs, Stephanie.'

'What a good idea,' she said. 'I'm sure he'd like to see them.'

'I'm certain he would,' said Cave, his voice thick with sarcasm. 'Why not go the whole hog? The whole bloody hog.'

'Take no notice of him,' Stephanie reassured me. 'Arthur can go into the most dreadful sulks. I'm used to it, and know how to deal with him. Don't I, Arthur? So behave yourself.' She already had a leatherbound album on her knee. Our shoulders touching, I looked down as she lifted back the embossed cover. The first page contained four neatly spaced postcard-sized black and white pictures of Mrs Cave posing among reedy sand dunes wearing nothing but a smile. Under each scene a caption was written in white ink.

'South of France, last summer,' said Stephanie matter-of-factly, as if showing me nothing to get excited about. 'We go to a haven of nudism on that coast. One goes about free as nature intended.'

'And flaunt your body for every damn Tom, Dick or Harry to ogle,' Cave chipped in sourly. 'I've seen them staring at your breasts and pubic area. Your big tits and cunt,' he spat out. 'And don't you just love it.'

'I'm warning you, Arthur,' threatened Stephanie. 'And we can do without the crude descriptions.' Cave growled and dug his hands deeper into his pockets. His wife carried on flipping over the cardboard pages, each one revealing her prime nakedness to my eager eyes. Suddenly I realised it was all a game they were playing, one scripted to give them the utmost pleasure in a situation of mistress and humiliated male. I'd never heard of sadomasochism then, but their roles were defined clearly. I was that special ingredient, the necessary other male. Arthur meanwhile paced and seethed, putting in the occasional snide remark and being threatened calmly but menacingly by his wife with dire consequences if he persisted.

I was in the delightful position of not only perusing page after page of Stephanie pictured naked, but the hand hidden under the album was giving my prick rubs and squeezes. The photos left nothing to the imagination. She was taken posed upright with arms and breasts raised, reclining with those ripe tits lolling on her chest and thighs parted to reveal a fine forested and curved cunt, and rearward to feature the splendid mounds of her arse, twin moons, with her thatch of pubic hair hanging between the cleft. In a few scenes other nude people were seen, including husband Arthur. I was happy to observe his flaccid penis looked a mere tiddler, at least compared to mine. Near the last section of the album a smiling group in slanting sunshine included my ex-schoolfellow Dinky Pettifer.

'You know him,' Stephanie observed. 'The boy Pettifer. He happened to be on holiday there at the same time –'

In The Mood

I'll just bet he did, I grinned to myself, horny bastard. No doubt too Dinkie had been in this very rented cottage and had experienced whatever lay in store for me. 'You're wasting time,' Cave suddenly announced nastily. 'I'm sure the boy has been shown enough to suit your purpose, Stephanie. Don't forget he's to be back at school for prayers and supper. Isn't it the Grand Tour next?'

Stephanie fetched him a resounding smack across the cheek, making him step back and blink tears. 'Arthur, you asked for that,' his wife informed him. 'Let's have no more of it. If you can't stand my having a visitor, go out.' He made no move and she turned to me, calm as ever. 'We are considering buying this property,' she said. 'It has an interesting olde worlde character, don't you think? Come, I will show you the upstairs.'

I was led off, leaving Cave to nurse his face and glower as his wife led me through a thatched door to a narrow stairway. Another door at the top opened to a small bedroom with beamed ceiling. The bedstead had tall brass ends with acorn-shaped knobs. 'It is delightfully snug,' my guide smiled, pulling my school tie to bring me face to face with her, those big ripe breasts nudging my chest. 'What did you think of the holiday pictures? Did you like them?'

'You were ... were marvellous,' I said in awe. 'I have never seen anything so beautiful. Really.'

'Sweet child,' she smiled.

'I'd like,' I bolstered my courage to say, 'I'd really like to see you like the pictures now. I mean without your clothes.'

'That would be extremely naughty, wouldn't you say?' she chided me. Then she kissed me, a light touch on the lips. 'All right, but just for being so kind, spending your money on a present.' She went to the door, closed it firmly, turning a large iron key. She stood beside the bed and began to unbutton her blouse. I

In The Mood

stood as each item of apparel was discarded as if she were undressing for a bath, placing each article neatly folded over a chair. Even her large owl-eyed spectacles were laid on her dressing table. So I saw the vision of Stephanie, her skin so white and curved, the full breasts hanging delightfully, the wide hips and fork of her thighs so forested with hair.

'Now you must give me the same pleasure,' she told me. I shed my school uniform in indecent haste, standing just apart from her with an erection that thrust up level with my navel. 'It always looks so painfully stiff, dear thing,' Stephanie said, her hand going to clasp the shaft. 'I suppose it needs relief? Do you think we should relieve it? I could show you a special way, if you like.'

She'd relieved me by hand and mouth so far. 'Oh yes, please,' I said. 'Then you must do exactly as I tell you,' said my mentor. Going to the bed, she lay across it, legs parted and hanging over the edge. 'Come to me,' she said. 'Kiss me, then kiss my breasts, suck the nipples. I know you like to.' All this I did happily, bending over her in between her thighs. She sighed, returning my kisses with wet mouth and tongue, cupped her breasts for me to suckle, toyed with my prick as we fondled. 'Now, you must feel me – there! Put your hand down and touch me, put your finger in.'

I felt that whether she knew I was even a little experienced or not, she was going to go through the whole seduction scene. And I was going to let her, dutifully obeying her commands. Her cunt was warm and moist. I found a clitoris stiff as a fingertip and circled it, bringing a moan to her lips. I wanted now to fuck her, determined too I'd bring her to a climax, have in my thrusts up her the means to make the ice-lady cry out and lose control. She had other ideas. Her hands were on my shoulders, gently guiding me down over her smooth belly. My face arrived between her legs, eye to eye with her curved mound and the pink

In The Mood

cleft surrounded by hair. 'Kiss it for me, my darling. Kiss it sweetly.' I did as required with a will, kissing her outer cunt as I would her mouth. I then lapped with my tongue, drawing it over the pouting slit. 'Yes,' she said, 'yes. Oh, do it. Do lick me out. Lick my cunt. Put your tongue up me – '

Nose and mouth smeared with her lubrication, I delved in, feeling her limbs stiffen and shudder, hearing her low moans. 'Lovely, lovely boy,' she uttered, her hands in my hair. I had done my part, I considered, now my balls and pulsating prick ached to fuck her, take her, fill her cunt with more than a tongue. I came up over her and as if with a will of its own my knob, my crest, my helmet, pierced her outer lips, nudged into the velvety passage, and went in to the hilt. She raised her body and gasped, then clung, her legs encircling my waist, her hands going down my back to cup my buttocks and haul on them. Her cunt tilted and she fucked, fucked back, her pelvis heaving to take my strokes. 'Say "fuck me",' I told her savagely. 'Say "fuck me hard"!' Her agitation increased. 'Yes, fuck me,' she cried. From beyond the door a shout rang out, followed by a flurry of hammering, a fist banging on the woodwork. Our pace slowed but I stayed in.

'What the devil's going on in there? I demand to know,' Arthur Cave ranted. 'Stephanie, I want to be let in. Let me in this very instance.' Below me his wife smiled up at me benignly, and I knew she had come, climaxed. 'Stay here, it's all right,' she assured me. I lay back and watched her lovely bare arse joggle as she went to the door and opened it.

Arthur entered looking about with eyes alight. 'What the hell is this?' he asked. 'What is that boy doing naked on that bed?'

Stephanie closed the door behind him. 'He's just fucked me,' she said calmly. 'And much better than you've ever done. And we haven't finished yet. If you must stay and watch, then you must behave.'

In The Mood

Arthur slumped in a corner chair as if resigned to his fate as Stephanie returned to me.

Chapter Ten

Stephanie climbed back on the bed beside me as calmly as if her husband was anywhere but sitting a few feet from us. He was, of course, what's now commonly termed a 'wife-watcher' and protest and act up as he may, this was his bag, his thing. I felt secure in the knowledge the more his wife and I did to put on a good show, the more he'd like it. Stephanie meanwhile had draped her full breasts over my face, looking down on me towards my toes. She swung her tits over me like church bells ringing, both stiff nipples brushing my lips.

Even as I tried to draw one of them into my mouth, she moved forward almost in a crawl over me until I looked directly up into the deep under-cleft of her fine arse. A pouting cunt was poised temptingly above, the curved bush a tongue-tip away. At the other end she had taken hold of my prick, now a slackened version of its full potential, between what felt like a thumb and forefinger, straightening it upright as it were. Something wet and warm that could have only been a tongue lapped my crest and I responded. The magic worked. My shaft reacted, filled, stretched and thickened out to an 'aagh' of approval from my manipulator.

Looking down from below the arch of her open thighs, across my stomach and in between her lolling breasts, thrusting round teats that became elongated as they reacted to gravitational pull, I watched her lower her parted lips over my resurrected cock. Her

In The Mood

cunt bore down over my nose and mouth, wriggling into the desired position. We were, as I knew, in the 'sixty-nine' position. It became hard to breathe as Stephanie covered me, pressed vigorously to get the full effect of her lubricated cunt rubbing on my features, my ears imprisoned by the upper flesh of her thighs. A fine judge, she raised her cunt the necessary inch or so at the moment prior to suffocation. I'd manfully managed a creditable period of lapping at her and now drew a deep breath to see me through a further bout of queening.

It was in that intermission that I peered down again across my prone form and between her splendidly pendulous tits to see her raise her mouth from my prick. Wet with her saliva, hugely excited by being held captive between her tongue and the roof of her mouth, by the suction exerted upon it, the shaft reared mightily. It stood engorged, proud, a veritable ramrod. As if by itself, throbbing with pulsating lust, it seemed to stretch up to her lips, the warm wet recess where it might vomit its thick volley. Instead she raised her head, releasing the prick from her steadying hand, letting it stand like a pole on its own.

'Isn't it a good specimen?' Stephanie enquired of her husband. 'Look how it positively rears, and what a splendid length and girth it has, Arthur. We have a find here. I believe it's my best one yet.'

'That should please you,' Cave said grudgingly.

'Very much so,' Stephanie answered brightly. 'And he fucks with it so very well. Do you want to see him fuck me, Arthur dear? I'm quite ready for him again – '

I was feeling my presence a mere formality, my prick the main attraction and their conversation conducted as if they alone were in the bedroom. I made to heave myself up. If she required a fucking, and her husband wanted a spectacle, I was more than willing to mount her right then.

'No,' Stephanie said firmly, pushing me on my back

In The Mood

again. 'This time we'll do it another way. You'll like it, won't he Arthur?' She then swung a leg over my middle, poised above me with her knees each side of my waist. 'This way I ride you,' she directed. 'You should lie perfectly still and let me do the work, so control yourself for a while until I tell you.' I lay back looking up to the two prominent cones of her tits towering above me. 'This way the woman becomes almost the man,' she added. 'Can control her pace and movement, alter the depth and angle of penetration. You must allow me the dominant role. A woman gets greater pleasure being in the superior position, mounted and in charge of her lover.'

'You do, that's a fact,' Arthur sneered. 'And what a load of nonsense you talk. Why not just ride the boy?'

'You're being offensive again,' Stephanie reprimanded him.

'Ride the boy,' Arthur said again. 'That's what you want, why make a speech about it. Go on, masturbate yourself on his prick, for that's what you do.'

'Leave the room and leave us alone if you can't stand to watch us,' she warned him. 'It is a beautiful position, and more women would insist on doing it if they weren't so repressed. Are you staying?'

'I suppose so,' he said.

She directed my glans to her nether lips, rubbing the knob on her cunt's entrance, then pressing down with a satisfied sigh as my prick entered her. It penetrated straight up, deep into her and she bore down her pubic bone upon mine. 'Remember you must lie perfectly still,' she reminded me, moving in a variety of down-thrusts in a corkscrew manner. She leaned far back, then crouched forward, shifting the angle of her pelvis to receive my prick at all tangents and levels. She became outwardly excited, vocal. 'Oh, I must have it,' she groaned. 'It's so fulfilling. So *fucking* good. Lie still now, you!' This last was as my hips rose in response to her thrusts. Her pace then increased.

In The Mood

She fell forward, put her tongue in my mouth, her breasts flattened on my chest, riding as if on the home stretch.

I caught a glimpse of Arthur pulling off his clothes, eyeing us avidly. He revealed a grey body with slack flesh, a prick that stood from a mass of dark hair. 'Your buttocks, Stephanie,' he told his wife, 'tilt them more, get your bottom raised for me!' He climbed up behind her. I saw his head and shoulders appear above her back as he crouched behind her.

'Oh,' she murmured suddenly. 'Arthur! Do you know where that is? Oh, you beast – ' Her movements above me became all at once more agitated. She reared back, threw up her head. 'Aaaagh!' she cried out. 'Beast, beast, Arthur. Oh, what you are doing to me. Beast!' Arthur in turn grunted and puffed in his exertion. 'We're all beasts!' he exclaimed, 'and it's so damnably good up you. Bitch, bitch! Take it, bugger you!'

I was well aware of where her husband was, and what he was doing. Its effect upon Stephanie was electric. She keened and whinnied and brayed, as the juddering, shuddering woman was the sandwich-filling between us. I grasped her breasts, which were bobbing and bouncing like live things above me as her lower torso jerked and see-sawed between the two of us in her. 'Beasts,' she cried out again, this time in the plural. 'We are beasts aren't we? All of us. Go on, go on, both of you. Have me, take me all ways – '

Arthur was doing his thing. In the spirit of the group I thrust up into her hard. Stephanie was lying prone over me by then, lopping about like a landed fish in her climaxes, a long series of spasms. Arthur had rolled sideways and lay huffing and puffing on the bed. My own contribution had been made some time before, a series of spurts that must have filled her. I had to ease myself out from below the sated and deadweight Stephanie, feeling drained myself as never before from

In The Mood

the hectic bout. We dozed quietly for what must have been almost twenty minutes to recuperate.

Stephanie was already up and in her dressing gown, covered now as if to notify the fun was over. 'Wash and tidy yourself up in the bathroom,' she instructed me. 'Time is moving on. Get dressed and we'll have tea before we take you to get the bus back to school.' It was said in the most matter-of-fact way. I washed and returned to the bedroom to get my clothes. Arthur was bent over the bed and Stephanie was whacking his bare bottom with a length of leather belt cut to a shorter length. I counted six of the best before Stephanie ceased.

'He likes that?' I asked. 'I've heard of someone else who likes to be strapped,' remembering what brother Ed had told me of my father taking a belt to my mother's bum. I looked from Stephanie to the reddened buttocks of her husband and she nodded calmly.

'It's our little ritual. I insist on it if Arthur had misbehaved. He did a very naughty thing. Didn't you, Arthur? Took advantage of me. Buggered me while you and I were making love. That wasn't very nice, was it?'

I thought from the way Stephanie had reacted, the intense pleasure she had been unable to conceal during the threesome, that it had been *very* nice. Seldom was I ever again to see a woman so aroused and excited in the throes. So we dressed and sat before the parlour fire to take tea, the conversation on the latest crisis in Europe and the chance of taking their usual holiday in France being stopped by the growing situation. I ravenously ate several slices of cherry cake. 'Stephanie does all her own baking,' said Arthur. 'It's rather good, isn't it?' I agreed while she poured me more tea, smiling at the compliment. We were all so civilized, not a word said referring to what had passed.

Arthur Cave drove me to near where the boys gathered to get the bus back to school, stopping where we

In The Mood

would not be seen together. As he leaned across to open the car door for me he said casually, 'You enjoyed the afternoon?'

'Yes, thank you. Very much indeed.'

'Most people would not approve of what we do, but we like it, as you observed. If I may say so, you have proved an able and obviously willing addition to the little games my wife and I play. We're free-thinkers, you know. Got no time for stupid inhibitions or such. It is never to be mentioned to anyone, of necessity of course. They wouldn't understand. Mark that, my boy. There could be other visits by you. But mum's the word.'

'I would never breathe it to a soul, sir,' I promised.

'I know,' Cave nodded. 'Stephanie has kept me informed of your intimacies over the past month or so. We feel you are entirely trustworthy. She's a fine woman, isn't she?' he smiled. 'You are a lucky young man.'

But within a week or two, before the chance of another threesome was offered, Hitler marched into Poland. The school was taken over by the army as a barracks, the pupils sent home. I never saw or heard of the game-playing licentious Caves again. I soon turned seventeen and, following Roger's wedding, was accepted for pilot training in the Royal Air Force.

Chapter Eleven

Before becoming a dashing pilot in a smart RAF officer's uniform there was the little matter of undergoing basic training – square-bashing, being shouted at by superiors and roused for physical training at an unearthly hour before breakfast, plus menial tasks like making our beds and sweeping the parade ground and barrack rooms. After boarding-school life this was not too different so I settled in quickly.

The training depot had been a peacetime seaside holiday camp and the all-male regime of drill, lectures and sport was supposedly rigid and strenuous enough to tire us rookies so that all thoughts of sexual activities were kept at bay. Of course they were not. Taking oneself in hand, or letting someone else do it for you, were the only available ways for the trainees to gain relief. Of several thousand personnel in the camp, there were no more than a dozen or so servicewomen stationed there on administrative duties. These Women's Auxiliary Air Force members were considered the property of senior members of staff. 'Cockpits for RAF officers' was the title given to the WAAF on base.

Once a few weeks training had been completed to knock us into a semblance of airmen, recruits were allowed evening leave to venture into town, famous for its tower and kiss-me-quick hats. It was during a stroll along the seafront that I met Lucy, a curvaceous little thing of nineteen, two years my senior and a

In The Mood

local aircraft factory worker, probably the most naive girl in that town. The Air Force erks were out in force and the famous prom really became a promenade. Boys walked one way, civilian girls strolled in the opposite direction so the two sexes passed face to face. This way they could size each other up as potential partners and make a date for the cinema and dance halls, courting as it was known.

Lucy passed me several times and I was attracted by her big tits jiggling so provocatively under her cheap cotton summer dress. She noted my eyeballing her, smiled after several passings, so I stopped and said, 'Hello, where have you been all my life?' This was considered a pretty smart opening gambit in those times, on par with 'Do you come here often?' when meeting a girl at a dance. Lucy giggled and made fun of my 'proper posh' way of speaking to the several girls she was with. Her accent was broad Lancashire. After the preliminary chat-up, she agreed to go with me for a drink. With barely a glance at her friends, she strolled off beside me, slipping an arm through mine.

At a nearby pub she wanted an orange juice whereas I had been prepared to fill her with drink, lower the resistance and have my wicked way with her. Later we walked the prom and she allowed kisses under the dark underside of the town's main pier. She refused further liberties even though all around us dozens of couples were copulating in the sand within yards of each other, a heaving mass of RAF uniforms rising and falling on prone female bodies below. Lucy refused to lie down, but I had progressed to deep tongue kissing and dry-rubbing my stiff prick nicely in place against her cushiony little lower belly, all the while pressing her up against one of the seaweedy iron stanchions that supported the pier. I noted while engaged in this quite pleasurable smooching that Lucy's eyes, wide as saucers, took in the sexual athletics going on all

In The Mood

around us in the gloom. She was entirely fascinated by viewing the humping, engrossed, so much so that her return kisses and general response to my attempts to work up her passion were merely automatic. She'd hardly noted I'd completely unbuttoned the front of her dress and fished out one luscious tit to suck on the red nipple before she protested and tucked it back out of sight.

Soft, sweet-smelling, cuddlesome as her nubile body was, I decided if she wasn't coming across this would be my first and final date with her. I didn't have time for half measures. She slapped my hand several times while fondling her or trying to get into her knickers, complained I was a dirty beast. So we returned to the prom, me with a sizable and urgent hard-on, which she'd refused to handle earlier, and I intended to dump her. She announced that her Auntie Beth lived across the road from us and she was going to call in. I escorted her to a deep porch fronting a terraced house. There I tried another assault, kissing her, flattering her, my hands roaming. It brought the usual protests, mild slaps and entreaties that I behave. I had my upright prick positioned to rub against her fat little cunt when the door suddenly opened and we both fell backward onto a carpeted passageway. I looked up at a tall well-built woman of perhaps forty who grinned down at us.

'Did I interrupt something?' she asked in amusement. 'That is our Lucy I see below that young man, isn't it?'

'The dirty beast wouldn't leave me alone,' Lucy complained.

'Well, lucky you,' said the woman, whom I'd rightly guessed was Aunt Beth. 'Now you're in, you might as well come in the parlour.' She escorted us into a cosy, overfilled lounge, where beside the usual furniture was set a double bed. I knew it was a practice for people to sleep downstairs because of air raids. Beth said, 'I

In The Mood

was having a drink, fed up with my own company,' and nodded at a small table whereon sat a selection of whisky, gin and port bottles. 'This was a holiday boarding house before the war stopped all that. All the booze was stock for the bar so I'm my best customer these days. Fuck 'em all, I say, let's make the most of what's going these times. What'll you have, boy?'

I took a large whisky; such a selection of spirits one would only see in a black marketeer's home in wartime. Beth had evidently decided it was for her own use. Lucy asked for another orange drink, laid down the glass and departed for the toilet. In her absence her Aunt Beth added a good slug of gin to the orange. 'Don't worry, she likes it,' said Beth. 'She's coming the goody-goody with you here, that's all. Some girls like to think if they act virginal and good they impress the boyfriend. She's all for getting married that one. You known her for long, whoever you are?'

'Only met her tonight. My name's Tyler. Ty.'

'Unusual name. And you didn't get anywhere with her?'

'No. You don't seem to mind if I had.'

'Bugger no. Get what you can, I say. Make the most of it.'

The woman spoke like a true fellow spirit. I looked her over with admiration, one of those tall well-proportioned types. Her size attracted me. She eyed me back as interestedly. She was about five feet nine or ten, tall for a woman. Her hips were wide, her body plump yet with not an ounce of fat. Her arse was broad and had firm round cheeks, her arms and legs nicely rounded. She wore a black dress that bulged with a full bosom, both breasts thrusting and well matched in size and shape. 'Are you sizing me up?' she said. 'Like what you see, do you?'

'Very much.'

'Bit young to tackle me, aren't you?'

'Give me the chance.'

In The Mood

'I believe you would, cheeky young beggar. My old man's at sea, merchant navy cook. He's somewhere out in the Atlantic.'

'Fuck his luck,' I said.

'Fuck his wife, more likely,' she laughed. 'It's been over a year since he was home so you might say I've been neglected. Only I don't want some inexperienced young boy that only knows to put it in and get so excited he finishes before I've started. When I take on someone it's for my satisfaction.'

I closed to her, put my mouth to hers, and meeting no resistance, hugged her closely. She opened her mouth and I tongued her. My prick rose with the arousal gained by the talk and through being cushioned against a pliant form. We kissed several times more, my cock rising to its full power. She moved her pelvis so that we were cock to cunt, grinding slowly at each other. She fell back, or rather went back, dragging me over her onto the bed. We were kissing, I had groped one of her large breasts and her breath was coming heavy as she lifted her crotch hard to mine, when Lucy came back into the room. She took a seat and said nothing, lifting her gin and orange to sip it.

'Is that Lucy?' breathed the woman into my mouth. 'Shall we get rid of her and get down to it?'

'She likes watching,' I said, telling of her interest in the fucking under the pier. 'I don't mind her if you don't.'

'She's no virgin, believe me, I know her. She's brought blokes here before. Here, what're you trying to do?'

'Undress you. Let's give Lucy a treat and do it naked, the only way.'

'Give you a treat, more like,' Beth laughed, but she sat up and began to pull off her dress. I unbuttoned my uniform jacket, delighted with the turn of events. The fact we had an audience added to the occasion, and I had hopes that Lucy could be persuaded to join

103

In The Mood

in. She came across to stand by the bed as we stripped off. 'You pair of dirty sods,' she said, giggling. 'What am I supposed to do now?'

I had stripped to my underpants, service issue, which bulged with the cockstand I'd gained. Beth lolled back naked, her big breasts lolling on her chest, her fleshy cunt mound covered in black hair, crisp and thick. Her lips were thick, like twin rolls of fat but as she put her legs apart they widened, showing crimson facings, a glistening orifice I intended to fuck deeply. 'Lucy,' she said. 'Bring me over my drink and make yourself useful. And for fuck's sake get out of your clothes. Don't be the odd one out.'

'Not with him here,' Lucy replied, which I took to mean she had stripped with her aunt before for some reason. I just wanted at it, so stepped out of my underpants, revealing a goodly eight-incher standing like a bar, rigid and ready. Lucy squealed and went into peals of laughter. I stood rather proud of myself, well aware Beth's eyes were fixed on my rammer.

'Stupid bitch,' she said, referring to her niece. 'My God, son, you weren't at the back of the queue when they were dishing out pricks. It's a bloody giant, makes my old man's chopper look like an acorn. Can you use that thing?'

I crossed to her, eased her from the sitting position and went over her splendid body. I kissed her mouth, went down to her nipples and sucked each in turn. I slid lower, coming face to face with her cunt, whispered to it lovingly and kissed that. Then, determined to make a job of it, prove myself, I parted the lips and tongued deeply. Beth groaned, reached for my head and raised her knees high. 'Oh yes, oh fucking yes,' she moaned. 'Do that, do that to me.' She shuddered like having a fit.

'You dirty beast,' Lucy said, hovering beside us. I had her aunt going strong, hunching her back, lifting her buttocks to me, moaning her pleasure. I came up

In The Mood

to her, her hand seeking my shaft, guiding it, then it was in, to the balls, and I rode her with a slow deep grinding of my hips. 'Don't hurry, I want it, want it,' she breathed, locking her ankles about my waist, clutching my buttocks to draw me in closer. 'Turn over,' I ordered her. She stopped in mid-fuck to regard me with amusement. 'You're fond of it,' she chuckled. 'You've done this before,' but she complied by rolling over and offering up her arse. Her backside was solid and smooth. I gave it a good slap for its cheek, then closed to get behind her. She had reached back and parted each buttock cheek for me. My prick went up like a knife through butter. 'Oh yes,' she cried. 'Fuck it up me, do,' and with that plump arse in my lap, grasping a tit in each hand for leverage, we went at it until her cries became continuous, she calling out for more, harder, then finished in a paroxysm of wild jerking as I loosed gouts of come well into her.

'Who taught you?' she asked mischievously when recovered. 'That was what I'd call a good going over.' She fanned her reddened face and laughed. 'Do you fancy taking on Lucy now? I need to recover.'

I patted her thigh, remembering how she had waggled her big arse while coming. 'Do you think she'll let me?'

'I want to see it,' Beth declared. 'Damn, she won't always get the chance to take such a big prick. You hear that, Lucy?'

'I don't want to. It's too big,' Lucy replied.

'Come on, you'll like it,' I encouraged her.

'I can't with my aunt there.'

'Well, I'm not going anywhere,' said Beth. 'Bloody stupid girl. I've seen all you've got to show often enough.' This made me ponder just what I had been fortunate enough to get into, meeting these two. Beth rose from the bed, gloriously naked, and went to her niece. Lucy tried to twist away from her but Beth pulled at her dress. The girl nodded sullenly, then

In The Mood

started to undress. Nude, she was all tit and bum, a delectable prospect.

While I stood admiring these two fine examples of naked womanhood, Beth led the girl to the bed – for me, I assumed. My cock was rising again, if not at full size yet, but I reckoned some play with Lucy's plump young tits would bring on the necessary.

'What are you two whispering about?' I asked as their heads were together in secret talk.

Beth laid Lucy on the bed and got on top of her, kissed her lingeringly and got between the girl's thighs. My two beauties became like a man and woman in each other's arms, kissing and fondling, breasts and nipples rubbing together, the thatch on their pubic mounds grinding against each other. Lucy soon threw up her legs until her heels were on her aunt's back. So they nestled belly to belly, churning, thrusting, the hair of two cunts intermingled. I had heard of two women making love, of course, read of it too in tattered pornography passed around at school and in the barrack room, but this was my first time to be privileged to witness it. Terribly aroused, I held my prick, stroking it gently but not wishing to interrupt the voluptuous coupling between the pair. Obviously it was not their first time.

Beth, arse-cheek muscles contracting, began to increase her pace in the dominant position. Her opened mouth and tongue sought Lucy's, their kisses clung and Beth's legs stiffened and she shook bodily before she lay quiet. 'You've come!' I said in some amazement and she laughed at me. 'Of course,' she said. 'If you can't get it one way, you have to get it another. Look at Lucy now. I've made her ready for you – '

Lucy, it was true, was lolled back as if in a stupor, half-fucked, aroused, legs apart and uncaring of offering a nice tight fat little cunt. I covered her and she guided my prick to her outer lips, drew my knob in while still holding the shaft, got into position to receive

In The Mood

the prick up her and raised her legs again. No protests now, she acted like any woman hot for the cock, randy-arsed.

'Shove it all up,' she groaned. 'Finish me. I'm all worked up.' She thrust her tongue in my mouth, lifted herself to get all my length, shoulders only remaining on the bed. In moments she began to climax, heaving herself up out of control, crying out, her hands tearing at my back. Beth stood beside us, encouraging us with bawdy remarks.

Thus I had them both, and so it continued throughout that night.

I crept out of the house before dawn, making my way through deserted streets back to camp. My leave had been evening only; I should have reported back at ten the night before. Now I went into the guardroom to be met by a stern-faced Flight Sergeant sat drinking tea. He fingered my station card. 'You are Aircraftsman Wight, I presume?' he said ominously. 'You know you are in deep shit, boy. Where the hell have you been all night?'

'I had the chance to sleep with a woman, Flight,' I said, deciding the truth was best. 'Two women, in fact.'

'Dirty, rotten, lecherous, lucky young bastard,' he grinned. 'Too good a chance to miss, eh?'

'Right, Flight,' I said.

He tossed my card into the box that showed I was in camp. 'No charge this time, then,' he decided. 'Get out before I change my mind. You'll just make it in time for reveille.'

There were several more occasions when I called on Beth and Lucy and our threesome romps continued. Then it was time to move. I had been selected for training as a bomber pilot. The next six months were spent in the wilds of Canada, gaining my wings in sub-zero temperatures on the plains of Winnipeg. Little chance of fun there with the female sex. I looked forward to my return to England, even if the grim tales that were told of the short life of a bomber crew over Germany made going on active service little to be commended.

Chapter Twelve

Returning to England, a Pilot Officer with wings over the breast pocket of an equally new uniform, was an anti-climax. Arriving at the depot in pouring rain I was granted leave and left undecided where to spend it. London was the obvious place, but the few pounds pay I'd been given would barely see me through an evening in the kind of nighteries I intended to frequent. There was only one thing left to do. First a duty call home to see my mother, sting her for more cash, then make for the fleshpots of the city.

She was delighted to see me, a lonely woman in a large house with little to occupy her. When I mentioned I might spend a few days in London, she reminded me the family owned a flat there and she would love a few days in town herself. She had been more than generous coughing up a decent cheque for me to squander, so reluctantly I had to agree. I would ship her back home after a day or two. London was getting nightly air raids. She wouldn't want to exchange the relative safety of a Sussex country house for a blitzed city. For her own good I'd insist she return.

We journeyed to London by train, first class of course, mother exceedingly proud to show me off in my RAF finery. She did not let me down either, looking exceedingly handsome and shapely in her chic costume and matching hat, as ever her hair and face made-up to perfection. I had to admit she was a fine figure of a woman, in her prime and exceedingly desirable, as

In The Mood

evidenced by the admiring looks she received from officers sharing our compartment. Arriving at the flat in the early evening, she got out sheets and blankets from the airing cupboard to make up two beds while I departed hoping to strike oil. I drank a fair bit in several almost deserted night clubs. The women all seemed to have come with partners. I danced with a few, the closeness of their perfumed bodies increasing my frustration and randiness. Anything I suggested to them, like leaving with me for an hotel, was turned down flat.

Around midnight I conceded defeat and made my sullen way back to the Belgravia apartment. My mother was still up, curled in an armchair in nightdress and negligee, drinking a gin. Not the first, I deduced, from the almost empty bottle on the coffee table before her, or the tipsy smile and the hiccup she gave on my return. 'Oh, I'm so glad you're back, Tyler,' she said, relieved, 'The air-raid siren has sounded. It's all quiet now but do you think it will come to anything?'

'Probably,' I said, not in a good humour. 'I told you that you'd be better off at home, mother.'

'But I see so little of you,' she complained. 'Life is so dull for me in this awful war. And now you'll be going off on flying duties like poor Eddie did before he was shot down.'

'Thanks for reminding me,' I said nastily, realising I was taking my frustration out on her. 'I'm off to bed. Goodnight.' Once there, I decided, it would be a handjob to relieve myself, the best there was in the circumstance. I had hardly settled down to the task when the crack of anti-aircraft fire sounded overhead and the crump of bombs exploding. There came a tap at my door and my mother entered with a glass in hand, her figure outlined through the flimsy night attire by the light from the room beyond. 'Should we dress and take shelter?' she asked.

In The Mood

I assured her I wasn't moving, somewhat annoyed for my prick was at that stage where the induced throb in the shaft had spread to boiling heat in the loins. 'There's little we can do about it anyway,' I said snappily. 'Not if a bomb has our name on it.' I reached for a cigarette from the bedside table and lit it. 'You can go down to the basement if you like.'

She sat on the edge of my bed, clasping my hand. 'No, I would sooner stay with you, son. Light me one of your cigarettes, and I'll fetch a bottle. You do like a drink, don't you? I know you do.' She giggled almost happily, going to return with a full bottle and another glass, settling herself again on the bed and pouring two full measures. Clinking her glass to mine, she said, 'Let's die happy then. Here's to good times.' She leaned forward and kissed me, her perfume and nearness arousing.

Believe me, I was almost tempted to reach for her and prolong the kiss. But she chatted on, the gin, shared out equally, relaxing us both as old times, when the family had been one, were recalled. Mother grew more gregarious as the bottle emptied. She referred to the many parties held in the old days. I was reminded here was the beautiful county woman so admired by father's friends, men she'd been flattered by and flirted with. How much I wasn't sure, but her life now must have seemed dull. She was also the woman, I recalled with a wry grin, that brother Ed had seen bent bare-arse up over an armchair while father had caned her prior to giving her a shafting doggy-fashion. That, I considered, looking at her now so rounded and shapely, must have been worth seeing. She leaned forward to make some point and her loose night attire fell open to reveal the firm swell of big creamy breasts, the nestling cleavage and rounds even to the thick prominent nipples so rubbery brown. She saw my eyes upon her, smiled, but did not cover herself.

'Did you ever,' I asked carefully, 'see or hear any-

In The Mood

thing of our maid Molly Dewhurst lately?' It was said in the full knowledge that my sexual romp with the widow had been observed by my mother.

'She's got a good war job, I believe, in a factory at Horsham. Married again too.' Mother gave a little wicked smile. 'Not before time for the poor woman, I'd say.'

'Do you ever see or hear of your friend Margaret?' I asked, pursuing the line of questioning. 'The one we boys called Aunt Margaret – '

'No, and I don't want to ever again,' mother replied firmly. 'She's taken herself off to a farm her husband owns in the Irish Republic. Dodging the war, if you ask me. I never really liked the woman. A perfect slut.'

'Is she?' I enquired, as if surprised.

My mother took a long drink, regarding me with a sly look. 'You know very well she is. Who better? Didn't she throw in my face that she'd seduced you on the night of Rodney's wedding? With that wet fool of a husband of hers, I shouldn't blame her too much, I suppose. But you were a mere boy.'

'Old enough and big enough,' I grinned. 'It was hardly a seduction.'

Mother clasped my hand and nodded. 'We had a terrible row over something and she positively crowed that she'd taken your virginity.' We both laughed aloud, mother even wiping the tears of mirth from her eyes. 'You're a bad boy, you've made me forget the air raid with your talk. Virginity indeed, she was evidently too late to get that. I well remember the shock of seeing you with Molly. It really looked as if the two of you had been hard at it – '

'Molly was better than Margaret.'

'Then I'm glad. Margaret always boasted about her prowess in bed, fucking bitch.' The word, coming from my mother, sounded with more feeling and emphasis than I'd ever heard it used. We both laughed again, she squeezing my hand. 'You are a wicked one. I know

In The Mood

Molly wouldn't have seduced you. However did you go about it with her? Plump Molly, why she is my age!'

'All the better to make love to,' I said, returning her hand pressure. 'Some flattery and a few kisses and cuddles. She was built for loving, just like you, and she was needing it badly.'

'Who doesn't, when it's not available,' my mother said quite pensively, her big breasts rising in a sigh, her thoughts of good memories of the past. I reached out with my hands, delved into the vee of her nightdress and cupped both breasts, bringing them forth in full view, cupping and weighing them in my palms, my thumbs flicking each nipple and feeling them tighten, firm up and grow out to definite projections. She sat up unmoving, and I bent my head and kissed each nipple, sucked on them. She held me to her then, sighing. I managed to push the bedcovers aside and take her hand, placing it around my swollen prick. Like an electric shock to her, she drew back, looking down at my erection, which sat bolt upright as if begging a favour.

Her hand slowly uncurled around the shaft. 'Oh no, Tyler,' she said. 'Not that. Not with you. Please – '

I clasped her to me, her bared breasts flattening against my chest. For a long moment we regarded each other's faces, then we kissed. It lingered, our mouths fused. I pulled her closer, lowered her head down to the pillows. My tongue probed her mouth and she responded. We clung for long moments kissing deeply, my hands on the orbs of her breasts, pinching her taut nipples. 'We can't. We mustn't,' she protested in a hoarse whisper. At that precise moment the guns banged out again, followed by the roar of aircraft and a screaming stick of bombs that exploded with roars and a rush of wind. The building shook, the windows rattled and plaster came down from the ceiling. As if surprised to find ourselves alive we stared at each other, her splendidly prominent breasts rising and fall-

In The Mood

ing, then we huddled together, her body trembling under mine as if for protection. Her face was raised to mine and my mouth clamped to hers again, glued to her lips, kissing madly.

The urge in my loins now would not be denied. I had the most bursting erection, demanding its right. Below me was a woman, warm and pliant. I drew her hand down to my prick, made her clasp it. Now she held it as if for dear life, stroking and squeezing. My hand went on to draw up her nightdress, revealing the strong thighs and the fork of them, the plump raised mound with its thatch of hair, the lips and cleft. I fingered in to the knuckle, seeking her clitoris, the nub, finding much moistness. I played with her, kissing her breasts, sucking upon them, my fingering bringing a moan and a response by the lifting of her pelvis. 'Do it if you must,' she said, her voice low and strained. 'I want it too. I want you to – '

I directed my glans, the peeled helmet, against her opening, forcing an entrance, inching my way in. Her body tightened as if to resist, relaxed, and her knees rose either side of my waist, affording penetration to the hilt, the balls. I withdrew almost completely, heard a muffled protest, then thrust hard and deep, repeating the process until her soft grunts were matched by her return thrusts. Her feet crossed behind my back, her hands cupped my buttocks as if for leverage. It became a magnificent fuck and I intended to play her for all she was worth, have her want to be given full measure. Her body heaved to mine, lifting from the shoulders as she arched up from the mattress. 'Yes, yes,' she muttered. 'Oh yes. It's there, I can feel it there – '

Her motions increased strongly to match my pace, stomachs slapping, thighs heaving in unison. 'Yes!' she exclaimed again, this time a cry of relief, an exultation, and her lower torso thrashed and heaved in an unstoppable climax. Then I allowed myself to unburden, groaning over her as the series of spurts shot out

In The Mood

from me in spasms and jerks, she still gripping me, meeting my thrusts. We rolled apart. I lay beside her, the two of us gasping our relief and exhaustion. When at last she spoke it was to say in a subdued voice that she was returning to her room, adding that she would leave in the morning for home. Her hand reached out to touch my back, almost an assurance that she did not blame me for what had occurred.

I turned, pulling the sheet and blankets over us both. The air raid had quietened, I noted, and I did not want her to go like that, filled with guilt perhaps. Lying face to face, I played the sympathetic character. 'It just happened, didn't it?' I said. 'Neither of us meant it, I'm sure, but I'm not sorry. It was beautiful, for me at least. Do you regret what we did?' Her reply was to move as if to get out of bed. I held her arm to stay her. 'Stay the night,' I begged. 'I want you to stay. You didn't seem to find it so awful –'

She lay on her back, looking at the ceiling. 'That is the worst of it and I can't deny it. God help me, it was as good as ever I've known. I think I needed that. I loved it. But not from you, surely? Oh, certainly not from you, love.'

'Why not?' I said. My hand sought to touch her breasts and she clasped my wrist. 'If you needed it and you say you loved it, what's so terrible?'

'I'm supposed to be your mother.'

'That didn't put me off. It was bloody marvellous.'

'Do you know why I finally allowed it?' she said. 'I mean apart from our closeness in the air raid, and too much drink as well, I suppose. And to be completely honest, my own weakness?'

'We both were at the point of no return, I guess. I'm more to blame than you. It will stay our secret.'

She smiled and touched my cheek. 'All that, yes, but there is another thing. It's something your father and I should have told you years ago, perhaps. You are our

In The Mood

adopted son, Tyler. We got you when you were just a month or so old – '

Strangely, the confession seemed no great surprise to me. 'I used to wonder why I was nothing like Rodney or Eddie,' I said. 'That is the truth, so help me. Eddie used to drop hints at times too – '

'He was warned against telling you.'

'So you're not my real mother. What we did was not wrong then. You're not my mother!'

'I feel like your mother,' she affirmed. 'I am your mother. Who brought you up from a baby? Who else is your mother?'

'It's not the same. I mean if we make love, and I want to again – '

I took her in my arms and she did not resist. Her body was so pliant, warm and comfortable against mine that I felt the stirring of arousal returning, my prick lifting, nudging her thigh. 'I should go,' she said, but didn't move. 'You surely can't think of me in that way, as a lover, can you?' I kissed her and resumed cupping her breasts. 'I don't know as you are nice to know, young man,' she chided me with a wry smile, 'or what I've allowed myself to get into with you. It must be this awful war and the separations. To think, making love with you, my son. And wanting you to – '

'Adopted son,' I corrected her. 'And you did say you loved what we did. Go on, say it again. I want to hear you.'

'Certainly not,' she said, returning a kiss. 'I may have, but you're not getting the satisfaction of hearing me say it. You are a young scoundrel, you know that? I shall feel eternally damned being here like this with you and what we're doing.'

'We make a good pair though,' I dared say, proud of my prowess for making this splendid woman forget herself in the throes of an orgasm so strongly. For having her remain in my bed. 'We were good at it weren't we?'

In The Mood

'You seem to think so.'

'Come on,' I challenged. 'You were all for it. I brought you off a treat. You went hammer and tongs.'

'It was all you, was it? While admitting it was very good, there were two of us. It wasn't just you.'

'You were a marvellous fuck,' I complimented her. 'Best I've had.'

'Strong language now,' she observed. 'Is that how you talk in your Air Force mess? Was I as good as your Aunt Margaret, the bitch, or Molly Dewhurst?'

'And all the others,' I boasted. 'And I haven't finished with you yet.' I remembered I had prowled London to find a good fuck and a special one was waiting for me. Drawing her into my arms she folded her body to mine. 'I want to fuck you,' I said. 'Tell me you want me to fuck you – '

'You know I want you to, isn't that enough?'

Her plump mound was pressed nicely against my rejuvenated prick. I rubbed the outer lips with my glans, poised to enter. 'Say it,' I threatened.

'I shall regret this all in the morning,' she said, 'I'm sure. But it's so cosy cuddled up like this, isn't it? You'll be going off to war soon, too, won't you? So fuck me. There, I've said it. Fuck me again, Tyler. You really did do it so well – '

Six weeks later, after twelve bombing operations over several German industrial centres, I was in the bag myself, shot down and a prisoner of war for the duration.

PART TWO

Chapter One

Despite her reserve at the outset, we had just met for the first time, the girl below me was starting to come. No doubt about it, the unstoppable urge was welling up from the inner depths of her cunt, giving vent to utterances and hoarse cries, increasing her convulsions and pelvic thrusting. To give her full measure I increased pace, looking down upon her clenched features, pleased with my effort. I could bring her off twice, perhaps more, and withheld my own approaching climax. She came with a rigid heave, lifting bodily, groaned as if finding great relief, then fell back for a moment before going hard at it again. In that brief interlude she opened her eyes, looked at me and muttered 'Yes, more – '

The backs of her knees were cradled in the angle of my elbows, feet splayed either side of my shoulders, arse tilted, her whole weight balanced on the back of her neck and head as she arched to me. Her hands groped at my buttock cheeks for extra leverage. I was crouched over her on the narrow old divan like a question mark, pistoning away. The second coming was as powerful as her first, her cunt thrusting wantonly to the shaft filling her. Against me, the pubic bone grinding on mine, hair to hair. The shy, quiet Moira loved it. I was not the only one to see to that.

'Jeez,' said Gus. 'She's fucking mad for it. Gone nuts.'

I heard Manny laugh. 'So would you with *that* going up you. Get the spare camera ready, I'm running out

In The Mood

of film. This is just too good to miss, the way they're going at it. Don't stand gawping, hand me the bloody thing.'

'They should be posing,' Gus complained jealously. 'They're not supposed to make a meal of it. That bastard up her is just having a good fuck – '

'But look at her face,' Manny pointed out. 'That's not an act and I've seen the best. You don't get an expression like that in many shoots – ' He moved around us, bobbing and weaving, on his knees, almost between our thrusting backsides, snapping away with the Leica, no doubt one 'liberated' during the advance into Germany. 'This is bloody good stuff,' he enthused. 'None of your run-of-the-mill half-hard posturing. You can tell Q we've got a find with these two.'

The morning had not started on such a high note for me. The cheapest lodging I could get for the previous night had been a room with paper hanging from the walls and a sagging bed. I couldn't even afford that for the night ahead. It had poured in the morning and I had not enough money for the bus, let alone a taxi for my appointment. I had been made to pay in advance so I left the run-down house with its smell of boiled cabbage and helped myself to an ancient umbrella from a chipped china pot in the carpetless hall. At the Suzy Q club all was shuttered. A repeated knock brought Gus, a skinny young spiv with a cigarette dangling from his lips. What else did I expect? He opened barely enough to allow me through, leading me up three flights of ricketty stairs. He gave three tentative respectful knocks on the frosted glass of an office door, then led the way in.

'Ever done it before?' said the enormous fat man I faced. The word sleaze came to mind. He was a sleazeball if ever there was one, belly nestling against a big desk and his bulging waistcoat, fawn with pearl buttons, spotted with cigar ash. This is what I'd been reduced to consorting with. I no doubt deserved it.

In The Mood

'I've had my share,' I said modestly.

'Who hasn't?' he scoffed. 'But this is on camera. It's art, boy. You not only got to be good at it, you got to look good. And no going off at half-cock. You got to *act* it.' He turned to the character beside me, who leaned forward in the classic pose of lackey to master. 'Take him down to the studio, see if he's any good. Tell Manny not to waste film. A few stills will do. We can always flog them no matter.'

While this one-way conversation was conducted I looked out across the fat man's domain, beyond dirty windows to a low grey sky, incessant rain and the grimy rooftops of Soho. 'Right on, Mr Q,' said the lowlife, but who was I calling names? I was part of them, as servile to the gross bastard sat so confident behind his desk as the little weed who now plucked at my sleeve annoyingly. 'Move,' he ordered, his attitude changed when addressing me, someone presently even lower down the scale than himself. 'We got people waiting. Mr Q's paying good money to help you out.'

Q grinned behind his desk, studying his cigar, enjoying my humiliation. 'Officer class,' he observed to no one in particular. 'Pity the war's over and everyone's equal again. Only some's more equal than others, ain't they? Not that the war wasn't good to me. Let's see how you perform, loverboy. You came recommended. It's your last chance – '

I was taken down narrow winding stairs lit by cobwebby naked light bulbs. No expense wasted, I noted, where show wasn't necessary such as in the drinking club on the ground floor. Each landing was stacked with boxes of black-market treasure: whisky, American cigarettes, radios and impossible-to-obtain electrical goods, even shirts and shoes.

'Regular Aladdin's cave,' I said to my guide. He gave me a sharp look of hatred, no doubt considering me getting off lightly. 'None of your bloody business,' he warned. 'Just see you're good at what you're here for,

In The Mood

mate. Mr Q's doing you a big favour. Your kind are two a penny.'

'Fuck Mr Q, the fat slob, and fuck you too, creep,' I said amicably, intending to annoy. 'I may owe him money but he doesn't own me – '

'Don't be too sure. He could have your face altered. I seen it done.'

I had no doubt about that. Beyond a cellar door was the so-called studio, a windowless room glaringly bright with arc lights. It was sparsely furnished with a divan, a wardrobe and dirty sink with a ragged towel on a nail. There was at least a camera on a tripod and a man adjusting another one in his hands. On the one kitchen chair sat a very pretty girl with startling red hair, dressed in an open tweed overcoat over a woollen frock revealing a full figure. A shopping basket with groceries sat at her feet and she twisted her hands as if in a state of nervous apprehension. She looked up enquiringly at me as I entered.

'He looks okay,' said the photographer. 'Get undressed, chum. Busy morning. Another session after this.'

'Where,' I asked, 'do I undress?'

'Right here. You can hang your clothes in the wardrobe or on the floor if you like.' He was adjusting his camera but spared me a second look. 'First time? You can get it up, I suppose? After that, just follow my directions.'

'Fucking by numbers,' I suggested.

'Something like that.' He smiled at the girl as reassuringly as his world-weary face would allow. 'You too, dear. Get 'em off. Time's awasting. You're not shy, are you? Think of the lolly, easy money.'

Aware of her unease I opened the wardrobe door to its widest angle, making a sort of screen. 'Go behind there. It's a little more private.'

'Stone me,' said Gus. 'A bleeding toff. Only he ain't no gent. Owes everbody. What he stands up in is all –'

'Shut your face,' I told him, 'or *I* may do a little altering.' I said to the cameraman, 'Does that sewer rat, that underfed slimeball, have to be here?'

Manny's look became somewhat more respectful. ''Fraid so. He loads my cameras, moves the light if need be. You're stuck with him.'

I looked at the girl, who had followed this exchange with interest. To her I held out an arm as if to offer her the privacy of the protective door. She went behind it, taking the chair to fold her clothes on in one hand and her shopping basket in the other. Gus was now sullen but silent. I stood before the open wardrobe and stripped to the skin.

When I turned around, Manny gave a long low whistle. 'Well, lucky old you,' he complimented me. 'I can see why you've been picked for this line of work.'

Even Gus looked grudgingly impressed. I sat on the divan waiting for the girl to reappear. Manny approached chewing his lip, deep in thought. 'You got a little beaut today. Moira here is hard-up keeping a boozy father and eight or nine snot-nosed kids fed back in some Irish bog. That's the only way I got her here and I want her back regular. She's special. Go easy on her.'

'Don't tell me she's a virgin?'

'She's done a trick or two for money. Didn't like it, or the kind of customer you get around here. She's a good Catholic girl. She don't do it for herself.'

My heart bleeds, I was about to say, but Moira came around the door, naked and hesitant, unsure whether to cover her nestling pointy tits or the titian-bushed prominent mound between her lovely white thighs. I thought her the most exquisite thing I had ever seen. Shapely as a statue, full and firm young breasts thrusting proud and defying gravity, the nipples red and like fingertips. A narrow waist curved out to rounded matching hips and she had the legs of a film star. 'I see what you mean,' I said quietly to Manny, 'about wanting to use her.' Right then I wanted to use her myself.

He took her hand, led her to sit beside me. She glanced at me nervously. I was intrigued with this new experience. If I owed Mr Q, this was a reasonable way to be let off my debts. 'Relax, girl,' Manny advised surprisingly kindly. 'You got a nice young man as your partner and it's not hard work. Put an arm about her shoulders, chum. Look into each other's eyes.' He took his first shots, a pair of naked strangers together like young lovers before mating.

'Great,' he said. 'This is a pleasure after the beat-up pros and old cows I usually get. Now start with a kiss, you two. Make it like you're enjoying it. You, chum, hold one of her tits. That shouldn't be hard. But *that* should be harder. Moira, love, give it a couple of shakes. Rub it up, dear!'

He shook his head. 'Don't look at me,' he told us both. 'Get on with it. That's better. Hold her like that –'

Moira looked into my eyes for a long appealing moment before offering her mouth to mine. The breast I cupped was both firm and pliant, as only young bursting-with-rude-health maids can boast. Her mouth was sweet. Her cool hand grasped my prick and gave it tentative strokes; the stalk thickened and stretched, she looked down at it with what I took to be a mix of alarm and approval. I heard Manny's camera clicking away but was lost in the utter sweetness of kissing and fondling such a lovely creature. For a moment she resisted my tongue against her lips, then her mouth was open and crushed against mine.

'Good, good!' Manny enthused. 'Now lower her under you, whatever your name is. Kiss her tits, go at it. Suck her nipples. Moira, keep hold of him. Lower your grip so a few inches of his prick can be seen. That's right. Jesus, two decent lookers for once, this is the best yet. Lift up a bit, chum, let me get shots of that

In The Mood

gorgeous body. This is nice work if you can get it. Hey! Who told you to get it in – ?'

Get it in I did. I considered it was at that stage. Up the slippery slope into a moist tight fleshy channel. Moira gasped, clutching at me, her knees rising and bending. 'Oh, you lovely thing,' I told her mouth to mouth, hot breath to hot breath. 'Let me fuck you.' As I penetrated her cunt it opened like a flower's petal in sunshine, leading me to the inner sanctum, gripping me. I felt the solidity of her body, slid my hands under to cup the rounds of her buttock cheeks. She gave me a deep sigh, moved to adjust the angle of penetration, making a cradle of her thighs, raising her cunt.

'Oh no, no, yes, yes, fuck me,' she agreed. Her two climaxes came and went and still she took me; shook me with her increasing spasms. 'The horny little minx,' I heard Manny say and Moira cried out 'Yes, yes!' I could hold out no longer as her body thrashed against mine belly to belly, loosing a thick volley deep up her begging crack. Subsiding, we clung to each other.

'Bloody disgusting,' said Gus.

'There's no doubt you'll be hearing from us for more of the same,' said Manny, rewinding his camera. 'What I got should go down very well. Pity it's black and white with Moira's colouring. Next time though. This was supposed to be a dummy run, not the fuck of all time. Give Moira her money, Gus. She's earned it. Did Q give you anything for this bloke?'

Gus could not disguise his delight. 'He can shag for ever and still owe the firm. We own his cock.'

I reached for my clothes, giving him the friendliest grin. 'You should be so lucky, Gus,' I said amiably. But one day I would have his guts.

Chapter Two

It still poured outside. I left the studio such as it was with the girl Moira, using my stolen umbrella to shelter her. 'What did that horrible man mean, you owe somebody money?' she asked, appearing concerned. I was touched.

'A few debts, nothing serious.'

'He made it sound a lot, like you were in trouble.'

I went with her through the mean streets of Soho, having nowhere else to go. I took her shopping basket and she did not object. 'I'm paying for a spell of high living,' I said. She was patently a kind heart, a soft touch, the sort one can appeal to and be thought more of for speaking the truth. 'I got in over my head with the wrong people. I'll sort it out.'

She stopped, facing me under the umbrella. Her voice was more concerned, the Irish brogue pronounced. 'Have you no job to go to? Do you do just *that* – what we did?'

'It was my first. Like you.'

She looked embarrassed. 'I had to do it. I needed the money. I'm glad it was you.'

'Me too,' I agreed, not adding that she had been a marvellous fuck. Behind her quiet, even shy, exterior was an ardent girl, but perhaps not the sort to be reminded of it.

'I think you're educated,' she said. 'Anyway, not the likes of those back there. What do you do?'

'When I've got work, a pilot. I seem to be grounded

In The Mood

at the present. We're getting wet. Better move – ' The umbrella leaked.

She did not seem to notice, more interested in my plight, it seemed. 'What about your people, your parents? Or have you got a wife?'

'No wife, nobody. As for my parents, well, I'm not really in their good books any more. I do them the consideration of staying away when I'm in a mess of my own making. When I write I tell them I'm doing fine,' I said heartrenderingly.

'Then there's some good in you,' she said approvingly. 'Would you like a cup of coffee, something to eat?'

I looked around at the cafés surrounding us, their windows steamed with customers' breath and cooking vapours. 'I've no money.' When broke, London in a downpour must be the most miserable place on earth. 'Otherwise I'd have asked you to join me.'

'Never mind that,' she said. 'Have it on me.'

'Wouldn't that be using your hard-earned cash?'

I detected a saucy smile. 'I suspect you're a bit of a rogue, Lord forgive me. You know very well it wasn't so hard-earned. It was shameful. I shocked myself. I suppose you are very good at it – '

'Not difficult with such a beautiful girl.'

'That's blarney if ever I heard. Come on then, we've to catch a number thirty-four. I live in Kilburn.'

'You're taking me home?'

'I'm not wasting money on café prices. As for home, it's a bed-sitter as the English call it. But it does have a gas ring and I can cook you something.'

The place was not much roomier than a bed to sit on. A nurse's dress, apron and cap hung from a nail behind the door. On a piece of clothes line stretched between a corner of the room was her entire wardrobe, a few poor dresses hanging from wire coathangers. But the cluttered space was neat and quite spotlessly clean, as was the bed. She filled a kettle at the one brass tap

In The Mood

over the tiny sink. 'We'll have that cup of coffee now,' she said. 'Do you take sugar?' This as she put out two cups from the shelf.

'One,' I said. 'Manny says you support your family back in Ireland. How old are you to take on that responsibility?'

'Eighteen. That Manny should mind his tongue. It's none of his business.' She saw I appeared sincere. 'My mother passed on, may she rest in peace. Father is not the best at seeing the family is fed and clothed. I send what I can.'

'If I can help to make you some money, count on me,' I offered grandly, as if that would be a chore! 'Manny seems keen to use us again from what he said. Would you mind?'

She studied me over the rim of her cup. 'I was a fair bundle of nerves going there. Now it doesn't seem so bad. Not with you. I wouldn't want to do it with anyone else. Here, I don't even know your name –'

'Wight. Call me Ty.'

'Short for Tyrone? Are you Irish?'

'If you want me to be. My name's Tyler. I know you're Moira –'

'Moira Lafferty.'

I held out a hand. 'Then hello, Miss Lafferty. I too won't do what we did with anyone else,' I lied. I had little choice and knew whatever prospective partner was obtained for me in the photo sessions, I would perform. She had put on a frying pan and poured two eggs in beside some rashers of bacon. I realised I had not had a proper meal for two days. 'This is very kind of you, Moira. I see you're a real sister of mercy, a nurse.'

'Probationer,' she corrected. 'I was on night shift last night and came home and went shopping, bracing myself to go to see Manny like I promised. I hung about the place for more than half-an-hour making up my mind if I could go through with it.'

131

In The Mood

'That food smells delicious,' I said. 'I'll leave soon as I've eaten. You must be ready for bed – '

'Cooking pollutes the whole room with its smell,' she complained. 'And the window won't open, it's stuck. But it's the best I can afford. Where do you stay? Have you a place?'

'Not at present. I'll try the Savoy or the Ritz to see if they'll take me.'

'You can stay here if you like,' Moira said surprisingly. 'I don't mind. Sure, we've done as much as any married couple. And I've a drunken neighbour on this landing who tries to break down my door every time he comes back. I'd be glad of your company.'

'Where would I sleep?' I asked hopefully.

'In the bed with me, of course,' she said. 'Where else? It's big enough for two – ' She looked at me with a smile in her eye. 'That's if you've no objection.'

It was a lifesaver, never mind the pleasure of sharing a bed with such a delightful creature. 'You're a good soul, Moira Lafferty,' I praised her.

'I'm not so sure of that,' she said seriously. 'I'll have to go to confession and do penance for ever, I'm thinking. You will use the time you are here to get work and share the expenses? I can trust you not to take my things while I'm on duty?'

There was nothing worth taking. 'There's a flying job in the offing. Meanwhile I can earn a pound or two helping at the street market. Soon as I've helped you wash-up I'll see what's going, get out of your way – '

'It's not fit for a dog out there today,' Moira said shyly, looking at the pelting rain beating against the window. 'Pouring buckets. I'm thinking bed is the best place to spend such a day.' She added impudently for her, 'So long as you let me get some sleep. I do have another night shift tonight – '

The lady wants more of the same, I decided. I sat in her one rickety chair and watched her undress, revealing that perfectly proportioned lush young body.

In The Mood

She did not try to conceal any part of herself, her gravity-defying full breasts, the thick reddish bush on the bulge of her cunt. 'Sure, and your greedy eyes are everywhere,' she chided me. 'Have you never seen a person naked as nature intended before?' I had the definite feeling she was enjoying flaunting herself before me, standing beside the bed and making no attempt to get in it.

'None so nice as you,' I told her. 'What a lovely figure. You have the best tits – breasts – I've seen.'

'Oh, and you've seen plenty I suppose, Tyler Wight?' she teased. But she cupped her breasts in her hands, studying them proudly. 'Look at my nipples, they're so big today. Aren't you going to undress? You've seen all there is of me – '

She slipped into the bed, covers up to her chin, watching me. I was already hard from eyeing her inviting strip and the thought of what was to follow, or to come to be more precise. And the thought brought an implication. 'I'm sure you don't want to be lumbered with a kid,' I said, meaning I didn't want to be. 'What do you do about us?' I know you're a Catholic girl – '

'I'm also a nurse, so don't worry about that. Sure there's enough Lafferty brats in this world.'

'So another mortal sin of the flesh to confess,' I grinned. She did not find that funny. I peeled off my jacket intending to join her quickly. God knows that such a beautiful girl was lonely, welcomed my companionship in her need for some kind of human relationship, but I realised it was so.

'You should meet a good Catholic boy and marry him,' I said earnestly. 'I don't think this kind of life is you. Even I'm just using you, letting you take me on when you've got more than enough dependants – '

'Come to bed and stop talking nonsense,' she giggled. 'You'll have me feeling sorry for myself. Come and cuddle up to me. I never felt more like a cuddle – '

I was down to my shirt and underpants when a loud

banging sounded from the door, a fist beating on the wood. 'It's himself and drunk already at this time of day,' said the Irish girl. 'If we ignore it long enough he'll go away when his hand hurts.' All the same I noted a frightened expression in her eyes. 'Don't antagonise him. He will go away.'

'One day he's liable to break down that door,' I said, seeing it straining at the lock. 'Who the hell is he, anyway?'

'An Irishman from home. He's a Catholic too. Maybe I should marry him,' she attempted to joke.

'I know you're in there, Moira me darlin',' came a call from beyond. 'It's me himself, Pat, wanting to talk to you –'

'We'll settle this once and for all,' I told the nervous girl. I opened the door and a carrot-headed young man of about my own age nearly fell against me as his words trailed off, 'Let me in, dear.' He was unshaven and his shabby suit was soaking wet.

'Bless you, my son,' I said, even making a quick sign of the cross across my chest. He stared glassily at me in my shirt-tail and underpants. 'It's Pat, isn't it?' I went on. 'Now you wouldn't want to disturb a young girl at her devotions, would you? And I haven't seen you at church at all. When did you last make a confession?' I took a bottle from his hand and shook my head before giving it back. 'The devil's in there, my son,' I warned.

'Yes, Father. Sure I know it.'

'Good. You must fight the temptation, and if you ever hammer on this door again I'll damn you to eternal hell.' He nodded dumbly. 'You got the message then?' I said, closing the door. Back in the bed Moira was sitting up, biting on the edge of her patchwork quilt to stop her mirth. 'How did I do?' I asked. In answer she raised the bedclothes, offering her nakedness to me. I got in and ran my hands over her smooth body; breasts, belly and down to the thatch between

In The Mood

her thighs. She put her arms about my neck, nestling close, put her tongue in my mouth, pressed the firm fullness of her tits against me.

I felt the still-warm slit of her cunt, lowered my mouth to come level with her hard nipples, sucking each in turn, my head cradled in her arms. Without further foreplay I rolled on her, bodies as one, my prick seeking and finding its niche of its own accord. She rose her entire cunt from the bed to receive me. 'Lord help me, I want it, I have to have it with you,' she sighed resignedly. 'I think I love you. Fuck me do, please –'

Tyler, old son, I told myself, embedded hard inside her, looking down upon a beautiful face, concentration on the pleasure being received twisting her features, you have done it again. Landed on your feet, or better still, in the bed of a most fuckable wench. One, too, whose evident enjoyment of coupling with me boded well for the near future, all I ever considered worth settling for. During the next nine months I was domiciled with the delectable, honest and still charmingly naive Moira who, apart from a habit of hinting about marriage, was the perfect partner. We did everything that could be sexually achieved and not always before Manny and his cameras. And when we did, we enjoyed the sensuality of our fucking every bit as much.

I imagine even now those postcard-size poses and copies of scratchy-surfaced black and white one-reelers exist and are viewed as classics of pre-video days. We made a good-looking couple and our pleasure in each other came through on film. Things had got much improved; we moved to a decent flat. I flew aircraft again, even some paying cargoes of Scotch and cigarettes to country airstrips on the continent. Then one evening I left Moira with a farewell note and was off with my case packed while she was on night shift at her hospital. East Africa beckoned, an RAF friend had told me of life in Kenya and the freedom of the sky as

In The Mood

a bush pilot out there. I was leaving an austere England still in a post-war depression and rationing for sunshine and new adventures, new women, new cunt.

Not that the past years had not had its compensations. Even my time in the prisoner-of-war camp had not been entirely wasted. I learned fluent German, boned up on navigation and flight engineering in the classes formed to pass captivity. There had been work for the escape committee, avoiding the more strenuous tunnelling by gaining a skill at forgery. A third attempt at escaping had proved successful but by then the Third Reich was crumbling before the Allied advance. Over two years back pay that I received was squandered entirely in the pursuit of pleasure in London, Brighton and the South of France.

Looking back again they seem youthful escapades, almost innocent crimes by today's standards. In a post-war Europe devoid of all luxuries, the whisky, cigarettes and other hard-to-obtain items smuggled in seem harmless contraband. Today it is lethal drugs. Even the series of short erotic films that I appeared in were strictly male-female fucking scenes, a mere stage forward than what is almost shown in modern films today. I had escaped sliding further down the slippery slope, perhaps, by my fortunate meeting with Moira. But as the months went by I had felt her possessiveness. It was time to go.

So it was with my passport ready, a single ticket to Mombasa on the British-India liner Uganda, that I set out with little money in my pocket for the next stage of my rude lewd life. From what I had heard, East Africa had great possibilities for a young and up-and-coming schemer. I eagerly anticipated investigating them.

Chapter Three

Leaving England for Africa and yet another phase in my life was just the sort of thing that kept my pot boiling. I needed change and thrived on it, which was just as well. So often it had been forced on me in circumstances of my own doing. Call it the luck of the devil, something or someone had always turned up in the nick of time to save my neck. Moira had appeared at a crucial moment when I was broke and homeless in London. An earlier unlikely saviour had been Uncle Joe Stalin, the despotic Russian dictator. He had decided that post-war occupied Berlin should be wholly under his Communist sphere of influence. In the early summer of 1948 he ordered a blockade of the city to get the Western allies to pull out of their zones of occupation. It was the start of what became known as the Cold War.

This fact, and the threat of starving Berlin into submission to get the allied powers to withdraw, was of no more than passing interest to me. I had troubles of my own, namely for those days a huge £2000 debt to Gino's, a London club whose proprietor did not approve of money being owed to him and employed a squad of heavy characters to remind you, usually by breaking your legs. I never seem to learn. Later I got into the same fix as already recounted, working my way out of debt by fucking before Manny's camera. This earlier time there seemed no way out. All back pay from my years as a prisoner of war had been enjoyably frittered

In The Mood

away, my shoes were down at heel and the rent in arrears. Even for me, accustomed to living on a razor's edge, things did not look good.

In this dark hour an official letter had arrived from the Air Ministry offering a continuation of my commission in the Royal Air Force. Pilots were needed, all that could be found. The Soviet occupation zone of Germany surrounded Berlin and all access by road or rail had been cut off. The West's response to the Russian blockade was to airlift all goods and material necessary to keep the allied sectors of the German capital surviving. My previous experience of flying to Berlin had been to bomb the place by night. Flying again appealed greatly, as did going from down-at-heel to well-paid officer and supposed gentleman. More, it meant I could disappear from my rented room where Gino's gorillas called regularly to beat down the door. Such was their persistence I hardly dared go there, having to beg a bed and a night's shelter from a diminishing band of acquaintances rapidly tiring of my dependence on them.

A generous allowance was granted to kit myself out as befitted an Acting Flight Lieutenant and thereafter was posted to the wilds of Norfolk for a pilot's refresher course flying an old dependable Douglas Dakota transport. I became skipper of a veteran aircraft of the Normandy and Arnhem airborne landings. For over two years the Dakota had languished in a hangar; with the emergency she was back into service with a complete overhaul.

All was hectic at the airfield, with little time or opportunity to indulge in my favourite sport, hunt the cunt. What few WAAF's there were around worked around the clock. The local village was made up of a few cottages, church and church hall, where ultra-respectable ladies ran a canteen for us brave servicemen off duty. I'd never bothered to go there. My one success at this time was a barmaid I'd fucked after

In The Mood

chatting her up all evening in her pub on my one run into Norwich. Even that was a fumble up against a wall after closing time and a knee-trembler during which she was worried about laddering her one pair of nylon stockings; well, at least until she got the length of me and began to grunt out her responses. To show my gratitude I paid for the fish and chips she was taking home to her husband on her return from work.

Within two weeks of reporting for duty I was ordered on my first delivery to blockaded Berlin. I was briefed the evening before the flight by Wing Commander Nigh, a stuffed shirt and real pompous ass if ever there was. As I was leaving the briefing rooms, hoping for a quick nip back to Norwich and another session with my buxom barmaid, Wingco Nigh collared me.

'There'll be some little extras I want you to fly into Berlin tomorrow, Wight,' he said. 'A few luxuries for the crews stopping overnight in a little rest house we've set up for you chaps. Get yourself over to the motor pool and sign out a vehicle then toddle off to the village hall where my wife will give you some packages to take with you to Berlin tomorrow – '

I'd intended to visit the motor pool anyway, to borrow a car to get me to Norwich. 'I had other arrangements made for this evening, sir,' I complained. 'Won't it do in the morning?'

Wing Commander Nigh fixed me with an icy stare. 'You will collect the packages tonight and return them to me. As they contain bottles of wine and spirits, plus a quantity of cigarettes and chocolate, they will be kept here under lock and key until given into your charge before take-off.'

I drove off to the village church hall mumbling about Wing Commander Nigh and his no doubt uppity wife that I had to contact. Inside I found a scene reminiscent of wartime, servicemen and women being served pies, beans and chips by dedicated voluntary service women.

139

In The Mood

My eye was immediately drawn to a woman in a flowery blouse who was facing away from me at a table. Her waist flared out from a violin-curved back to broad child-bearing hips and the neatest rounded arse that moulded her grey skirt to the provocative cheeky mounds. Below the skirt hem were strong legs, trim ankles. I judged her as younger than the average among the women serving, and was interested to see if the front view of her was as enticing as her rear.

Circulating around until facing her, I noted the flowery blouse positively bulged with a fine upstanding big pair of tits, thrusting and tipped with nipples that proved their precise position by impressing each tip through the silken material. I was helplessly and rudely ogling this most beddable woman when she noticed me, saw well my lewd stare, and smiled.

'What would *you* like, young man?' she said wickedly. The lady was teasing me with her sense of humour, which I liked.

'I'm afraid that has nothing to do with it,' I had to say, taking off my cap. 'I've been ordered to seek out a Mrs Nigh. She wouldn't look anything like you, I suppose?'

'Exactly like me,' she laughed. 'Will I do?'

My look at her magnificent breasts answered her query, but I had to inform her I was there on her husband's instructions to collect some packages for Berlin. She led me off to a small room off the hall, and I followed admiring the sideways movements of the firmly muscled cheeks of her bum. On a table sat four boxes all sealed and labelled stating 'Duty Exempt Goods, Airman's Rest, Royal Air Force, Berlin.' I told her I had a car outside and would load the parcels in the boot.

'Where do I find this Airman's Rest place?' I enquired.

'Not a very original name, is it?' she smiled. 'It was

In The Mood

my husband's idea. I do the supplying at this end and Cuthbert's sister runs the club at the Berlin end – '

'Cuthbert, Mrs Nigh?'

Again she smiled, her attractive face lighting. 'Silly name, isn't it? My husband doesn't mind. His sister that you will meet in Berlin is a Letitia. Their parents had some strange ideas about naming children. Thank goodness I'm just plain Susan, to you if you wish. Your name is Flight Lieutenant – ?'

'Tyler Wight and pleased to meet you Susan,' I said, shaking her hand and holding it just that moment longer and giving it a suggestive little squeeze. 'You were about to tell me where I'll find this Airman's Rest joint.'

'Corporal Fox will no doubt show you. He's to be your load-master so my husband informed me. I think you should watch him. He has made a few Berlin trips and I'm not sure all the supplies I've sent out arrived as intended. I make an inventory list of all I forward now and Letitia checks it at the Berlin end.'

'Very wise,' I agreed, while making a mental note that this Corporal Fox sounded like a man after my own fashion. I had loaded the cardboard packages into the boot of the car when Susan Nigh came out and stood beside me as heavy rain began to fall. She had on her coat so was obviously leaving. 'Can I give you a lift?' I asked. 'No sense getting wet.' I drove her to the end of the village until told to stop outside a single cottage. There she thanked me and wished me a good flight, saying wistfully she wished she did exciting things.

'I could think of a few exciting things you could do,' I said, considering the chance worth taking. Susan Nigh was a likely lady in my book. I wondered however she'd come to be married to such a wet husband, adding meaningfully, 'And I don't mean flying to Berlin – '

She gave a little tinkling laugh. 'I'm well aware you don't, Flight Lieutenant. I saw the way you looked at me in the church hall canteen. Don't you think I'm perhaps a little old for you? I could almost be your mother – '

The less said about that relationship the better, I thought. Susan Nigh was making to get out of the car beside me so I had to act fast. 'Don't I at least get a goodbye kiss?' I asked. 'Just for luck, seeing as how I'll be off tomorrow, risking life and limb – '

'Rubbish. I suspect that, like a bad penny, your kind always turn up. And would you stop at one kiss?'

'Let's find out,' I said, taking the cuddlesome Wing Commander's wife in my arms. Her lips were soft and moist, her mouth parted for our tongues to meet, I felt the pliant warmth of her body as she leaned into me. My prick responded by erecting during our long passionate kiss. Then she drew away, holding me at arms' length, her breathing heavy.

'Phew,' she said. 'That's quite enough for you. I'm going in before things get out of hand.'

'I'll see you to the door,' I said, at which she laughed again, saying it was just yards away. But in the darkness of her arched porch before the front door I kissed her again. Now she held me with her arms around my neck, allowing lengthy opened-mouth kiss after kiss, repeating between our pausing for air that 'We mustn't, we shouldn't, this must stop now – ' while the bulge of my prick found the fork of her cushiony thighs and I began an insistent little rub-rub against her. I heard the slight moan she gave with each pressure, recognised the almost imperceptible movement of her body she made to align her cunt mound against the upright stalk pleasuring her. I considered I was on a certainty, and then the telephone rang beyond the door.

'Saved by the bell,' she said, pulling away and opening her front door. As she put on a light in the little hallway I saw her hang up her coat and turn to lift the telephone from a low ornamental table, bending to

In The Mood

do so, and from where I stood, seeing her standing sideways to me, saw a heavy breast fall forward and her rounded buttocks thrust out the seat of her flowery dress. I was not going to be denied so easily and followed her, closing the door behind me. My arms went around her again, this time from her rear, hands cupping the droop of her tits, my rampant prick now pressed hard to a most ample and yielding arse. She did not try to shrug me away.

'Oh, Cubby,' I heard her say. 'Yes, he came to the church hall. A young Flight Lieutenant.' She was speaking to Cuthbert, no doubt, and did not attempt to stop me as I unbuttoned the front of her dress and delved in a hand. I felt a quite overflowing bra holding prisoner two most succulent firm tits, giving them a fond squeeze, testing their weightiness. My other hand went up under the dress. Did she part her legs for my better access? I went far up between her thighs unimpeded, met the warm dampish crotch of her briefs with my fingers, felt the hair-covered mound under the thin silk. Susan Nigh was talking again to her husband, sounding remarkably composed. 'He went off with the stuff for Berlin some time ago, that's all I know,' she lied. 'Look, I've got to have a bath. It was pouring when I walked home and I got soaked. I'll see you in the morning then. Goodnight, dear, something has just come up I must attend to – '

That something had just come up was the full length of my prick penetrating her receptive cunt from the rear position. During her conversation with dear Cubby I had eased down her briefs and watched her step out of them by lifting one shoe at a time without stumbling over a word. I'd lifted her dress up over the polished white moons of her glorious backside and entered her. Now began the first see-sawing movements as I shafted her quite slowly and gently, letting her get the feel of it. She bent over to grip the little telephone table, thus raising her arse and tilt her cunt

In The Mood

to receive deeper entry, grunting somewhat in her pleasure and her arse starting to grind back into my belly as her aroused state craved more fucking.

'Don't you dare come yet,' she warned me as I increased my thrusts up her. 'If you're going to fuck me, see you do a good job of it. Oh Lord, oh Gawd, whatever has got into me – ?'

'About nine inches right now,' I told her joyfully, 'and all hard up a nice juiced-up cunt. Oh, Mrs Wing Commander Nigh, what a lovely fuck you are!' I began to buffet her arse like a battering ram as I sensed she was reaching the brink, poking her hard and fast to take her over the top. Her rear jerked back against me violently. She craned her neck and muttered hoarse noises in her extremity, in the throes of a climax that went on and on. I had her good, as I'd intended, all constraint and reserve thrown to the wind in her heightened state. As her convulsions eased she went forward on her knees, body across the telephone table, her shoulders heaving. I waited until she had recovered somewhat and turned her head to face me, her hair down and across her face. Her eyes were level with the massive erection I'd managed to retain, bursting to get relieved.

'My God, was all of that up inside me,' she said. 'Why is it still hard after all that – ?'

'Just wanted to make sure you got enough of it. Now you can return the compliment.'

She twisted around on her knees, clasping the upright shaft. 'It is a very good one. Do I rub it for you?'

'Messy,' I told her. 'I'd like you to suck it.'

Her eyes lifted up to my face, her head shaking as if in disbelief. 'You are a forward young man, aren't you? Do you always make your intentions known so strongly? My husband would never ask me to perform fellatio on him. Never.' She still grasped my prick nevertheless, stroking gently, my gorge rising danger-

144

ously. She giggled, 'I don't think I could get this in my mouth – ' and as if to try she covered my crest with her lips, sucking in the first inch or two.

I stood legs apart, my hands each side of her face as she took more in. I could feel her tongue below the shaft, the roof of her mouth above, and the suction as she drew sensations up from my balls. My legs trembled, I bucked from the hips, unable now to stifle my own grunts as she sucked on me avidly, a soft hand cupping by balls and gently squeezing the sac. Full as her mouth was, I distinctly heard a little triumphant sound from the depth of her throat as my spasms began. I had brought her to wild excesses of lewd behaviour; now she had me going out of my senses. In all truth I began fucking her mouth, thrusting hard into her in my urgency while she gobbled and gargled away, her nose to my pubic hair. I must have drenched her throat with a series of jets as I exploded my come to the back of her mouth. Even then she continued sucking, draining me to the last. 'Oh you lovely cow, cocksucking bitch that you are,' I praised her in my subsiding moments, for praise indeed it was for the use of her nice mouth.

While I stood adjusting my dress she sat up on the low table, regarding me with a curious little smile. 'I must have needed to let myself go like that for once,' she said. 'Cuthbert is not really the greatest lover on earth. Will you come and visit me again sometime?' That was an offer I could hardly refuse and we kissed fondly in her doorway as I left.

Back at the base her husband demanded to know what had kept me. I told him I had to change a tyre on my return trip, wondering why with such a good wife he'd never asked her to suck him off. I had left the borrowed car parked near his office. Wishing him goodnight, advised to get a restful sleep before my flight next morning, I drove back to his cottage and knocked on the door. Susan Nigh opened it, in a dress-

In The Mood

ing gown and ready for bed, welcoming me in. Sleeping together often means anything but that, I find. What hour or two we did snatch after exhausting ourselves ended with her awakening me around dawn. 'Fuck me,' she whispered, 'and then you really must go,' draping her warm comfortable naked form across me. 'I want to do it on top of you –' That's what I call being roused in the morning.

My first take-off for Berlin went well, soaring up with the old Dakota heavy ladened with sacks of coal, drums of diesel fuel, cement mixers and a variety of spares for army vehicles. My crew consisted of a sergeant navigator and a corporal load-master, a gingery Liverpudlian youth whom I'd been warned about by Susan Nigh. With his natural crafty look he was well-named Fox. The approach to Berlin in an air corridor over the Russian occupied territory was like Piccadilly in the rush hour. At any time, above and below me, I could count as many as a hundred aircraft coming and going. Bombers were being used as transports, there were civil airliners chartered for the emergency, dozens of Dakota aircraft like my own and even flying boats which landed on the city's lake. Fighter aircraft buzzed around us all the while in case the Ruskies got any big ideas about stopping the aerial lifeline.

Berlin's airport was overcrowded with planes landing, unloading or taking off. I was directed to a landing space on the grass strip between two concrete runways and impressed my crew with a good approach and smooth touchdown. I was the new boy and they watched to see how I performed. The navigator disappeared at once as if he had an urgent appointment. I strolled aft from my cockpit to see Corporal Fox zipping up a large service holdall which bulged with whatever it held. That I intended to find out, but mainly by gaining his confidence more than by pulling rank.

'Where the hell did the navigator vanish to, corp?' I

In The Mood

asked, offering him a cigarette. He took it with a grin as if accepting we were buddies.

'Sergeant Grey's got a ladyfriend here, sir. Not bad, either. He'll be back in the morning before we take-off, don't you worry.'

'I don't worry. The way the sky is filled with aircraft from here to England, who needs a navigator. Good town for women, is it, Foxy?'

He nodded as if pleased at the use of his nickname and my casual attitude as an officer. 'Great town if you got the old wherewithal, sir. Full of hungry young widows with kids by Jerry soldiers knocked off in the war. They'll do anything to eat. I've been on the Berlin run from the start. It's a great town. Best thing that ever happened, this blockade.'

Coming in from the air, Berlin had looked a ruined town, the skeletons of buildings stretching for acre upon acre. 'So just what is the "wherewithal" and how does one get it?' I asked.

His crafty look returned. 'The odd packet of ciggies, tin of coffee or bully beef. Sugar's a good thing to bring. For things like that you can fuck yourself ragged if you want.'

'So what's in your holdall, corporal? Barter goods?'

He immediately became wary, defensive. 'It's my weekly wash, sir. You can get all your laundry and ironing done here for a few cigarettes – '

'So open up,' I smiled, indicating the holdall. He sullenly unzipped the bag and I saw several wrapped packages, all with the same label as the goods for the Airman's Rest. 'Where did these come from? The stuff I was given last night is still on board. Did you nick these? Better come clean, Fox.'

'Only the labels, sir. The other stuff I got in England from a mate. It's all honest-to-God paid for, sir. Just stuff used for bartering like – ' He appealed to me as if for justice. 'I got the labels from where Mrs Nigh keeps them in a drawer in the church hall. It gets you

In The Mood

through customs, see, if there's any eager beaver on duty.'

'Very crafty, but I don't think Wing Commander Nigh would approve of your initiative. What did you bring with you?'

'Whisky, some cartons of ciggies, packets of tea, coffee and sugar. Are you going to report me, sir?'

'I think we may come to some little arrangement, Fox,' I said, much to his relief. 'Shall we say a split fifty-fifty on the goodies you've got there, and any in future. From what you say, one could live like an Oriental prince with what you've got there. Have we got a bargain?'

'Have I got a choice?' he complained.

'Not really. I'll foot my share of any goods you obtain in England, of course. Increase the amount we bring in, don't you think. Where do you unload your loot?'

'Any nightclub, sir,' Fox said, brightening. 'Every cellar in town that's still standing has been turned into a whorehouse or night spot. Proper dens, all of 'em. It's the life.'

I decided it would be as we drew a jeep from the United States Air Force motor pool and headed out of the airport. At the customs post we were waved through and drove on. 'They don't always let you away with it like that,' Fox said. 'The Airman's Rest labels have saved my neck a few times. This time it's the pilot's wings and war medals you got up, Skipper. Very impressive. Straight down the old strasse now to drop the delivery for the Airman's Rest then we can go to town.'

'What kind of joint is it? Worth a look in?'

'Avoid it like the plague,' advised Fox. 'Who'd want to go there with the civvie night spots catering for everything, and I do mean everything. You know who runs it like a church canteen? The Wingco's sister. Now if it was his wife, that would be a bit of all right – '

In The Mood

'You know Mrs Nigh?' I enquired.

'Only to collect a delivery from her,' Fox said. 'But what a built woman. Wasted on the old Wingco, I'd say. What a pair of fine tits. I could drag my balls across her fanny any time.'

That's what I had done the previous night and Susan Nigh was all that Fox claimed. I went into the Airman's Rest to find it not surprisingly half empty. Fox and I carried the consignment through to a side office behind a facsimile English public house bar and waited while Letitia Nigh checked it out. She was in her middle-thirties, short and plumpish with large spectacles. When Fox left to return to the jeep she seemed keen to retain my company, asking about her brother and sister-in-law. I had fucked worse, I decided, little plump naked women made good bedmates. In my own way I thought too it would be fun to screw both my Wing Commander's wife and sister. I excused myself saying I had to return to the airport. 'Don't be a stranger to us, young man,' she said as I departed.

'Where to now?' I asked Fox as I got back into the jeep. He directed me through a maze of streets until telling me to pull up before a seemingly derelict building. Through a heap of rubble I was led into rooms that had been made into an apartment. Fox stood back proudly while I surveyed the scene in what I supposed to be his domain, a well-furnished bed-sitter with four-poster bed, a sideboard laden with bottles of whisky, gin and sherry, and gilt-framed oil paintings decorating the walls.

'Lord of all I survey, Skip,' he boasted. 'And you ain't seen nothing yet. Marlene, come out and pour a drink for our guest,' he shouted into what was the kitchen. A moment later a German girl came in smiling at us, wiping her hands on a floral apron. She was about seventeen and pretty, if a little slim for my taste. Fox made a great display of kissing her roughly for my benefit. I took an armchair while she brought me a

In The Mood

double whisky on the rocks, proving Fox had even found a working fridge in his scouting out what was still working in Berlin. He spoke to the girl in good German, asking her if she had unloaded the last load of contraband he'd brought in. I spoke better German, learned from my time as a prisoner in that country, but decided not to let on. It soon paid off.

She asked who I was and he laughed, saying I was a shit of an officer who hoped to get in on his lucrative trade. Not a chance, he said, if he couldn't see that cunt of an officer off and make out of him, his name wasn't Fox and he'd give up. While saying this he grinned across at me in a show of great fellowship, so I raised my glass in reply and nodded. At that precise moment, if I hadn't thought of it before, I knew I would do Fox, take him for all he possessed including the apartment we were in. Just for starters I spoke to the girl in my fluent German. I saw their eyes open wide in surprise.

'Come over here and sit on my knee, Marlene,' I invited. 'I'm sure you and I could be very good friends. Don't be shy, Foxy won't mind –'

The girl giggled, then crossed the room and sat down on my lap. I kissed her and she returned the kiss, allowing me to fondle her small firm round tits. When I reached up under her dress she opened her thighs and I felt the warm fork of her upper legs, a neat little bulge of a cunt under the nylon material. 'I'm fixed up for the night, corporal,' I said. 'If a busy little operator like you has business in town, you can borrow the jeep. I won't need it until the morning.'

'But that's my bloody girl,' Fox protested wildly.

'Tough,' I said, 'but this shit of an officer ain't going anywhere, Foxy old boy, so fuck off and be back with the jeep bright and early. I'm sure you'll find plenty to amuse you in Berlin. It's a great town, so you claim.'

He snatched up the keys of the jeep and stamped out of the room, with Marlene covering her mouth to

In The Mood

suppress her giggles. 'What does he mean to you?' I asked her.

'Nothing,' she said firmly. 'He feeds me and I fuck for him. He is not good at that either. I think you will be much nicer.'

I decided that having a nice willing young slip of a thing for a change would be rather good. 'What's cooking in the kitchen?' I asked. 'It certainly smells good – '

'Steak,' she said. 'Steak and onions and potatoes.'

'Good. We'll dine on Foxy's ill-gotten goodies.'

She had an arm around my neck and suddenly looked worried. 'It was not for him,' she admitted. 'Please, sir, I did not know he was coming. I made the food for me and my friend Greta. She is in the kitchen – ' Marlene lowered her eyes. 'Sometimes when he's not here I bring my friend for a meal. There is always food here, he doesn't miss it.' She jumped off my lap and went into the kitchen, returning with another young girl, a very blonde miss with her hair down her back in plaits tied with ribbons. She looked apprehensive and clutched at a school satchel.

'How old are you, Greta?' I asked. 'You're still at school – '

'Sixteen, mein herr,' she said. 'I go to the academy. It is my last year.'

'How come Fox didn't spot you when he looked in the kitchen when he came in?'

'She was hiding in the big cupboard,' Marlene answered for her, hopping back on my knee and replacing her arm around my neck. 'Don't worry, she fucks too. We all have to, even our mothers – '

'You must bring them along for a meal sometime,' I suggested, and both girls giggled, relaxing. It seemed I had struck gold. The food was delicious, and Fox's stock of Rhine wines were given a good sampling and declared palatable. In all, the meal was a pleasure made all the more enjoyable by my two young companions, eating ravenously and having their fill for

151

In The Mood

once and chatting happily at the table. When it came to them insisting on doing the washing up, I went through to the bed-sitting room to see what treasures Fox may have stored away. His cupboards were empty but for a few clothes and apart from the selection of drinks on the sideboard and some packets of cigarettes in the drawers, there seemed little of value. Only a slightly turned-up fringe of a carpet in a corner under an armchair gave a clue. I peeled back the carpet, lifted several loose floorboards and looked down upon a veritable trove of bottles, cartons of both American and British cigarettes, tins of coffee, ham, corned beef and packets of sugar. I removed a few tins of coffee and some sugar to give to my two girls, then carefully replaced the planks and carpet. The pair of them, all work done in the kitchen, came through and stood beside the bed undressing. It was expected, I supposed, so I got out of my uniform and joined them.

Their bodies were supple and of that skin texture that only young girls have. I fucked Marlene first with Greta sitting up watching closely. Later when she mounted me, her little tits bobbing over me as she worked up to her climax, Marlene sat over my face, lowering a tight-lipped little cunt onto my mouth. They giggled over the size of my prick, jiggled above me, both giving heartfelt sighs and moans as their arousal gripped them. On Marlene occasionally rising her crotch off my face, I caught glimpses of the two minxes kissing each other, grasping at the others budding tits. We all came off splendidly within seconds of each other and I was left on the bed, glad of the rest after my previous night's exertions and the flight to Berlin. They dressed and left with their booty, both giving me a passionate farewell kiss, still giggling.

I slept like a log, awakened only by a hammering on the door. Corporal Fox stood there when I opened up just enough to let him in, naked as I was. He looked across at his rumpled bed, his shifty eyes filled with

In The Mood

hate. Two empty wine bottles were at the bedside table with three glasses.

'Made yourself at home, I see, sir,' he said with heavy sarcasm. 'Better make the most of it while it lasts, which ends right now. I've got as much on you as you have on me –'

'Then we're in this together then, aren't we?' I said easily. 'I don't see why we can't both benefit by a bit of private enterprise, old chum. I thought my first night in Berlin rather successful for a new boy. I do hope you found a place to spend the night. It was rotten to be turned out of your bed –'

'I have contacts here that could have you disappear,' he threatened. 'Disappear out of sight –'

I caught him by the front of his uniform jacket and lifted him to his toes. 'Then I shall have to leave a sealed letter with my solicitor, won't I?' I said. 'A signed affidavit made on oath to be opened in case of said threatened disappearance by me. It would make interesting reading about stolen duty-free labels, the horde you keep under the floorboards. I think we understand each other, Foxy. Don't think I don't admire your ingenuity. I fully intend to recommend that you be promoted to sergeant, for services above and beyond the call of duty.'

'Get fucked,' Corporal Fox snarled viciously.

'Oh I do, every chance I get,' I assured him. 'Now let's make for home and another cargo of the wherewithal, as you so rightly call it. You'll have to introduce me to your best customers next trip out. I think this Berlin run is going to suit my lifestyle very well.' And very well it did over the next six months.

Chapter Four

In time the Berlin airlift became known as a 'Milk Run' and it was the norm for pilots like myself to make as many as four or five flights a week. There were casualties, as there were bound to be with so many thousands of aircraft in regular use with the same destination. From the air one could spot crashed planes around the approaches to the city; at the airfield itself a crash landing was a daily occurrence, arrivals lumbering in overloaded with everything you could name to keep a population alive and public amenities operating. By the end of the emergency, when the Russians gave up and lifted the blockade, over one and a half million tons of goods of all kinds – food, coal, fuel and medical supplies – had been flown into Berlin. You can add to that thousands of cigarettes, loads of booze, coffee, tea and sugar and other luxuries in short supply brought in by Corporal Fox and myself in our bootleg business dealings.

The result was, in a cut-off community with even the bare necessities in short supply, my partner and I in crime lived the life of Riley. Corporal Fox and I maintained a relationship of mutual loathing while being necessary to each other's success as providers of luxuries where none existed. Within weeks I had obtained an undamaged apartment in the best area of the city, was on terms with the top black marketeers around, had my pick of women and was a big-spender in the best night spots in town.

In The Mood

Most of my deals were accomplished in the aptly named Club Sixty Nine, a cellar den presided over by Helga Stolz, a noted beauty of a noble pre-war family now reduced to operating a strip joint attended by the most successful crooks in besieged Berlin. Helga had dropped the 'von' from her name but did not drop her knickers it was said. This made me all the more determined to have her. Her club never closed until dawn each day, during which time she would sit at her private table overseeing her business, always with a young girl rumoured to be her slave.

Some said she was out-and-out lesbian, others that she still remained faithful to her dead husband's memory, a Panzer colonel executed for his part in the plot to kill Hitler. She was tall, blonde and classy; I itched to give her one and brought gifts of silk underwear and stockings to tempt her. I was one of the few privileged to be invited to sit at her table with her girlfriend, a beautiful young creature with long blonde hair and milk-white skin who greatly resented any man joining them. I sat with them one night talking business about the latest contraband I'd brought in on that evening's flight, and when Helga excused herself for a telephone call to a likely buyer, I was left with the girl.

'You will never fuck her, you know, Englander,' she taunted me. 'Why don't you go fuck so many of the whores in here?'

'I can but try,' I said easily, pouring champagne into her glass to show there were no hard feelings. 'I'd throw a little fuck in your direction too, given the chance. I'd make it well worth your while.' I gave her a wink and she glared hate at me. That was encouraging, it meant she feared my eventual success. Helga returned to take her seat, nodding at me to say a deal was on, then noting the girl's sullen features.

'Take no notice of him, liebchen,' Helga soothed her.

In The Mood

'He teases you. Flight Lieutenant Wight is a good friend – '

'He wants to fuck you,' sobbed the girl.

'Every man in here wants to fuck me,' Helga said while taking her in her arms and smoothing her hair. The girl dipped a hand into the low cut vee of Helga's evening gown, bringing out a luscious big creamy teat and sucking upon the nipple contentedly. That was the Berlin scene I'd got into.

So I determined to nail the aloof Helga, but meanwhile there was no shortage of willing women to keep me going, both at home and abroad. Back at base Wing Commander Nigh was rumoured to have his sights set on an O.B.E. at least, plus a promotion to Group Captain by dedication to duty during the airlift by remaining at his post through all hours. He was always in his office no matter when I looked in there, working out the flight schedules. This left his wife at a very loose end.

Like a good service wife she encouraged her husband to do his duty, and kept a light in the window for me to visit and console her between outward-bound flights. I did not need to look farther afield than the supple Susan Nigh when in England. We slept together every available chance and it was lovely to awaken those summer mornings to birdsong and the soft warm nakedness of the eager lady beside me. Often that awakening came with her bending over me, bedclothes thrown back, sucking on my prick to arouse me for yet another bout of the fucking that she'd grown inordinately fond of. She never bothered to dress when I stayed with her, rising in the morning to bring me tea and toast in bed, sitting on the edge with her big tits hanging so nicely before me.

I had rarely met such a vocal female, delighting in crude talk before, during and after a fuck. 'Is this the nice lady who presides at the church hall canteen?' I used to tease her as her body bucked and thrust under

In The Mood

me during a screwing. 'Does your husband fuck you like this? Does he know what a hungry cunt his wife's got between her legs?'

'Just shut up and fuck me with that big prick of yours,' she'd grunt back, further aroused by the pillow talk. One of her favourite expressions when right in the throes, on the verge of a strong come, was to cry out, 'Give me a baby, give me a baby! Oh, shove it all up my cunt, give me a baby –' And afterwards, while side by side recovering, she'd say things like, 'You fucked me, you beast. Fucked your commanding officer's wife. Was that a nice thing to do?' To which, of course, I'd reply it was a very nice thing indeed.

Perhaps we got careless through the ease which allowed me to call upon her. A month or two into my Berlin airlift time I left her house at the usual early hour before the village came to life. My car, a sporty little MG I was now solvent enough to own, was kept hidden up a track in a clump of trees some way from the back door of her cottage. When I reached it, Corporal Fox was leaning against the bonnet, the smoke from his cigarette curling up into the morning air. The smug grin on his ratty face told me all I needed to know.

'I was just passing, Skip,' he informed me. 'Recognised your car and thought I'd hang about and get a lift back to base –'

The lying bastard had been spying on me, but I wasn't giving him the satisfaction of seeming perturbed. 'Hop in,' I told him, 'and say what you're bursting to come out with, Fox.'

'Is the Wingco's wife a good ride?' he asked maliciously. 'I'll bet she is just is, all that nice tit and arse –'

'You should be so lucky.'

'Now it's my turn,' Fox said casually, 'for you to ask me if I'll report you. Just like that first time you caught me with the goods in Berlin, remember? The RAF's

In The Mood

going to take a pretty dim view of you fucking your senior officer's missis, much as I'd like to get across her myself. I think to shut my mouth we ought to consider our business partnership for starters.'

'So what do you have in mind?'

'No more fifty-fifty split. I'd reckon on a bigger share for me now, wouldn't you? And there's your flat in Berlin. Nice, very nice. I suggest we make a swop, your place for mine – '

'How did you suss out about Mrs Nigh and me?'

'Kept the old eyes peeled. Saw you wasn't staying on the base at nights. Followed you, couldn't believe you were making out with her, not her. So I thought I'd give you a little surprise this morning.' He could not disguise the smirk of triumph on his face. I decided it was time to wipe it off.

'Fox,' I said, deliberately and slowly. 'I have been in the shit more times than you've had hot dinners. All my life. One more time is neither here nor there, you spying scumbag. Go ahead and report me, see if I care – '

'You don't mean that,' he claimed.

Neither I did, more for Susan Nigh's good name than for my own, but I wasn't letting on. 'Try me,' I offered. 'You drop me in it and I'll drag you down so far you won't come up for air. Got me?'

'Is that all you got to say?' he grumbled.

'Not quite,' I said. 'Now you can get out of my car and walk back. And if you're late for our flight, I'll slap you on report – '

'Thanks a bunch, you bastard,' said Fox. 'I thought I'd got you, but I haven't, have I?'

'Nice try,' I admitted. I saw his sly face crease into a grin, even an admiring look. I could only grin back at him.

'Two of a kind, you and I, sir. No sense falling out.'

'Get back in the car,' I told him. 'What goodies has your spiv friend supplied us with this trip?'

In The Mood

'A real treat for Jerries, tins of Frankfurter sausages. Yank army supplies that got lost in transit – '

'I don't wish to know that,' I laughed. 'Anything else?'

'Dried-egg powder, the usual ciggies and stuff, all safely stowed aboard. Does the Wingco's wife really like the dick, sir?' he asked enviously. 'Fuck like a good 'un?'

'Let's say she has no complaints,' I said, and left it at that.

For all our agreeing not to disagree, I still did not trust Fox as far as I could throw him. My making up with him was simply because I believed it was better to have a friendly enemy than a real one.

That same evening in Berlin we were supposed to make a return night flight back, but a reported dicey port engine on the Dakota gave us an excuse for a stopover. I went to my flat to shower and shave before heading out on the town. Waiting on the landing outside my door were Helga von Stolz and her girlfriend, both of them dressed in street clothes for a change and with a small suitcase apiece. I invited them into my parlour, of course, asking why I had the pleasure of their company. Normally, I was sure, they never surfaced during daylight hours. Helga seemed aggravated and her young friend sullen and sulky, as usual. They took off their coats as if meaning to stay when I poured them a stiff whisky each. They seemed in need of a boost. The girl slumped in an armchair, glaring at me, tossing back her drink and reaching for the bottle for more. Helga too knocked back a second drink, for once not her usual cool self.

'Yes, we shall stay here for a day or two,' she announced suddenly, as if deciding without consulting me mattered at all. I knew she had an apartment much larger and grander than mine, so asked why I had been so honoured. 'The police,' she said. *Politzei*

In The Mood

schwinehund was what she actually said. 'For all the protection money I have paid them, they want more. So they close my club, search to arrest me. Me! Me that let them fuck the girls in my club for no charge. That let them have imported food and drink for free. Now they say I'm to be made an example of, to be charged with supplying prostitutes and black market goods – '

Running a brothel and making on black market deals was precisely what she'd be doing, but I couldn't laugh while she was so on her high horse. 'What can you do about it?' I asked.

'Pay them, of course,' Helga snapped. 'My lawyer, Herr Doktor Himmelstoss, will negotiate with them for me. You'll see, in a few days all will be business again. Until then I must stay here.'

'What made you decide on my place?' I wanted to know.

'They will never look here, an English officer. You will move out, of course, while we stay here.'

I don't think so, I had to tell her. 'Stay if you wish but you'll have to put up with me.' I said it deliberately, having been giving the cold shoulder from the imperious Helga often enough, despite giving her presents with the sole intention of fucking her. 'I'm going out, but I'll be back,' I told my two guests. 'Make yourself at home, there's more drink in the sideboard.' I found the situation intriguing, seeing as how there was only one bed in the apartment, and I had no intention of kipping on the settee.

I spent the evening with Corporal Fox unloading our stuff successfully in the back room of the first cellar club we went to. With a suitcase of loot safely locked in the back of a pre-war Volkswagen we used for our sales' outings and guarded by an ex-paratroop glad to do so for a packet of cigarettes, Foxy insisted I be his guest at his favourite nightery. It was a sleazy joint but really jumping as the saying goes. The booze was the best Scotch, brought in by ourselves, I was proudly informed.

We saw a succession of strippers through a haze of smoke, an amateur parade of hard-pressed women with families to feed willing to bare all for the prize of some tinned food. There were big tits revealed, small tits, wide-apart ones, danglers, pear-shaped and nice nestling-together ones. As many types of cunts and buttocks were uncovered too: wispy-haired mounds, tight little girlish quims, fat bouncy arses all getting applauded by the drunken throng.

Later Foxy drove me back home half-pissed. I invited him in for a share-out of our pickings, quite forgetting that Helga and her sulky girlfriend were there. We found the pair huddled together on my settee, obviously drunk, Helga with her blouse and brassiere off revealing a large pair of fleshy tits being fondled by her friend, the rubbery nipples quite taut and glistening with saliva.

'Big Helga, by fuck,' Foxy said to me in awe. 'First Mrs Nigh and now Helga. You do all right on the quiet, Skip. Will we get a fuck at these two, you reckon?' He stared across at them through bleary eyes, hicupping. The girl fondling Helga's big tits stuck out her tongue at us before going on to continue sucking on a nipple. 'A couple of lesbos,' Fox decided. 'You into watching kinky stuff?'

'Landed on me, didn't invite 'em,' I said, as pissed as a fart myself. It was not my usual, getting drunk, but it had been one of those kind of nights that turn out that way. We emptied our suitcase onto the table. We had collected some prize items in our bartering: silver candlesticks, diamond rings Foxy had checked out with an eye-glass, pearl necklaces, brooches, bracelets, and a fine selection of Nazi memorabilia. There were SS daggers, Knight's Crosses with crossed swords and rubies, Iron Crosses, belt buckles and regimental badges – all valuable stuff with a growing collectors'

In The Mood

market at home and especially in America. We usually drew lots to see who got what but our eyes were drawn to the pair on the settee, kissing and fondling openly before us, Helga's hand up her girlfriend's dress working away nicely.

'Let's leave the dividing till the morning,' Foxy suggested. 'I can't concentrate with those two at it. I need a bloody drink.'

I agreed, getting out a fresh Walker's Black Label bottle and opening it. Across the room on the settee, Helga held out her glass for a refill. When I filled it, the girl with her took the glass and poured a few drips of the whisky over Helga's tits and began licking at them, turning every now and then to look at us two watching men as if to say, 'This is mine, not for you.' We stood fascinated as the pair aroused themselves with the added ingredient of an audience to give spice to their lovemaking.

'Lilly, liebchen, you are so naughty, we are not alone,' Helga moaned as if in protest while holding each succulent teat up for her partner to lick and suck. The pair arose and took off their clothes, the glorious Helga with her big jutting breasts and ample thighs, the younger Lilly slim with pert little tilted tits and a boyish arse. They fell back onto the settee in each other's arms, kissing lewdly between glancing to see if we were watching. I had gained a hard-on that seemed permanent. Beside me Fox was muttering his frustration. Lilly then slipped to the floor before Helga, who opened her legs wide as she lolled back to show her all, a cunt like a mouth with a hairy bush aimed directly at us. Lilly looked at it adoringly, sniffed it and kissed it, then plunged her face right against it.

'You going to stand for this, Skip?' Fox enquired. Before us now Lilly was slurping away on her knees, her back dipped so that her polished little buttock cheeks were tilted upwards daring us to resist the offering. As if reading each other's minds, Foxy and I

In The Mood

immediately began throwing off our clothes, the best civvie suits and shirts Berlin could provide. We both stood with massive erections and the women looked across at us startled, Lilly turning with her mouth glistening. Fox and I crossed the few yards of carpet, cocks in hands.

'Helga, you are going to get fucked,' I informed her, looming over the pair of them. 'You've asked for it – '

'Both of us then, but take her bottom first,' Helga said surprisingly equitably. 'Let her go on, don't stop her – '

That seemed a fair enough request, but Lilly paused in her lapping and licking at her mistress's cunt to protest, eyeing my rampant cock waving before her eyes with something like alarm. 'I can't take that! I won't,' she grumbled. 'Not in the arse – '

'You've had it there before, and bigger,' Helga snapped. 'And you know that you like it once it's in you.' To me she urged, 'Go on then, get on with it. I want her to lick me while you bugger her. I want to see you doing it.'

It was that kind of drunken orgy, all of us saying and doing things that our baser instincts crave at times. I felt between Lilly's arse cheeks, gave her cunt a little feel, felt the wetness of arousal in the velvety channel. I soaked my finger well with her own lubrication, then drew it back the inch necessary to finger and ease open her tight little bottom hole. 'Tight as a nun's bum,' I announced, still probing away while Lilly grimaced and drew in her breath.

'You'll never get your bloody great chopper up there,' Fox claimed. 'Let me in there first.'

'Do not talk so much about it,' an irate Helga cut in. In the absence of Lilly licking her cunt, she had a hand at her slit working away nicely. 'I tell you she will take it and like it. I have dildoed her there myself. She uses one on herself, so big it is – '

'That I'd like to see,' Foxy whooped, staggering about

In The Mood

in his inebriated state. I could have roared with laughter myself, the sort of silly drunken hysterics that comes over one, but young Lilly's glossy little bum seemed raised expectantly and she was beginning to writhe on my penetrated finger. I went closer behind her, parted the firm cheeks and guided my knob to the puckered ring. She gasped but actually pushed back against me, brought to wanting it without further delay. I went up surprisingly smoothly, feeling my shaft tightly clenched. At the same time Helga grabbed the girl's head and pulled her back into her crotch. My in-and-out movement grew easier to achieve as her arse relaxed. Her grunts and moans as I rode her were muffled into the cunt she sucked at her other end.

Glancing up in my thrusting I saw Helga looking down at the bum-tailing with eager eyes. 'Yes, yes,' she said meanly. 'Fuck the little bitch good. Split her naughty little arse. Do it for me. Oh, oh, how her tongue torments me. I will come, come – '

'Oh, bloody heaven,' I was grunting out myself, lost in the delight of a lewd threesome, tightly ensconced up the grip of Lilly's back passage, her pliant little bum jerking wildly back into my belly. I hunched right over for further depth, gripping her hard little tits for leverage, riding her like a monkey. The scene proved too much for Foxy to be a mere bystander. He held out his prick as if on offer.

'What do I do with this?' he cried appealing. 'You horny sods have forgotten me – '

'Helga's mouth,' I shouted. 'Fuck her mouth, Foxy.'

'Nein, nein,' Helga protested, but Fox was up on the settee, his legs planted firmly each side of Helga's thighs, standing directly over Lilly's bobbing head. I saw him feed his prick into Helga's lips, rub his knob over them, then saw Helga find the temptation too much and puff her cheeks as she sucked him in. I can't say how long we continued, in our state time seemed a moment, an hour. When we collapsed against each other it was in a heap of naked sweating bodies, sated and drunk.

I remember staggering through to my bed sometime later in the night to find Helga there and climbed in beside her to fall fast asleep in moments. When I awoke dawn was already lightening the curtains and the bed was bouncing with frenzied movements. Lilly was on hands and knees with Foxy shafting her vigorously in true doggy fashion while she squealed out her pleasure. There was nothing else for it. Beside me Helga lolled naked and inviting. I sucked on her thumb-like nipples and brought her to a drowsy understanding that she was being used. She pushed at my head and I went below to lap at her cunt. When her arousal was such that she was lifting herself against my mouth, moaning in extremis, I raised myself and penetrated her nicely first go. Surprised as she was, she continued her thrusting as she had when receiving the tongue, her legs circling my back.

Such was life for us in Berlin as the months proceeded. That it would all end one day as the Russians conceded was rumoured as each week passed. For me it had been good while it lasted. I had paid off my debts back in England, got myself a healthy bank balance, and had a great time in the whole of the airlift period. To stay in a peacetime Royal Air Force was not my intention, it would be too tame for the likes of myself. As always for me it was time to be thinking of moving on.

At home my affair with Susan Nigh had petered out as her husband had got his decoration and promotion, thus being moved on to command of another larger airfield in Gloucestershire. His wife wrote to tell me it was over and how good it had been for her while it had lasted, adding that she missed my prick and what it did to her 'in all orifices' as she cheekily put it.

My association with the Nigh family had not exactly

In The Mood

ended there, however. It was in my nature to follow up inclinations, and the plump little Letitia at the Airman's Rest in Berlin presented a challenge. It was easier than I'd reckoned. A few flattering remarks on my visits to her with supplies from home, an evening out together at a concert by the newly reformed Berlin Philharmonic Orchestra, tickets for which were hard to obtain but got through my contacts, broke the ice. That evening at my apartment I had her chubby bare body under me in bed, as eager to fuck as I.

The end of this halcyon time came with a call to present myself to the Group Captain's office at the airport in Berlin. I was summoned as I prepared for the flight back to England, my navigator aboard but no sign of Corporal Fox with less than ten minutes to go to take-off. That seemed an ominous fact as I tapped on the Group Captain's door and was bade enter. The senior officer sat behind his desk looking serious. I knew the man fairly well, he enjoyed the nightlife of Berlin like myself and I had once or twice had a drink with him in some nightspot.

'The last thing I want to do is throw the book at you, Wight,' he said. 'How many flights have you made in the Berlin airlift?'

'Without referring to my log book, sir,' I said, 'it's something like ninety-odd.'

'Ninety-eight exactly,' the Group told me. 'Twice at least coming in on one engine. A fine record. Pity you are about to terminate it – '

'Am I, sir?'

'I think so. In the early hours of this morning your loadmaster, Corporal Fox, was apprehended in the city with a vehicle loaded with contraband goods. He's in custody now.'

'So he implicated me,' I said. Foxy had had the last word.

'Never said a word about anyone working with him. He's been questioned for several hours now. I've

In The Mood

spoken to him myself and he claims it was nothing to do with anyone else.'

I said a silent prayer of thanks. 'I'd like to see him,' I asked. 'He's been in my crew from the start – '

'That's why I've been asked to conduct an enquiry into any part you may have played in this business. It's not gone unnoticed you've been living pretty high in Berlin. I could get a warrant to have your apartment searched. I won't. Not if you care to resign your commission now.' He pushed an official document across the desk to me. 'Sign, and no further action will be taken.'

So I scribbled my name on the dotted line. 'I asked can I see Fox, sir? Perhaps I could take him some cigarettes?'

'He was flown off to England half an hour ago under escort,' I was told. 'As you are no longer an officer of the Royal Air Force, Flight Lieutenant Stevely will fly your aircraft back. You will return as a passenger.'

I rose to leave. 'Is that all, sir?'

'Not quite,' he said. 'I believe you have a rather nice apartment here in Berlin. Pity to see it going begging – '

I understood, handing him the key.

'Now we've both done each other a favour,' he nodded. 'See you keep out of mischief in future, young man.' I couldn't promise that.

Chapter Five

Austerity there may have been in Britain. On the liners still plying the sea lanes of the world in the early 1950's all was as pre-war standards demanded. To step aboard was like Alice going through the looking glass into a different world. Stewards and waiters attended to every request. The menus were comprehensive and dining on unrationed servings an unhurried pleasure. The duty-free bars were stocked full of every conceivable alcoholic drink. They were floating luxury hotels, the faster aeroplane came a poor second.

I'd expended what little money I had on a first-class ticket, a decision not only to treat myself to the superior service assured but because one inevitably mixed with a more relaxed and well-off type. This was not snobbery on my part. More relaxed and well-off women, I'd found, were more likely to indulge in affairs, extra-marital or otherwise. Without Moira's knowledge I'd been measured for a new wardrobe of evening wear and sports clothes. I intended to look the part, even taking a selection of silk cravats as I imagined a suave man-about-town would wear. I was not yet thirty, six foot, an ex-officer with a DFC and more than presentable. I thought I should do all right.

On that last evening in London, luggage safely stowed in my single cabin at Tilbury Docks, I went to the Suzy Q club to say my farewells. In the elation of freedom to go my own way, do my own thing as they now say, I intended to tell Q what I thought of him and

In The Mood

sort out the snivelling Gus while I was at it. Manny I'd buy a drink, for he had proved to have a streak of human kindness under a seen-it-all exterior. Instead they treated me to drinks on the house, slapped my back, and I decided they weren't such bad fellows after all. Before they poured me in a taxi for Tilbury, the driver paid, I sentimentally made Manny promise to keep an eye on Moira, as if tearing myself away from her was the decent thing to do. This was pure bull. Little Moira was a survivor.

On board I slept the sleep of the just to awaken to a steward tapping respectfully at my cabin door and a definite roll on the ship. He came in balancing a tray of morning tea and informed me we were heading downchannel into a blustery gale. Did I want the tea, sir? 'Of course,' I said. 'Glass is dropping,' he said cheerfully, 'we're in for a spot of weather.' True, once in the open sea it worsened and for the next several days few passengers felt well enough to leave their cabins, let alone wine, dine and enjoy the shipboard entertainments which had been cancelled anyway. The ship was proving to be as dull as a wet Sunday in a provincial town.

I was left a good deal to my own devices. It seemed the majority of the first-class were farmers, senior colonial civil servants and their wives returning to East Africa after a visit to the home country. They seemed all very middle-aged and stuffy characters. A handful of the men who seemed unaffected by the high seas kept to a panelled mahogany salon playing endless games of poker, drinks and score pads beside wrists with the little piles of coloured gambling chips. From their concentration it was evident they did not welcome onlookers. I was in another bar contemplating what might have been when joined by one of the men I'd seen at the card table. 'You'll have a drink, young man,' he said, more of a statement than an invite, nodding to the white-jacketed barman to refresh my drink.

In The Mood

He wore an evening suit with wide velvet lapels, old-fashioned but immaculately cut for his bulky figure. In his late fifties, he was ruddy-faced with a clipped moustache, tight boiled-starched collar and bow-tie. He carried authority, the kind that comes with wealth and power. 'Gore-Blomley,' he introduced himself. I said who I was but he did not offer his hand. 'Hoping to make a good life in Kenya, are you? Ex-service?' I gave him a yes to both. 'You don't play cards,' he added.

I'd heard from the stewards about the stakes played for, sums beyond my means. I was no gambler. My money when I had some may have been recklessly expended but I'd always got great pleasure from wasting it on the opposite sex; less of a gamble too than the turn of a card. I stayed silent, wondering what he was getting at. 'You'll be in this bar a while, will you?' he said. 'I have a favour to ask. My wife was due in here to join me for a drink. She must have been detained with my sister, who's down in her cabin being constantly seasick, bloody woman. I don't know what gets these females so feeble in a little bit of weather. My wife is all right but should have been here by now. And I'm well overdue in the salon. Be a good chap, when she appears do be kind enough to explain for me. Apologise on my behalf to the old girl. I'd rather you handled it than the barman chappie. Buy her a drink and have one yourself. I won't forget the favour – '

He went off, eager to get to the card table, without giving any description of his wife. I was not delighted, fancying myself stuck for part of the evening with the kind of woman married to his sort. The sole occupier of the bar, I could only take the first female to appear as his 'old girl' and the description was not flattering. She was of medium height and no more than in her forties, the very prime for a woman who had cared for her looks. More often too at that age one did not have to waste time getting them to do what was expected.

171

In The Mood

She had beautiful wide hazel eyes under the lightest auburn hair crimped over her forehead. Dressed in blue-grey silk evening gown, she carried a stole which draped easily over nicely rounded arms. She was well-fleshed yet had not an ounce of fat. Her big breasts jutted out in front, tight cleavage starting where the V of her dress met. The diamond pendant that nestled at the cleft of those glorious tits sparkled for real.

She looked about with undisguised annoyance and sat down at a table, her ample shapely bottom filling the chair. I'd always had a strong lech for attractive older women, the very beddable kind. I beat a hovering steward to her and he drew back, giving me pride of place. She was about to light a cigarette. I flicked the lighter I always kept for such an occasion into flame. She drew on her smoke and glanced up at me with little interest.

'Mrs Gore-Blomley?' I enquired. 'Forgive my presumption. Your husband was here and asked me to explain to you that he was expected in the salon.'

'No doubt,' she said drily.

'He asked me to get you a drink.'

'He would.'

'I'd be more than happy to. Do you mind if I join you? We could be the only people alive tonight from the activity around here – '

'And who are you, may I ask?' she said. 'Do you know my husband?'

'We met here in this bar just now.' I confessed. As I seemed to be getting nowhere with a rather humourless upper-class bitch, I relaxed my manners. 'He asked me to tell you and I've told you, end of story. I didn't know him from Adam.'

She relented somewhat and smiled thinly. She drained the champagne cocktail I was told to order for her then indicated a refill by shaking the empty glass at the steward. I was caught out looking down her cleavage, admiring the full rounds of her shapely breasts.

In The Mood

'You're staring at my tits,' she said calmly. 'They are rather good ones, aren't they?'

I detected from her derisive look that Mrs Gore-Blomley was testing me after my previous direct reply. She was trying to shock me. 'They are better than good,' I said levelly. 'Great tits, in fact. I hope a look and a feel at them during this voyage is not out of the question?'

This brought a short laugh. 'You have possibilities. Do you always speak your mind?'

'Faint heart never won and all that,' I said, 'especially for two such magnificent reasons. You haven't answered my question.'

She glanced about the ornate bar. 'It is dead as a doornail in here. What do you suggest we do?'

'My cabin is a private one.' I was elated by the possibility of having this woman but remained deliberately calm to match her own studied nonchalence. 'It's on this deck, quite nearby. We could raise a glass or two, continue this conversation.'

'I don't think you're nice to know, young man,' she said, 'but it seems I'm about to find out. Anyway, my husband will be at that bloody card table until dawn. Serves him right, don't you think? He did tell you to amuse me, I gather – '

Locking my cabin door behind us and admiring my guest, I intended to do more than amuse her. She draped her stole over a chair, regarding me. 'Now that I see you here, you are very young,' she said. 'Perhaps I made a mistake coming here –?'

'I want to see you with everything off,' I told her. 'Naked and showing those big tits off. I want to see your cunt, too.'

'You've a greedy eye. There's quite a lot of me.'

'There's quite a lot of me,' I promised. She was a find, I congratulated myself. A handsome and voluptuously shaped woman and evidently one prepared to have

In The Mood

a sexual diversion as an amusement. 'Quite a lot,' I repeated.

'Don't boast. I've had the likes of you for breakfast.' She sat down. 'I'm waiting for that drink you promised me.'

I brought her the drink and in handing it to her, bent to kiss her lips. She allowed my mouth to linger, my tongue to probe between her lips, a hand going up to hold the nape of my neck. 'You'd better be good,' she warned. I took the drink from her hand, placing it on the bedside table, lifting her and taking her in my arms. I resumed kissing her with my tongue, my whole body hard to hers, breasts, cunt-mound and knees. My prick had attained a fine rigid erection, prodding against pliant flesh. 'Let's do this properly,' she said.

Drawing away from me, she began to undress, a woman of no inhibitions when the occasion demanded. She was evidently rich, married to wealth, self-assured but easily bored perhaps. A sexual adventurer like myself. I stood before her and disrobed as casually as she, retaining my Y-front pants to keep her guessing. She evidently intended to hold onto her status during copulation but I would fuck the bitch until she'd know it, fuck the arrogant superior look off her face.

Standing naked before me, I walked slowly around her, assessing her body. I lifted a tit, let it fall back, tweaked her nipples, noting that they were elongated and hard. She watched me with a shake of her head. It was like a chess game, each waiting on the next move. I went behind her, admiring her buttocks, broad and well-rounded, firm, with the divide tight as a clam. I caressed both cheeks.

'I like what I see,' I told her, giving her arse a good feel and a friendly slap. To regain the initiative she lolled back on the bed, legs apart and draped over the edge. She parted the outer lips of her cunt with the first and second fingers of her left hand in an inverted V. I saw the pink inner lips glowing moist, a pronounced clitoris nub and the pubic hump raised to invite me to the core of her inner cunt.

'Lick me out,' she ordered sternly. 'Lick me clean. You do that, don't you?'

'It's been known.' I'd had enough of playing. She presented a fine pouting quim worthy of a good lapping and licking. I went down admiring what was before me, the hairy mound that bulged between the fork of her thighs, the cunt lips crinkled and dark brown against the creamy flesh of her slight tummy and the large tits that splayed apart across her chest. I began by kissing her inner thighs; led on by the tempting odour of her cunt I inserted my tongue. It brought a sigh and a 'yes' of encouragement. My tongue tip flicked around her clit. She settled her body to get full advantage of my probing, moving her thighs. I stood then, leaving her in midstream.

'Go on, don't stop now,' she said irately. 'Damn you, I was just beginning to like it – '

I laughed at her urgency. 'Don't worry, I'm just getting into this myself.' I played what I thought would be my best move, stepping out of my Y-fronts to reveal a prick engorged to the full by my licking of a juicy cunt. She looked up at me with her neck craned. The cock she saw stood up rigid and level with my stomach, thick and menacing.

'I want that,' she said, her voice almost a plea, the first sign of a weakening of her resolve. 'Give it to me – '

'In good time,' I promised. I poured a glass of wine, kept a mouthful, then knelt down again, spreading her thighs to their widest, filling her cunt with the wine and swilling it around inside her with my tongue. She drew in her breath sharply, took hold of my head and squirmed her whole lower body to gain the utmost titilation from the slight sting of the wine and my delving tongue. I felt the first spasms shaking her.

'Good God,' she swore. 'You bastard, you horny bas-

In The Mood

tard, what you're making me do. Go on, don't you dare stop now – '

'Like it?' I taunted from her crotch.

'Oh, fuck me, it's lovely.' Her body thrashed and her cunt mashed against my face. 'Oh, I'm coming! I haven't had a decent come in weeks – ' And then she came, heaving, grunting, gripping. I sat back on my knees and watched her subside.

'Who with?' I asked. 'That last decent come?'

'In Paris. That's all I'm telling you.'

'Not with your old man,' I suggested.

'Never with him any more. Don't talk. I've still got the feeling. Use that damn thing you're threatening me with.'

'Get on your knees then,' I directed her. She obediently rolled over, kneeling on the edge of the bed backside to me, showing cunt and arsehole together. For a few moments I put my hand between the warm damp cleft, touching up both entrances. She waggled her bum at me in invitation.

'Go on, I want it again,' she urged. 'I've more comes in me yet. Put it in – '

My shaft slid up her easily to the hilt and she shuddered with the pleasure. I was told not to hurry, she wanted it to last. Her buttocks were solid and comfortable, smooth in the curve of my belly as I curled over her. My balls seemed jammed between the moons of her arse. She reached back to part the cheeks for my deeper access. Thus we fucked, like dog and bitch, I grasping her tits, both lost in the throes; grunting, muttering and mouthing oaths in our lust. She was as good a fuck as I'd known and I told her so in plain words. 'Ride me, ride me,' she cried out. 'Fucking ride me, you bastard!'

'Oh, I'll fucking ride you,' I assured her. 'You'll whinny like a horse before I'm through with you.' As if to prove myself her jockey, the whiphand, I gave her backside sharp slaps as I rode her down the final straight. She raised her head and cried out. I felt her body lift, judder uncontrollably and collapse back face down still undulating. The wad I fired into her went on in repeated jets. Each last thrust was gripped by her cunt as if reluctant to lose the invader, milking the last drops from me. When we parted it was to fall apart, she to loll back on the bed as if in a stupor, me to slide to the cabin floor. Above me I heard her regaining her breath in long gasps.

She said, 'It seems this voyage won't be quite the boring dull trip I was dreading.'

I felt the deck move beneath my bare arse. 'Weather's turning even rougher, I think,' said I. 'This ship's positively bucking tonight. Feel it?'

'That was us,' Mrs Gore-Blomley said wickedly. I realised I didn't even know her first name, or she mine.

Chapter Six

Magically, once past Gibraltar the weather turned tropical, the sea Mediterranean-blue and calm. The ship came to life with people, the dining hall filled with recovered passengers and games and evening entertainments resumed. The card school played on in the salon interminably, food and drink served at the table, oblivious to all but the gambling urge. It left Gore-Blomley's wife at rather a loose end, one I was more than ready to fill.

I discovered she was a Virginia, addressed by her colonial acquaintances as Vee, and an Honourable by title if not by nature. Every chance that presented itself she warned me by sealed messages delivered by stewards to be in attendance in my cabin at various times. On her arrival she would hastily disrobe and fuck like a wanton, a daily injection of sex before remaking her face and dressing to join her set on the upper deck. Sometimes she would leave gifts on my dressing table without mentioning she had. My spoils included a gold cigarette case, which, as I did not smoke, could be sold to aid my financial position, and a very good wristwatch I could use, having pawned my previous one to help find my fare on the ship. These gifts were no doubt purchased from the ship's shop, stocked with luxury goods that would have made Mr Q go green with envy.

As a first-class person myself I mixed on the edge of her set, not making our relationship in any way obvi-

In The Mood

ous, which would have been impossible anyway as she ignored my presence. During games of deck quoits, swimming, cocktail parties and dances that were arranged to keep us amused, it was easy to glean bits of gossip about Vee Gore-Blomley and her husband. He was a wealthy farmer in Kenya with an estate rivalling Delamere's, a first-class shot as his trophy room proved, a pillar of society and an autocrat and bigot from way back. I was glad I was fucking his wife. That may not have been unique.

I made a friend of a young woman returning to Kenya from university and found a good source of information about the Gore-Blomleys. Vee, it was rumoured, had been an enthusiastic member of the promiscuous Happy Valley set in the Kenya of the 1940's which had fostered a murder of passion.

My time became divided between fucking Vee Gore-Blomley and spending it with the plainish girl graduate, an outdoor type named Anne who dragged me into every shipboard activity. I had advanced to feeling her tits and trying my hand up her skirt in darkened corners of the upper deck. Shy, she allowed kisses, would not risk entering my cabin and, as she shared a stateroom with her parents, that was a dead end. The challenge of her intrigued me. Determined to fuck her, I sought out likely places from the hold to the lifeboats where I could finally nail her without disturbance. The evening before entering the Suez Canal we danced on the upper deck under strung fairy lights, the atmosphere romantic.

I had pressed a champagne cocktail or two on her. Our bodies clung close as we danced, yielding tits hard to my chest and the ever-ready erection I got in close encounters nudging her lower belly. She agreed to slip away with me. I had her up against a winch on the empty foredeck, safe in deep shadow, softened up with sweet words and long kisses, tongues touching, hearing her whimper with arousal. She had my prick in her hand, one tit free whose nipple I was busily sucking, and two fingers up a warm and moist cunt when her name was called loudly by Vee Gore-Blomley in an urgent and disapproving tone. The girl leapt apart from me, straightening her gown.

'Whoever this young man is, Anne,' warned the woman I'd been fucking daily, 'I'm sure your parents would not approve of him at all. No doubt many of his type will come to East Africa and we'll do well to avoid his kind. I shall forget this incident. You had better return to your parents – '

'Yes, Mrs Gore-Blomley,' said the embarrassed girl and fled.

'You bastard,' Vee said to me when alone. 'Lecher, seducer. I'm not standing for this.'

'I am,' I told her, taking her hand to my uncovered and erect prick. 'Standing like a good prick should. Jealous, are we?' She pulled her hand away, giving my stander a swipe in doing so. 'Is that the way to treat something that's been good to you?' I teased her. 'You haven't got exclusive rights to me, you know.'

'You will leave that girl alone,' she threatened. 'I say so.'

'And you won't tell me what I can do,' I said calmly. To my amusement she slapped my face. I drew her to me and kissed her deeply, crushing her mouth, preventing her struggles with a bear grip. 'If I can't fuck her, I'll fuck you. I'll be in my cabin waiting. See that you'll be there – '

'Fuck you,' she said and stormed off. I was not at all sure my invitation would be accepted, but it had been well worth the try. My dalliance with Anne had got me more than ready for a good ride at a woman, but neither was I going to let Vee order me around like her personal property. Dancing, and my other activities on a sultry night, had left me sticking to my clothes. In my cabin I used the shower and dressed in a kimono, which I thought rather fetching. I was mixing a drink

In The Mood

when Vee's usual light knock took me to the door. She entered quickly as I locked up behind her, taking the drink I'd prepared and seeing it off. Without speaking she began to undress like any woman preparing for bed. There was no false modesty about her. Once naked before me she said, 'Damn you. I don't know why I'm doing this – '

'Maybe because of this,' I suggested, showing her my prick. She went down on her knees before me, one hand cupping my balls, the other circling my shaft. She pressed several kisses to the helmet, licked up the length. 'And don't you ever tell me what I must do,' she said, as if continuing our conversation held on the foredeck. 'No one does that, ever – '

'Shut up and eat my cock,' I ordered her. 'I want to fuck your mouth first. Eat it!'

'Yes,' she said. 'Eat it. I've been thinking about doing this all evening. I watched you dancing with that damned girl.' She gave me several sucks, paused to see it stretch in her hand. 'God, it is a lovely thing, so big and stiff. She wasn't getting this – ' Her lips went an inch or two over the shaft, then were drawn back slowly until my prick sprang free. This was repeated several times until she moaned and covered it in her mouth to suck avidly. I looked down upon her head bobbing, grasped a handful of hair and used my free hand to hold the nape of her neck. Struggle she might, but for the first time I'd come in her mouth, something she had always forbidden.

I thrust with my hips, pulling her face to me, fucking it strenuously. She tried to gag a protest but I held her fast, my prick nudging the back of her throat, head buried in the fork of my groin. She reached up a fist to pummel my chest but I held firm, and then she sucked furiously, caught up in the wantonness of the act. My knees gave, I groaned and jerked as a succession of spurts hit the back of her throat. She choked and gulped; made to swallow before I released her.

In The Mood

'Lovely bitch,' I moaned. 'And don't tell me you didn't love it – '

'Pig,' she swore, rising to her feet. 'Bastard. I don't allow that to happen. No man does that to me. I suck but I don't swallow, damn you.'

'You do now.' I let slip my kimono, lying back on the bed with my hands cradling my head. 'You've met your match, I'd say, Honourable Mrs Vee. Your bit of rough on the side doesn't stick to your rules like a good boy, does he? I think you quite enjoy that too – '

'Go to hell,' she said. She crossed to my cabinet, pouring herself a glass of champagne, using it to rinse her mouth, her back to me. I told her she had a splendid arse and she wobbled it at me. She came back with two glasses filled and sat on the bed beside me. 'I really should have no more to do with you,' she said, allowing me to cup one of her tits. 'You are obviously a bad lot. Tell me, have you fucked Anne Bellinger? The truth, mind. Not that a good screwing wouldn't do something for that pasty-faced little goodie-goodie.'

'I take it you don't like her?' I grinned.

'Answer my question.'

'Not yet. I was about to when we were so rudely interrupted.'

She looked down at me and shook her head. 'I believe you'd fuck anything. If so, I've a candidate in mind. I'd make it worth your while. I do believe you haven't two halfpennies to your name, so that should interest you.'

'Devious bitch,' I told her. 'You want to compromise some woman, don't you? Have something to hold over her.'

'That's what I want,' she agreed. 'I want the bitch on this bed with you as many times as you can manage before we reach Mombasa. I want you to do all the things to her that's sexually possible. Everything – '

'How can you be sure she'll come across? I like the idea, but who says she will? Who is she anyway?'

In The Mood

'Leave it to me, you ask too many questions – '

'I've got to know who it is.' I had of course eyed up all the presentable women on board. 'Have I met her, seen her?'

'Not yet. She's my husband's sister, Marigold Gore-Blomley. Unmarried and itching for it. I know she masturbates because I've caught her at it before now. I've a strong suspicion she even let one of the house-boys screw her for some years. The fellow was sacked for no apparent reason – '

'But you don't want to do her any favours?' I said.

'She's always considered I married her brother for his money and position. She regards me as a slut – '

'I didn't say a thing,' I grinned, taking her hand down to my cock which was showing signs of reviving.

'Then don't smirk. Marigold has had it in for me for years. I want her screwed good and proper so that she'll know it. She's not unattractive. I'll be with you to help the introduction, get her to visit you here – '

'If we appear so close, might she not surmise we've been at it too? If she thinks you do a bit on the side?'

'Crudely put, but if you succeed in having her, what can she say or do? We'll all have something on each other.' Leaning over me, her tits draped in my face, I kissed a nipple. 'Do this little thing and I won't be ungrateful,' she said. 'You'll be new to Kenya, wanting introductions to the right circles. I can assure you the Gore-Blomley's are not without a great deal of influence there. What do you say?'

'I say it's time I fucked you.' I felt her cunt, saw her loll back on the bed and open her thighs, pushing herself against my hand. 'As for Marigold, wheel her on. I'll fuck her, too.'

'How crude you are,' she said, but pulling me over and above her, directing my prick to where she wanted it. I had her head down, legs over my shoulder, penetrated to the hilt and nicely fucking away when a knock sounded at my door. Vee cursed, stopped her

In The Mood

motion against me. 'Who the hell is that?' she queried. 'Tell them to go away, whoever it is – '

The knock was repeated almost furtively. I rose and put on my kimono, looking down upon the sprawled and naked Vee. 'Get in the bathroom for now,' I told her, bundling up her clothes and throwing them in my wardrobe. She rose sullenly, going to the bathroom irked. Going to the door I found Miss Anne Bellinger there, in her ball gown, clasping and unclasping her hands nervously. I greeted her warmly, invited her in. She entered cautiously, looking about, from me in the silk housecoat to the rumpled bed.

'I've disturbed you,' she said. 'Were you asleep?'

'No, no. Just resting. I was having a drink. Join me.'

I poured a glass of champagne for her, which she sipped. Again she hoped she had not disturbed me. She wanted me to continue where we'd left off on the foredeck, I knew. The fact that a furious Vee was in my bathroom naked added piquancy to the situation. 'Mummy and Daddy have gone to bed,' she announced, 'but allowed me to stay up at the dance. I had to see you, to say how awful it was when Vee Gore-Blomley found me. She's an awful woman really, and not the one to preach morals to others. Her reputation in Kenya for having lovers, well, it's been talked of for years. I just hope she did not embarrass you terribly.'

I glanced at the bathroom door to note it was slightly open, enjoying the thought that Vee would be behind it not missing a word and fuming. Not enough perhaps to burst upon us in her naked state, but the idea was tempting. 'Then such a person is obviously not worth worrying about,' I said. 'I only thought how embarrassing it was for you. Are you all right now? Won't you sit?' I sat myself and patted the bed beside me. 'Do stay. The worst thing that bloody interfering woman did tonight was to butt in when we were just getting better acquainted.'

In The Mood

'Now that I know you are not dreadfully upset over her seeing us together, I'd better leave,' said Anne.

I took her wrist and made her sit beside me, my arm about her shoulders. 'She's not here now,' I told her, 'stay a minute or two, please.' I added I hoped we would see more of each other in Kenya.

'I don't know about that,' the girl said. 'We live in the northern territory almost on the Sudanese border. It's very remote. My father is a district commissioner and we rarely get to Nairobi.'

As I had no intention of continuing our shipboard acquaintance, this was good news. I kissed her neck and she shivered somewhat, repeating she should leave. Then I turned her head, kissing her lips, saying how sweet she was, her kisses too. She returned them, allowing my tongue in her mouth.

'See what you do to me,' I whispered, opening my kimono and clasping her hand to my upright cock. As I kissed her further she retained her grip on my shaft. When I lowered her to the bed she resisted for a brief moment before putting her arms about my neck.

'Let me see you,' I begged, 'see all of you.'

She was hesitant, but finally helped me to get her gown over her head and discarded. She wore silk underwear, rolling over onto her face as if in modesty when I unclipped her bra and drew her panties over her feet. I told her she was lovely, and indeed there was a smoothness about the feel of her. I caressed her buttocks, kissed each cheek, felt between them and sought her crack, fingered it and found it still moist. About to mount her in that rearward position, she suddenly turned and faced me.

'Don't hurt me,' she pleaded. 'It looks so big. But I do want you to if you'll be careful. Promise you won't make me pregnant?'

'Not a chance,' I assured her. 'Relax and enjoy. This is not your first time, is it?'

'No,' she said shyly. 'There was one other, at univer-

In The Mood

sity.' She looked up at me wide-eyed. 'But he was quite old, one of the lecturers. It wasn't all I thought it would be. He couldn't really do it to me. You know, be like you are now – ' As if to prove her point she squeezed my prick. 'It feels so hard, yours.'

'That's what you've done to me,' I said.

This last I knew would infuriate Vee, in whose cunt my prick had been not ten minutes before. A quick look at the bathroom door showed part of her face glaring around it. Anne then took my attention. Her tits were small but neatly formed, a matching pair, and her nipples quite prominent. I sucked each one while feeling in her cunt among the soft folds of flesh, found a stiff little clitoris and made her jump and gasp titillating it. When I lowered myself down between her legs she asked whatever was I doing? I think the poor girl thought putting a cock up her was the be-all of it.

When I sucked upon her cunt she protested, made me push her knees apart for better access, then settled back as if helpless to intervene as I tongued her as deep as I could, nose buried in wispy cunt hair. As I knew it would, her hands came to hold hard on my head, pelvis writhing, muttering her pleasure. I intended to bring her off that way first, introduce her to the finer arts. She gasped loudly, cried out and shook to her toes in her spasms. The performances was not entirely for her benefit or mine. I hoped Vee would find the scene enlightening.

Then I was in her, easing in but finding it accommodating in the extreme, a snug fit but taking all I offered. As if the most natural thing in the world, and it possibly is, Anne raised her rump, clasped her legs and ankles around me and began humping. Perhaps it was all the orgasms she had never had, but she let herself go and had several in succession, her mouth seeking mine, her body thrusting up to me.

'I'm coming, coming,' she repeated several times, 'make me come again, won't you? Don't dare stop yet,

In The Mood

please – ' and being worried about getting made pregnant was long forgotten.

When the urge came to me, the fire that churns your balls, makes your arse faint. I withdrew and heaved myself over her, cock in hand and directing my load over her heaving lily-white tits. She glanced down over her chin, touched the gooey stuff and smiled at me gratefully. I didn't need to ask how it had been for her. She kissed me and said it had been lovely, she'd hardly known where she was and good job I'd controlled myself but now she must go. The sounds of the dance band was no longer heard playing out on deck, her parents would be expecting her, but it had been lovely, marvellous.

Anytime, I promised her. She sat up and shyly said she would like to clean her breasts before dressing. As they were dripping with my come, I had to agree. I told her if there had been time, if she hadn't had to leave, I'd love to give her a bath. 'I'll get you a towel,' I offered.

In the bathroom I found Vee standing hands on hips, her lovely big tits thrusting and hairy snatch so tempting I could not resist giving both a quick feel. She allowed this and seemed in a surprisingly good mood.

'All very funny, that display,' she said quietly. 'Now get her out of here.'

'Watching us at it has made you horny,' I challenged her.

'Get rid of her.'

I blew her a kiss and got a towel, ran my face flannel under the hot tap, and returned to Anne, still sitting nude and with a contented smile on her face. She let me bathe her tits, dry them, then kiss each nipple before standing up to dress before me. 'It's been a lovely evening,' she thanked me. 'All of it. And this nice thing too,' she added, holding my limp dick. 'I did enjoy him. And now he's gone all soft – '

In The Mood

'You could kiss him better,' I suggested. 'He'd like that.'

For a moment the girl regarded me with surprise, then bent over swiftly and pressed a kiss to my knob. The first throbs coursed through my balls and into the shaft in her hand. She felt it and looked up in surprise, liking the feeling, the wonder of resurrection from flaccid to fullness. 'It's growing,' Anne said. 'It's getting big again – '

'Suck it and see,' I suggested.

She tentatively put her lips over it, found it to her taste, I suppose, and sucked gently, then quite greedily. I was at full cock, filling her mouth with flesh, before I drew her up. 'You'd better go,' I told her, 'or we could end up back on the bed. Mummy and Daddy are waiting, aren't they?'

'Bother them,' she said. 'I could just stay here all night, but I had better go. We will see each other again, won't we?'

I led her to the door, looking out to see that no one was about in the passageway, and ushered her off. Before flitting away she pressed a kiss to my lips. 'What we did, that just now, you know – '

'Sucking my dick,' I suggested.

'Well, yes. It was my first time. I always thought no one could ever do that.' She lowered her eyes. 'But I did like it. Will we do that again?'

'Mummy and Daddy,' I reminded her, giving her bum a slap. 'Go before they're out searching for you. Off!'

'Yes, master,' she said sweetly, hugging me and getting in one more kiss before hurrying off. There were possibilities with that girl, I decided. It wasn't so much a case of seducing her as just bringing her basic urges out. Back in the room Vee was sitting on my bed naked and with a full glass in hand. She shook her head and regarded me with a look I interpreted as one giving up on a hopeless case.

In The Mood

'Kiss it better,' she mimicked me. 'Suck it and see –'
'I did it for you, getting it up ready –'
'You are without doubt, a vestige of doubt,' she claimed, 'the most aggravating, scheming, slimy toad of a young lecher it has been my misfortune to know.'

'But you like what I do to you,' I laughed. 'I take it you are staying awhile?'

'If you think I was made to watch you fucking that girl without wanting a fuck myself, you can think again.' She gave me her empty glass. 'Pour me another drink and have one yourself. You're going to need it. And then when you've fucked me good and proper, I'll tell you how I plan to lure the slanderous Marigold to this cabin of sin for your attention.'

'I'll look forward to that,' I promised, touching glasses. 'Is there no one else in the Gore-Blomley clan you want me to screw? I'm open for offers –'

'I have a daughter, Angela,' Vee informed me. 'You ever lay your lecherous hands on her and I'll personally have your balls.'

Chapter Seven

Over the next several days I made the acquaintance of Marigold Gore-Blomley, introduced to her casually by Vee in the first place while strolling past them in their deckchairs. The time and place had been arranged; I was in the correct dress for such an occasion, white shirt with cravat, shorts, knee-length white stockings and white shoes. 'Tyler Wight,' said Vee to her sister-in-law. 'A young man who has helped organise so much of the ship's activities this trip. He's going to live in Kenya after service in the Royal Air Force.'

I shook a firm hand and decided Marigold well worth a fuck. She was fortyish like Vee and, though sitting, I noted the good bust, spread hips and strong legs. A strapping shapely woman. As to organising ship's activities, if screwing came under that heading, I suppose I had. I was invited to join the ladies as coffee was being brought to them. I sympathised with Marigold about her sea-sickness, was led into talking about the RAF by Vee as planned, because our intended victim had not only served as a WAAF officer in Kenya in the war but her fiancée had been shot down over the desert. I commiserated, adding that I had been luckier. Marigold warmed to me on my best behaviour, and as the Red Sea day was intolerably hot, I suggested that the coffee be served in my air-conditioned cabin nearby.

So Marigold had set foot where the deed was plan-

In The Mood

ned. I saw her several times in the next day or two, had drinks at the bar with both her and Vee, was bored out of my skull playing hours of bridge as her partner, and gained her confidence. This sounds easier than it was, as Anne Bellinger had not given up on me and sought me out. Thankfully Mummy and Daddy kept a tight rein on their girl, but where there's a will there's a way. Two days out from docking in Mombasa, now in the balmy Indian Ocean, I was due one morning to meet Vee and Marigold for coffee. Going to my cabin to change into suitable clothes, I'd been swimming so was in wet trunks and dressing gown, waiting for me on my return was an expectant Anne. She threw her arms about me, saying her parents had heat stroke.

Evidently the ship's doctor had ordered them to their cabin to rest. I did not want to antagonise Vee in her plan and not meet she and Marigold, but Anne did look nice, young and fresh in a flowery dress and smelling temptingly sweet as twenty-year-old girls do. We kissed lingeringly with tongues entwining and wet open lips, so Vee was going to have to wait. 'I have so wanted to see you again,' said Anne plaintively. 'You don't have to be anywhere, do you? Don't send me away – '

It is not too often one gets that kind of adulation, and I was going to make the most of it. 'Shouldn't you be worrying about your parents?' I said sternly. 'They may need you.' Years of being repressed and bullied by her ma and pa had really had their effect on her. Rotten git that I was, I took full advantage of the fact.

'I would, but it's only a touch of the sun,' Anne pleaded. 'They fell asleep in their deckchairs yesterday. Now they are lying down in a darkened cabin. They did say I could go for a swim. It's all right really – '

'What would they think if they knew you weren't swimming, but invited yourself to my cabin? To meet

In The Mood

a man?' I made it sound the most wicked thing in the world, and as though I were not involved.

'I don't care any more,' she pouted. 'I wanted to see you –'

'And you know what will happen, coming here?' I was set to find out how far a modest girl would let herself go when pressed.

'Y-yes,' she admitted.

'Well, say it. I want to hear you use the right word.'

'We'll make love. Like we did before –'

I sat her on my bed, bringing her a gin and lime with more gin in it. 'Love is what's made on honeymoons. You're a nice girl, Anne, and I could get more than fond of you. But you'll be stuck up on some frontier outpost and I doubt if we'll ever meet after we've docked in Kenya. As for me, I've no money, no job, no place to live once we get off this ship. So what we do is fuck. Say it, and I'll lock the door, or else leave.'

She took a deep drink at her gin, swallowed, and said, 'I want to be fucked. There. Fuck me.'

'Then undress. I'll sit here and watch you. One day,' I added sagely. 'you'll meet a man and fall in love and marry him. He'll be grateful you had this tuition; got bloody silly notions of false modesty fucked out of you. Make sure you get what you want, Anne. You really are a sensual girl. That's nothing to be ashamed of –'

All the while I was spouting this arrant drivel, and revelling in it, she was undressing and nodding at the wisdom of my words. 'Yes, yes, you are right, I never liked to admit it to myself before,' she admitted, finally unhooking her brassiere and stepping out of her knickers. She stood before me, still a little embarrassed, but with her hands by her sides and appealing with her slender girlish body, the small neat tits and the slight cunt mound with the sparse wispy hair.

'Turn,' I ordered, and she went around, stopping when facing from me to reveal the curve of her back and the rounds of her arse, so unlike the heavy fleshy moons of the older Vee. I had a great lech to smack each perfectly matched buttock for their pert cheekiness. I told her how nice her bottom was, slipping off my dressing gown and swimming trunks while she looked over her shoulder. Her eyes went to my prick, standing semi-erect and therefore horizontal. I told her later; it would be all hers later. First there were a few preliminaries, I'd decided. I drew a chair to the centre of the cabin, sitting down and telling her to get face down over my knees.

She obeyed at once but giggled. 'Are you going to smack me?'

'I may do. Depends how you answer some questions I have for you.' I had one hand under her, hefting her hanging-down tits, and I looked directly down upon her tight little rounded bum. My finger trailed up the cleft and she shivered, clenched the cheeks. 'Relax!' I ordered sharply, giving her a light slap. 'You've had your bottom smacked before, haven't you? I want the truth.'

It was a wild shot, but paid off. 'My parents, my father, punished me if they thought I'd been defiant or naughty. I was quite young. Before I went to school in England,' she confessed.

'Like this? Knickers off and across his knee?' I asked.

'Sometimes – '

'Often?'

'Well, quite often.'

'Both your mother and father? Did they both smack your bare bottom when you were naughty?'

'Only father. Mother stopped certain privileges – '

'So Daddy had you across his knee, tanning this lovely little bottom. Did you like that?'

'No, it hurt. It stung. He used a cane – '

'Did he? And did he like beating you?'

'I don't know. He always said I deserved it.' She squirmed around somewhat to look up at me; and my

In The Mood

prick, hard as iron and pushing into her soft belly, was what she asked to have.

'In good time,' I promised. 'Confession is good for the soul, Anne. Tell me more about Daddy punishing you – '

'Do I have to? It's rather embarrassing.' She pleaded with her eyes. 'I don't mind you smacking me.'

'Because it excites you. Did Daddy's smackings excite you?'

'No. Well, sometimes. I don't know – '

'What was the procedure. Was your mother present?'

'No. Daddy would order me to my bedroom. I had to remove my knickers and pull up my dress. There! Is that what you want?'

'Why would he punish you? What terrible crimes?'

'Laughing with the servants, not eating all my dinner, answering them back sometimes. That was all.'

'This is all for your own good, Anne,' I told her. 'Getting things out in the open so you can live with them. Like I said, getting rid of stupid inhibitions. Do you want to stay a little mouse, under your parents thumb? I'm not doing this for my benefit!'

All the while I was saying this my hand caressed her smooth arse. She relaxed and I sought between, touching up a lipless split until my fingers found a moist inside. 'Don't you think I'm right?' I said. 'So how old were you when he last caned this nice little bum?'

'Seventeen,' she said.

'The dirty old bastard.'

'That's what I used to think too,' Anne suddenly said with spirit. 'I could even see he got aroused. And it made me quite aroused too – '

'Don't blame yourself for that,' I said. 'Did you masturbate afterwards? It would be the thing to do.'

'Yes I did. And I did it other times too, hating myself for my weakness – '

In The Mood

'But we all do that to relieve ourselves. Men and women, all the time. You're not ashamed of that any more, I hope.' Now my hand simply soothed and smoothed her arse. I did not want to smack her, rather felt a great fondness I'd have to be careful wouldn't even stretch to loving her. 'What will you do when you get to your old man's district?' I asked.

'Play with my cunt again,' she said, meaning I was to do what I'd been doing. 'I'll be working in the pharmacy at the hospital. That's why I qualified.'

'Then don't take any more shit from Mummy and Daddy,' I advised. 'Tell them to get off your back. Find a place of your own. Who knows, if I get into flying I could just come up and visit –'

'I'd like that,' she said, 'but you do talk a lot. I came here for you to fuck me again, but first I want to suck that big cock of yours –'

'Get on the bed,' I told her. 'Good old sun, burning up your parents. It couldn't happen to a nicer pair.'

'They can roast in hell for all I care now,' said the new Anne. 'Don't just stand there with that thing pointing at me. Use it. Just two days from Mombasa and we're wasting time.'

I ordered tea in my cabin when Anne had left, for the moment feeling somewhat sated after several hours with what had proved an insatiable partner. Bathed and in my kimono, I was not at all surprised to have an irate Vee come to visit. 'Where the hell were you this morning?' she demanded. Marigold had been all primed up with cocktails and Vee had had to sit it out with her unfavourite person. 'Damn you,' she said again, 'where the hell were you?'

'Right here, fucking Anne Bellinger,' I said.

'I thought as much.' Vee took that better than I expected. 'You still intend to go through with my scheme?'

'I rather fancy fucking Marigold if possible.'

She glanced at her watch. 'The captain is holding a

In The Mood

party tonight. You have two hours to be ready. Black tie – ' Vee gave her amused look. 'It's for VIPs, only the cream qualify. You are there solely on my patronage.'

'Thanks a bunch. Why me?'

'Marigold will be there. The drink is served as fast as one can swallow it. She needs little encouragement, but see her glass is never empty. Then you'll invite us both to your cabin for a nightcap. Oh, I intend to have one up on her! Let her throw my past at me ever again – ' She looked me hard in the eye. 'Rape her if necessary, only compromise the bitch.'

'I've never had to rape anyone.'

'You know what I mean. Anyway, stay with her at the party, flatter her, pour the drink into her. I'll help. And bring her back here with me. And have your bed remade, for God's sake. It looks like a battle has taken place – '

'It was hectic. Anne had hidden depths.'

'That's another thing,' Vee said severely. 'If you must fuck that girl I suppose I can't stop you – '

'You can't,' I agreed.

'Then let me know if she's coming to see you. I can be in the bathroom like before. You'll do that? I'm sure you're the kind that likes to be watched performing.'

'Maybe I am,' I had to laugh. 'One thing is certain though, that you like to watch. Gets you up, doesn't it?'

'Get me a drink,' she said, as if her throat were very dry. 'Just what did you do all morning and afternoon with that girl? I didn't think she had it in her, cowed little creature with those awful parents.'

'We're working on that. She's coming along nicely.'

'I can't imagine it. Tell me what you did – ' She drained the glass of wine I'd given her. 'I want to hear.'

'Everything,' I told her. 'Fucked, sucked each other, did all the permutations. You would have loved seeing it, watching through the opened crack of the bathroom

In The Mood

door. We were at it all the time, hours. She couldn't get enough.'

I talked in the lewdest terms, seeing the effect it had upon Vee. She sat back in the cabin armchair, rubbed her thighs together as I gave every lurid detail and a few more for good measure.

'You're squirming in that seat,' I said. 'I'll bet your cunt is sopping and throbbing. I'm saving myself for Marigold tonight. If you want to finger yourself off, wank, masturbate, whatever you like to call it, don't mind me – '

'You're disgusting. Do that in front of you –?'

'Why not? I'll bet you played with yourself the last time you watched from the bathroom. Go on,' I encouraged her. 'I'm just getting into the best bits. Like when I fucked her in the arse.'

'I don't believe you. Did you really?'

'Finger yourself and I'll tell you. Make yourself come.'

'You are a pig,' she berated me, but her right hand went up under her skirt. 'Tell me then, you promised – '

'We'd done all the things I've told you. She sucked my dick like it was a lollipop. I was up her front, back and sideways. I'd come in her mouth but not in her cunt, not wanting to get her preggy. She said it was a shame, me having to leap off to save coming in her every time. So I said there was a way.'

My words had Vee flushed in the face. The bulge of her hand working between her thighs under her skirt moved faster. 'Go on,' she urged me. 'Tell me – '

'Let me see your cunt then. I want to watch it when you come.'

'You beast, you really are a beast,' she swore at me. 'You know very well I can't stop now.'

'Go on, Vee. You'd love me to see it. Give you a better come too, won't it?'

She hitched her skirt as if in a mood, drew her silk

In The Mood

panties down and over one foot. Then she sat back in the chair, legs wide apart, showing her hairy cunt mouth thrust forward. It stared at me like a red eye. 'Satisfied?' she demanded.

As I talked I watched her hand creep back to her slot. It stroked, rubbed, then sought her nub, the clitoris. With her other hand she parted the outer lips. She seemed to sink lower in the chair, eyes fixed on mine as I ogled her. Two people, I knew, doing exactly what they found lewdly exciting. I described how I had positioned Anne on her elbows and knees, arse raised and how she had agreed to let me use an ointment to lubricate her anus. She had stiffened when my finger went up, the little tight nut-brown asterisk of her puckered arsehole giving way; but she settled to the feeling, agreeing it was rather nice, pleasant, and saying she now wanted it that way.

'You did, you corked her!' Vee exclaimed, stroking herself.

'Right up, finally,' I agreed. 'After a while the few inches up her wasn't enough. So I eased the rest up and she liked it. Said she could feel its actual shape, right up to her belly. Urged me on even. Took to it right away. So I fucked her and flooded her innards. Filled her backside and she loved it.'

Vee was gasping in her chair, in the last throes, her pelvis humping. Only when she had subsided, regained her composure somewhat and washed her hands in the bathroom, straightened her dress and got back in her pants did she deign to speak to me. 'I have never done such a thing before,' she said. 'You really are beyond redemption. Why I let you lead me into these situations I will never know. I don't wish to know you.'

'Not even if I do your dirty work for you with Marigold tonight?' I taunted her.

'That's business,' she snapped. 'Do it like I want it done and you won't find me ungrateful. You're hoping to get on in Kenya. The Gore-Blomleys are good people to give introductions, put in a good word, especially for someone in your position. The party is at seven o'clock in the captain's quarters. We call it a Sundowner in East Africa. See that you are there on time and suitably dressed in evening wear.' She drew an envelope from her handbag and laid it on my dressing table. 'That's your invitation. You can consider yourself very fortunate to have one.'

'Yes ma'am, or is it memsahib out here?' I said, throwing up a mock salute. 'I'll be there on time, in black tie, white dinner jacket and a very natty cummerbund. Oh, and one last thing. I'm glad you enjoyed that nice wank. I'll think about you doing that when I see you chatting with your posh friends tonight.'

'You really are an utter cad,' Vee said with feeling as she left my cabin. It was the first time I'd ever been called that. I thought the word had gone out years before.

Chapter Eight

Silver print, embossed ship's crest in gold, my name inscribed in copperplate hand, I placed the invitation on the silver salver held by a red-jacketed steward and passed into the captain's sanctum. It was spacious, dotted with comfortable chairs and occasional tables, a huge sideboard arrayed with bottles, deep carpeted and packed with elegantly dressed people. I could only feel wry amusement as I took my place among such an elevated throng, considering the ups and downs of my recent years. Such was my nature, even the downs had had moments to savour. What the hell, one must make the most of all times.

I had dressed fit to mix with the best, white tuxedo jacket and all the accoutrements. Whilst getting ready Anne visited, adjusting my bow tie, pouring me a drink, brushing imaginary fluff from my shoulders. I knew she had arrived hoping for another sex session, a further meat injection, but settled for a promise of at least one last romp before docking. The girl had certainly discovered her true self. She proudly informed me she'd told her parents she was out for the evening, not inviting questions but letting them just think on as she dolled herself up.

She sat with a drink and rapidly brought the subject around to sexual matters. It now obviously fascinated her. I must have had lots of women, she observed, as I was so very good at it. 'Well, going by the things you have done to me,' she smirked. The feelings I'd aroused

In The Mood

in her! She didn't mind either if I wanted to smack her bare bottom, she rather liked it. All this had the effect of making my prick stir, raise its cowl as if seeking the cause. I told her and she laughed and clapped her hands like a schoolgirl, delighted to have had that effect upon it.

She talked of her time in college. The middle-aged tutor she had slept with, his poor performance, his dick which was not half as nice or half the size of *that*, she said, giving the bulge in my trousers a fond squeeze. And it didn't always happen with him, didn't get beautifully big no matter what was tried. She had gone with him simply to prove a point anyway. To elaborate, for my telling her that confession was good for the soul had not only borne fruit but gone forth and multiplied, she disclosed that her sexual experiences prior to the inadequate instructor had been solely with other females, apart from a spot of self-abuse occasionally. My ears pricked up, like most males I was intrigued by the concept of lesbian love. Come clean, I advised, and she settled back for the telling. How women with supposed secrets enjoy relating their sexual histories once started!

Well, it had started at school. Nairobi. Another girl had played with her in the gymnasium showers, giving Anne an orgasm. An all-girl boarding academy for the daughters of white farmers and expatriates, the hanky-panky was more or less like the activities I'd experienced at Rossall Abbey. Sweet kisses were exchanged, hand holding, crushes, slipping into bed with each other. We had measured adolescent pricks. Anne described how budding breasts were contrasted, cunt hair compared. Their little tits had been fondled, nipples made erectile by nipping and sucking, tight virgin cunnies fingered. Nothing more sophisticated evidently, no licking or tonguing yet, or the use of artificial cocks, like carrots. The girl's father had been posted to Borneo, leaving Anne bereft, but the

In The Mood

sport continued with a circle of girls who indulged.

Then she had left for study in England. Seemingly attractive to tutors, a married woman lecturer had taken Anne under her wing and to her bed, seducing her. This lady had taken her protégée home for weekends, obviously with the approval of her husband who was present. So she spent nights initiated into serious mutual masturbation, fondling, fingering and licking. She'd had so many comes, one upon the other, felt so secure in the woman's arms, was roused to such passions that she needed to assure herself that she was not entirely of that inclination. Hence the affair with the male tutor, which had left her in even more of a quandary as to her sexual disposition. I assured her after what we'd managed, her enthusiasm with a good stiff prick up her cunt, no way. She really was wildly sensuous, randy for a good mount, but I had reservations. She was also a natural switch-hitter, strongly and irrevocably bisexual. Lucky Anne.

Which goes to show one never knows about quiet types on the surface when there's a cauldron bubbling underneath. I was privileged to be party to her confessions, or rather admissions, for she was in no way contrite in the telling. All in all she was my kind of girl, I decided. Pretty face, good figure and a lewd turn of mind. My kind of wife even, if I was in the market, which I definitely was not. Her strict upbringing would be an asset too in marriage, obedience and a desire to please being too deeply instilled by her parents to ever completely leave her. Coupled with her highly sexual nature, the combination was attractive.

To assure herself further that she was not entirely queer, I let her open my trousers even though due at the captain's shindig. I'm that kind. I stood before her chair and she fished out a prick made thick and stiff by her revelations. She smiled up at me, clasped the girth and bent her head to suck. There are worse ways

In The Mood

to start an evening out. I let her have her head, so to speak, standing quite relaxed until the inevitable surge came, the rush of heat, the groans of pleasure and trembling of limbs. She murmured her pleasure through a mouthful of cock, sucking happily until the final spurts of my emission went down her throat.

I was therefore a little adrift arriving at the captain's quarters. Vee marked my arrival with a look of relief, nodding sternly to remind me I was there on a mission. Marigold smiled, raising a hand to invite me over. We were definitely on good terms at least. I lifted a filled glass off a passing tray and went to join the ladies.

Gore-Blomley himself in his old-fashioned evening suit, prised away from the card table, intercepted me, taking my elbow to lead me to one side, muttering about damned cocktail parties. He was due in the salon at the poker game he said. Be a good chap, ensure his wife and sister had male company, for he was leaving. He'd heard I'd taken coffee with them, was Marigold's partner at bridge. I'd come to his rescue before, he remembered, and he might be able to do something for me getting settled in Kenya. You know, the right introductions. I seemed the right sort of young fellow. We were joined by the captain and Gore-Blomley excused himself, hurrying off.

'Landed you with us, has he?' Marigold said when I got to the ladies. They were splendid in evening wear, Vee's big tits shown to good advantage in a gown cut low at the neck so that the exposed swell of each full breast rose enticingly with each breath.

Marigold was dressed more conservatively, a form-fitting silver sheath that showed her fuller figure to great advantage, every ample curve. Her tits were if anything bigger than Vee's, the kind that not only thrust forward but round out sideways to her arms. A fine big woman, I itched to see her nude. Both had been at the sauce as they say, drinking steadily with

In The Mood

the trays circulating non-stop. Vee had no doubt primed her sister-in-law with cocktails in their stateroom prior to the party. We were certainly chummy. Marigold said how smart I looked. I flattered her in turn. Vee's eyes gleamed and she was all sweetness and light, sensing success. It augured well and I looked forward with eager anticipation to a seduction. Fucking the comfortable Marigold would be a pleasure. And who knows, once things had hotted up, maybe I could cajole Vee into the scene? The evening had great possibilities.

The party broke up around eight-thirty and my invitation to continue a pleasant time in the privacy of my cabin was accepted. I linked arms with both women as we went our way. The handsome aristocratic face of Marigold was flushed, she was animated as I'd never known. I sat her in my armchair and brought her a drink. The chance was there as I bent over to hand her the glass. Vee sat on my bed, watching closely, so I kissed Marigold on the lips lightly. She did not move so I put a hand on the nape of her neck and kissed her lingeringly, my tongue slipping into her mouth. She allowed the contact for a long moment, then drew her face away.

'Why did you do that?' she said.

'Because I had an overwhelming desire to kiss you. I have had all evening. You're a beautiful woman – '

'I'm almost old enough to be your mother.'

'Does that matter?' I pleaded. I dropped to my knees before her. 'I've never wanted someone so much. I mean to have you – '

'Really, Tyler,' she said, and when I had kissed her again she nodded at Vee. 'Silly boy. As if I could – '

'I'm meeting some friends in the bar,' Vee announced rising and putting her empty glass on the dressing table. 'Don't do anything I wouldn't do, you two.'

'I can assure you we will not,' Marigold said, as dignified as she could be, watching Vee leave. 'Do you

In The Mood

know I can't stand my sister-in-law? A bitch that has led Reginald an awful dance – '

'Reginald' I took to be Gore-Blomley, but I was still intent on the business in hand, and that was to slide one of them up the inside of her leg under her dress, past the knee and beyond. Getting no rebuff I put my other hand up too, on the outside of her other leg, circling a hip and sliding my palm between the seat of the chair and a cushiony buttock cheek. Her dress had risen and revealed a fine fleshy pair of thighs, silk stockings held by suspenders and between the stocking tops and silk French knickers several inches of white rounded meat. I pressed kisses on both sides.

'You shouldn't do that,' she whispered.

'It's your fault. You make me want to. I can't help myself.'

Was that a little giggle from her? 'I think you are, helping yourself, that is. This is ridiculous really. Well, at least lock the door if you can't control yourself.'

Oh, but I was in control if she only knew it, plan proceeding accordingly, although her compliance showed just how amenable a woman can be when the urge is there. I walked to the cabin door and made an Academy Award performance of pretending to lock it. Now that Marigold was evidently willing, however, I also feared the sudden return of Vee would halt the good work. So I decided to waste no further time on the niceties. I went back to her, kneeling again, parting her knees and putting my head between her thighs. The warm smell of a perfumed body, a hint of sweat, the odour of cunt, had me aroused. When I drew at the silk knickers she raised her arse. I drew them over her shoes. Although she never spoke, I noted she eased herself forward on the chair and widened her legs as if slumped.

She was, in effect, inviting me to get a good look at her cunt and do whatever that might lead to. It was one worthy of attention, full-lipped on a fine fleshy

In The Mood

hump of a mound with a thick dark triangular forest of hair that grew down either side of the quim cleft to meet her arsehole, a luxuriant copse. I kissed her cunt like it was a mouth, murmuring sweet nothings, nibbled at the crinkled lips, used the tip of my tongue to probe. Her hands went to my head and I buried nose and mouth hard to the spot. I curled my tongue like a tunnel to stiffen it and tongue-fucked her, chin tight to the V of her thighs, going deep into moist velvety flesh.

'Oh Lord, what are you doing to me?' she groaned. 'You're going to make me come. Come! I can't help it – '

At that moment as if waiting in the wings, Vee returned. Marigold stiffened, both with her climax impending and with alarm at the sight of Vee. She tried to push my head from her. Vee, the schemer, came forward smiling. 'Good for you, Marigold,' she praised her sister-in-law. 'I really didn't think you had it in you.'

'She hasn't yet,' I said bluntly. 'Leave us, please.'

'Sorry I interrupted,' Vee said. She picked Marigold's discarded knickers off the carpet. 'But don't let me halt what you both were evidently enjoying.'

'I don't know what came over me,' Marigold claimed. 'This young man practically forced himself on me.'

'Not from where I was standing,' Vee said wickedly. 'Good God, Marigold, you're a grown woman. I don't blame you for allowing yourself a little pleasure. And I can see Tyler didn't need you to force him. Pray continue do.'

'Certainly not,' Marigold said emphatically.

'Well what about me?' I protested. 'Left in a fine state of arousal while you two have a discussion. Is that to be it?' To show them how I'd been left I showed them a rigid prick. It reared under Marigold's nose, magnificently proud. 'Look at this! I can't stop now. It's going to be one or the other of you – '

In The Mood

'I'm a married woman, it's out of the question,' Vee said. 'Besides, Marigold is the cause of that huge erection. She should do the necessary –'

I took matters in my own hands, undressing completely before the two women, standing bollock naked with my rearing cockstand. 'Come on, Marigold, get undressed! You were all for it before.'

'I can't with Virginia here.' She looked at me. 'Tell her to go. I don't know what I'm doing. Tell her to go –'

I took a reluctant Vee's elbow and steered her to the door. I asked her quietly if she were satisfied. She complained she wanted to watch. I showed her out and she said as she left, 'Do whatever you like with her. Bugger her. I want her to remember this episode. I certainly will. And don't lock the door as I shall be back –'

'What was she saying?' asked Marigold. 'She'll hold this over me, you know. Never let me forget it.'

Fucking women, there was I desperate to get my end away and it had been like a bloody debating society. 'She's gone now,' I said. 'Let's get on with it.' I began to unbutton the back of her dress and she just stood. 'Forget Vee,' I said more kindly. 'It's you I want, not her.' I kissed her throat, her mouth, and held one of her weighty breasts. 'You don't know how much –'

She melted somewhat, allowed more kisses. I got her back in the right mood. She helped me get out of her dress. Off came a petticoat, a formidable brassiere, every stitch including the suspender-belt and stockings. I wanted her gloriously naked. Her tits hung heavy, slightly pendulous with their mass, big globes with their inside rounds nestling together, thick nipples in an aroused state. I suckled on them, my hand down in the forest of hair stroking the parted lips. She let me lead her to the bed to be laid flat, opening her thighs for me.

'That's a beautiful juicy cunt,' I told her. 'I'm going to fuck it rigid at last.'

'Oh do,' she agreed. 'I do want it now.' She craned her neck, looking down between the hills of her tits to her raised mound and my prick poised at her split. 'Put it in. Fuck me, Tyler.'

I told her that's what I liked to hear, easing my prick into her slot, intending to tease her a little with the first few inches. But Marigold grabbed my buttocks, her body rising and falling with increased fervour, as eager as I'd ever known a woman to want a fucking. She pushed her tongue in my mouth, grunted and bucked under me, completing the climax Vee had disturbed.

'Keep it in, don't you dare come yet,' she implored me, almost at once going into the throes of a second coming. I held back as I like to do, looking down goatishly at the distortion of her face in extremis, the rolled eyes, open mouth, stretched neck and head thrown back. Hoarse mumblings rose from her throat, rising into a shout. In the grip of continuous spasms she waggled her big arse vigorously.

Sitting up over her as she lolled back, I toyed with her cunt, feeling it throb like a heartbeat. She saw my prick still at full stretch. 'You haven't come yet,' she said. I told her I came when I wanted to, and what I wanted was for her to turn over, offering up her magnificent arse. She asked for a drink.

We sat and she saw off three glasses of wine, the pair of us naked and touching, kissing, her clasp on my stalk, my finger gently frigging her hot inner cunt. I placed her on her elbows and knees, her tits hanging down almost to the bedcover. The grand canyon of her arse was worth exploring, a tight brown ring and not an inch or so away a cunt like a hungry mouth set between such splendid orbs of rounded flesh. Out of interest, I asked if she had been had that way before, corked. I saw her nod her head.

In The Mood

On went some suntan ointment, all I had in that line, and in went my prick. She grunted, settled on her knees, bracing, reaching back to part her cheeks for my better access. I went to the hilt surprisingly easy, kneeling behind and working up to stronger thrusts. She moaned but repeated 'Yes, yes,' my arm around her, two fingers pinching her clitoris. We both cried out and she thrust back to me, my spurts continuing until it seemed my balls were drained. She collapsed under me, still clenching her arse cheeks as I rolled aside.

We must have slept. I awoke to a tapping at the door, was still regaining my composure when not Vee but Anne walked in. She looked at the scene before her, me sitting up with a flaccid dick hanging, and the large supine naked form of Marigold face down across my bed. I thought she might turn and flee. Instead she came forward, looking down with interest at Marigold. 'Get me a drink if you intend to stay,' I told her, my throat dry as a desert and my voice a croak. She went to the sideboard, searching among mostly empty bottles, saying there was not much of a selection. I told her in my reduced circumstances it was as much as I could afford, I had not banked on such a succession of visitors. Water from the tap would do. She giggled, coming back with a tumbler full of lime juice. I drank it down in one.

'You look awful,' she laughed. 'Like you've just done a hard day's work –'

'I just have. She's a lot of woman as you can see. If you want anything you'd better come back later. What gives with Mummy and Daddy that you're here so late as this?'

'Tucked up with the sleeping tablets I gave them with their cocoa. Can I sleep with you tonight? I promise I'll leave early, before anyone's about –' Then she nodded at Marigold. 'Or is she here for the night?'

'What about both of you?' I said. Suddenly I had an

210

In The Mood

urge to relieve myself. I went into the bathroom and peed, sluiced my hands and face. Coming back I paused at the door. Anne was by the bed, standing looking down over Marigold, her fingers trailing down the sleeping woman's spine and then caressing both cheeks. She bent over, kissed Marigold's bottom, the ample globes, each receiving a tribute before Anne pressed her face to the cleft. As I came to the bed she straightened up self-consciously.

'Go on,' I said, 'She's there for the taking.'

'What would you think of me?'

'That you like the best of both worlds. And why not?'

She hesitated a moment but the lech was on her. 'Do you think we could turn her over?' she asked. I tried not to smile, at the same time intrigued by the turn of events. I rolled Marigold on her back and she sighed, stretching her body, opening her legs as if to comply with Anne's wish. Her cunt pouted most invitingly, a mature woman's cunt. Her huge tits lolled part.

'Such breasts,' said Anne. 'I wondered if those things were real when I've seen her dressed. Then she was at the pool in her bathing costume – '

'And you fancied them? See how big her nipples are.'

'Yes,' the girl said quietly, then stretched out her hands and cupped them over Marigold's tits. As the owner seemed to slumber on, Anne held one and kissed around the large brownish circle surrounding the nipple before closing her lips over it. She sucked gently for a moment or two, leaping back when Marigold stirred and sighed in her sleep as if in a pleasant dream. 'I'd better stop,' Anne decided. 'This is like rape, isn't it?'

'She seems to like it,' I encouraged her. 'Go on and see what develops. All this is getting me worked up too. Take off your clothes. I'll play with you while you play with her.'

Anne nodded as if I'd suggested the most natural thing in the world. Her slim young body revealed, she bent over Marigold again while I felt up between her arse. She kissed both tits, went down to lick at the belly button, then with a little moan of resignation went between Marigold's thighs, sucking on the curled outer lips first and being unable to resist, putting out her tongue to the pink inner folds. I bet it tasted like nectar to her. She forgot herself and lapped, with her face buried in Marigold's pubic beard. The woman awoke, craned her neck to look down, asking who, what? I knelt on the bed, bending to kiss Marigold, to soothe her, assure her. She relaxed, even tilted her cunt for Anne's benefit, or more likely her own, grasping the girl's head, writhing her pelvis.

Anne was making mumbling sounds, pushing Marigold's thighs further apart. My prick could not stand much more of this. I went forward on my knees, holding it to Marigold's face. She looked at me with somewhat glazed eyes but understood my intention. Turning her face she opened her mouth and let me feed it in. We were all happy. Anne lapping like a cat at the cream, her hands stretched up to clasp Marigold's tits; Marigold herself being nicely tongued and her nipples pinched, and myself helplessly and suddenly lubricating the back of Marigold's throat with my load.

I left them still at it to get more lime juice. I was at the sideboard surveying the pretty scene when Vee appeared, peering around the cabin door first, then sidling beside me. 'What's going on?' she said quietly, delight in her face. 'I don't believe it. What *is* she doing?'

'Eating cunt. Marigold's cunt to be precise.'

'I can see that. Anne Bellinger of all people. Did you arrange this?'

'These things just happen,' I said amicably, 'but it's turned out better than you expected, I'll bet.'

She even kissed my cheek in her elation. 'And did you have Marigold first? Of course you did.' Looking back on the pair across the bed, their feet towards us,

In The Mood

she added, 'I've enough on Marigold to keep her quiet for ever now. I'm going to remind her of this little lapse if ever she goes to my husband with some tale. Do you think I should disturb them and tell her?'

'Leave them at it. They're enjoying each other so much. You've got the goods on Marigold now, what more do you want?'

'And you intend to leave them here? Why not dress and come to my stateroom for a drink. My husband will be at the card table all night as usual. The stakes have got astronomical and he won't stop playing until we dock in Mombasa – '

'I think a walk on deck first,' I said. 'A bit of night air to refresh myself.'

'I'll await you then,' Vee said. She leaned forward on her toes to press a light kiss on my mouth. 'For such a young man you are the most completely immoral, corrupt and dissolute male I have ever known. Do you accept money even?' Before I could answer she slipped out of the cabin, holding her lips to prevent a laugh. I dressed while Anne and Marigold lay in each other's arms, kissing wantonly, fondling, Anne on top and cunt to cunt. They would not have noticed me if I'd played a trombone over them. I was off to sleep with old Gor-Blimey's wife in his bed. Lucky at cards, unlucky in love, so they say. He ought to be on a winning streak.

Chapter Nine

Mombasa is the gateway to East Africa and its sights and smells appealed to me the moment we docked. I had started the voyage with so little money to spare that I thought my activities might be curtailed, but it had been a more than memorable trip. My sexual encounters with Vee, Anne and Marigold had kept down any weight I may have gained through wining and dining so well over the weeks. Before I left the ship a steward brought me a small package and a sealed envelope, giving me a knowing look. In the envelope was a sheaf of notes for two thousand East African shillings, the equivalent of one hundred English pounds. There was no note with it, but I knew it was for services rendered to Vee.

The little package contained yet another gold cigarette case, purchased from the ship's luxury shop, and with it on a little card the simple initial M. Marigold's contribution no doubt. Anne had phoned my cabin earlier, thanking me for the loan of my bed, on which she and her lady love had romped until dawn. The money and the cigarette cases, when flogged, would be my sole fortune. My first-class ticket on the liner had included rail travel to Nairobi. Once there I would have to fend for myself but had high hopes. In such a vast region pilots would be at a premium, I imagined. There was also the oft-repeated promises from the Gore-Blomleys that introductions would be made to the right people. I quickly found out that these were

In The Mood

as so many empty words, given freely at the time and never meant. They were big league, rubbing shoulders on shipboard perhaps, but far above my station on their own ground.

This I discovered at Mombasa railway terminal. The Gore-Blomleys, with every official and a throng of native porters to see them and their luggage aboard, specifically ignored me although I stood just yards away on the platform waiting to board the train. Vee looked past me. I had been effectively paid off and that was that. It was my first lesson in coping with the arrant snobbery of many old Kenyans, the rich estate owners and senior civil servants, the kind that kept their clubs exclusive and lesser mortals in their place. Fuck you then, I thought, looking at Vee giving a boy an ear-bashing for dropping one of a matching set of pigskin suitcases.

The train journey itself was a pleasure. In those days, crossing the Athi plain it was possible from the carriage windows to see Samburu tribesman with spear and shield on the hunt or trek, and plenty of gazelle and giraffe, even the odd lion and leopard.

On arrival in Nairobi I took a room in an Asian-run hotel, the cheapest reasonable accommodation but hardly considered the done thing by the settled white community. Without membership of a European club it was not easy to break into the social round. But luck favours the bold, I think. On my first night in the hotel, the only white face in the bar, a hearty approach was made by the owner, a rotund Gujarat in a white cotton gown, hair jet black with pomade and a pencil-thin moustache. He looked a rogue so I took to him right away. Every word he spoke was a question, sussing me out, a poor white who might be useful to him. When I told him I was a qualified pilot looking for a flying job, his eyes widened. Would I care to go to Nairobi airfield in the morning? I didn't have a car. 'But you will when you have got on your legs,' he said,

In The Mood

meaning on my feet. It would be his pleasure to drive me. Who knows? he claimed, perhaps he could find me a job, slapping my back.

We drove next morning early to an old hangar on the edge of what is now Nairobi International Airport. Inside was an aircraft I instantly recognised, a DH 90 Dragonfly, circa about 1935, and I had actually flown one. We were joined by two Sikh mechanics and discussed the aircraft. They were impressed I seemed to know my stuff, talking of de Havilland biplanes, the Gipsy Major I inverted in-line engines, its history on airline and charter work, or even as an executive plane for the wealthy.

'This one,' said Nizar Ramji, my hotel host, 'once belonged to King Feisal of Iraq.' It still looked in fair nick to me. The words on the fuselage proclaimed 'Athi Airways'. It could take four passengers, I knew, one sitting beside the pilot. We wheeled it out and I took my new friends for a flight over Nairobi, landing confidently.

So I found work, mostly flying passengers down to Mombasa for holiday breaks on the Indian Ocean. The aircraft handled well, I was making money, and several return flights a week was not hard work. As a new boy, I was making little headway with the local society who counted: the wives and daughters I saw shopping or taking coffee under the thorn tree with its pavement tables, or leaving their cars dressed for a ball at the club. Ramji, however, was delighted with the success of his one-plane airline and its pilot. The old Dragonfly got a fresh coat of paint, a repair job on seats which had their stuffing sticking out. I was given a uniform, a white overall with shoulder insignia and wings over the breast pocket. So it was I got to fly four young men and girls of the Kenyan top bracket on a private charter to a barbecue on an estate near Thompson's Falls.

The two girls and their boyfriends, typical children

In The Mood

of the local white landowning fraternity I imagined, carried on like kids on an outing during the flight. I had to warn them to keep to their seats and was booed. We landed at an airstrip near a grand colonial-type residence, where white-robed Kikuyu servants waited to take any hand luggage into the house. I got out to take in the scene, the swimming pool, the barbecue fire, a roasting pig and tables of salads and wine. The party had already started, young men and women were laughing and drinking together. I was dry and hungry myself, but was not invited to join in. There was shade under the aircraft so I sat there watching how the other half lived. One day, I knew, give me time, I'd take to the life in the manner born.

The girls were pretty, flighty females, silly but self-assured with wealth and breeding. I singled out a girl circulating in a two-piece swim suit, obviously the hostess. She was maybe seventeen, I calculated, but with the tits and arse of a mature woman. The tropics had that effect on young girls, fleshing them out early.

I saw legs by the plane's wheels, two shapely ankles and very neat calves. By craning my neck I saw a girl inspecting the Dragonfly with interest, crawled out from below and stood, dusting my overall off. She had copper-gold hair tied back in a ponytail, a pretty face that seemed somehow familiar. A white shirt, tied in a knot under her breasts showed a smooth flat expanse of stomach and a neat indented navel. An open neck had been unbuttoned enough to reveal tight cleavage between breasts that bulged the cotton shirt and pert nipples made points in the rounds filling the stretched material. Her shorts were filled as nicely too, snug fitting over matching curved hips. I liked what I saw and did not attempt to hide my admiration. She tilted her head and laughed.

'The people you flew up were saying their pilot was a miserable old so-and-so. You don't look so old to me.'

'They carried on like idiots during the flight. I had

to warn them to calm down. Do you live in this pile, this grandiose monument to colonial living?'

'No, I don't. I'm a guest of Bettina's. Actually I live in an even larger, more grandiose pile, as you call it. I take it you resent success? I take it you are all for independence when it comes, everyone equal?'

'No. I'm all for me. I just haven't eaten that's all, and the food looks bloody tempting –'

She ignored the hint. 'I want to fly,' she said. 'I shall take lessons at Nairobi one day.'

'It's not inexpensive. You'll need to pay for quite a few hours before you even solo.'

'That doesn't matter.'

'Daddy's lovely money?' I suggested.

'None of your fucking business,' she said calmly. 'Take me up for a flip so I can see what you do.'

I would do so, never one to refuse a beautiful female. First I asked what was in it for me? 'You are hired to be here and do as required,' she said, in the manner of one used to ordering servants and lesser mortals to do her bidding. 'It was I who actually ordered the charter for Bettina for her barbecue –'

'So let her order me about. Who is she? The girl with the huge tits and good arse. Send her over.'

'I know your employer, Nizar Ramji,' warned the girl. 'Would you want me to report your insolence to him? Rest assured I could get you fired if I have to.'

'I've no doubt of that,' I said, 'so get in the aircraft and we'll have a couple of circuits over this joint in what fuel I have to spare. Understand, two circuits only.'

She sat beside my pilot's seat and to make it look good I handed her the take-off checklist, actually a grimy sheet with oily thumbprints obliterating most of the instructions. She religiously checked off and called out each sequence and we rumbled along the sunbaked murram strip and soared into the air. I explained this and that, she nodding and noting every word and action. I already had a terrific lech to fuck her, making a resolution to try by all means I could conceive.

'You really can fly well,' she said in surprise. 'I expected from your surly attitude you'd refuse me, even with the threat to have you dismissed. Do you really fancy Bettina, the one you described with the big tits and good arse? She's a fat cow.'

'Given the chance,' I risked, 'I'd much rather fancy you.'

'You mean fuck me?'

'As we're down to basics, yes. Very much yes.'

'But I don't fuck in public, thank you.'

'Who says it would be public?' I questioned, liking the way the conversation had turned.

'They do, down there,' she nodded out of the cabin to the pool below. 'Once they've drunk themselves silly they'll dismiss the servants and anything goes. Naked bathing in the pool, groping, screwing. It's always the same when Bettina's parents are away for the day. Do you find that disgraceful, the rich young indolent at play?'

'Sounds good to me.'

'You would. It's all so contrived, even boring. They've all fucked each other so many times. When I want to get laid it has to be at my choosing. The male, the time and the place.' She gave me a cool look. 'So that includes you out, pilot.'

'You don't know what you're missing,' I told her, banking the aircraft sharply and flying down over the pool, buzzing it so low that the startled guests, many still dressed, jumped into the water. The girl clapped her hands and laughed with great delight, not the least disturbed by my sudden aerobatics.

'I think you'll make a flyer,' I said. 'You enjoyed that, didn't shake you up at all, did it?'

'Do it again.'

'Can't.' I tapped a gauge. 'Fuel consumption, remem-

In The Mood

ber. I've got to get this crate back to Nairobi this evening. Before Bettina's parents return, I bet. Do they know their daughter throws orgies?'

'They may suspect. They were famous for the orgies they arranged in their time.' She glanced at me knowingly. 'In a small and close well-knit white community quite often there's not much else to do – '

'But amuse and entertain among yourselves,' I finished for her. 'I can think of worse ways to pass the time.'

'When we land I'll get you to join the party then,' she said. 'They'll welcome another man, the males are outnumbered today. Someone new should go down very well with the girls.'

'I have been known to,' I smiled. 'Go down, I mean – '

'I know what you mean,' she said, not amused. 'Your mind is a sewer. You think every female is there to be screwed – '

'When they dress like you are, yes. The goods are on display. You bloody know it.'

'I thought we were getting on very well when I saw the way you fly,' she remarked icily. 'Evidently I was right in my first impression of you. A complete lout.'

'Your estimate is a little generous but otherwise correct,' I told her. 'Do complete louts still get invited to the party?'

No more was exchanged between us. We landed, taxied in, and walked to the poolside, hearing wild shouts and screams as the fun proceeded. I noted all at the party had now cast off their clothes and the males' idea of great fun with naked girls was to hurl them into the swimming pool when chased and caught. I paused at a table to make up a thick sandwich of pork and help myself to a bottle of Tusker beer, the local brew. The girl named Bettina came up to us, gleaming wet and bared to the buff. Her fat young teats were big as balloons. Her cunt hair lay flat with the soaking, long and dark between ample thighs.

In The Mood

'Angela, you mean thing,' the girl said. 'Sneaking off and having a flight with this yummy young chap. Why didn't you let me know? I would have liked to have gone up –'

'I'm Ty,' I introduced myself, shaking her hand and making her big tits wobble. 'Angela here says I may join your party. That's if you agree, of course.'

'The more the merrier. You'll have to take off your clothes though,' she giggled. 'To see if you qualify –'

'What about her?' I asked, indicating Angela. 'I'm game.'

'You think I wouldn't?' Angela snapped. She untied the knot of her shirt, revealing perfectly formed uptilted tits. Stepping out of her shorts, she then peeled off her tiny briefs, draping them over my head. I held them to my nose, sniffing appreciatively before handing them back. Bettina went into gales of laughter.

'Admit it, Angie,' the plump girl said. 'You've met your match.' She swayed with the effect of whatever drink she'd consumed. 'Are you going to let him fuck you?'

'It's your party, he can fuck you,' Angela said. 'He evidently likes big girls. He said so.' She made a face at me, her dislike showing. Why? Who knows what can upset some young women so violently. Taking some frustration out upon me for not towing the expected line? Perhaps she was just a bitchy girl, peeved too at my evident ability in the air. 'He referred to you as the girl with huge tits and a big arse actually, Bettina.'

I could have said you called your friend a fat cow, but that would have been unforgivable even as a riposte. Bettina as it happened laughed it off. 'I know I've huge tits and a big arse.'

'And that will do nicely for me,' I told her, taking her elbow. 'It's too crowded and noisy out here. Come into my aircraft.'

'Let's,' Bettina agreed. 'It's called a cockpit, isn't it? Will there be room?'

In The Mood

'You know the rules, Bettina,' Angela warned. 'No sneaking off at these parties. Everything done with the full knowledge and in sight of everyone else. Don't you dare go with him.'

'Angela,' I said, 'belt up. If you're jealous, I'll fuck you next. Right now Bettina and I are going to christen the old Dragonfly. I'm sure she'll soar like an eagle after it.'

'He hasn't even stripped,' Angela protested. 'That's another rule you seem it to ignore, Bettina. You know the penalty.'

'One strip coming up, so hide your eyes, girls,' I said. 'What gives with your bitchy friend, Bettina, all this stuff about rules and penalties? I thought this was a free-for-all – '

'No going off alone,' repeated Angela. 'Everything in full view of others. That's the rule for anyone who gets invited to our private parties. Bettina knows that very well. She was present when the rule was agreed. It prevents anyone being left out. Like Bettina, for instance,' she added meanly. 'Some people are more attractive than others – more in demand – '

'You cow, Angela,' swore Bettina. 'You rotten beast! This is the last time you'll ever be invited here. That was hurtful.'

'Girls, girls,' I interceded as they squared up as if to scratch each other's eyes out. Much as the thought of two young shapely naked females, one nubile and one plumpish, wrestling on the grass, was inviting, seeing the pair of them showing off their tits and cunts had got me in the mood for a fuck. I had shed my flying overall, leaving me in just my Y-front pants. When I had stepped out of these my prick was already at half-cock; not quite its full length and girth but still formidable. Both girls stopped glaring hate at each other and stared. 'Come on, Bettina,' I urged her. 'Screw the rules and screw Angela. We'll make up some of our own.'

223

It was cramped in the aircraft. I had to bend to avoid the overhead but as Bettina was shortish, and I was kissing her mammoth tits while feeling her cunt, that was acceptable. She was as eager for it as I, pushing herself against my fingers deep in a soft plump quim as juiced up as I'd known. I backed away, still holding a tit, finding a seat and lowering my arse to sit down, pulling her with me. No messing about, she wanted me to fuck her without the frills, wanted the weapon she grasped in her hand to poke at the itch in her tail.

She squatted over my lap, poised to lower herself, impale her cunt on the rigid shaft held upright between her thighs. It went right up as she squirmed down on it, straight as a flagpole, nudging who knows where deep inside her works. Wherever it was she began to whimper with pleasure, facing me on my lap, using the purchase of the floor under her feet to rise and fall over her tormentor. My face was squashed by enveloping teats, sucking and biting them. My balls lay in a hot hairy pocket between her comfortable arse cheeks. I heard her cry out and bob up and down more furiously in her orgasm, the old aircraft swaying with her effort. She collapsed face on my shoulder, breasts heaving with each gasp, our sweat mingling in a pool at our laps.

But the aircraft still rocked. I heard shouts and cat-calls beyond, saw through the cabin window at my seat that we were surrounded by the partygoers. 'Out, out,' they shouted, pushing at the fuselage and wing struts. I heaved Bettina off my lap, opened the starboard cabin door and leapt out.

'Crazy bastards,' I shouted, but then I was seized by four pairs of strong male arms, held tightly. I was too hot from the writhings of Bettina's ample body against mine and the heat inside the fuselage baked under the African sun to care to struggle. Bettina emerged from the Dragonfly after me, looking sheepish but pleased

In The Mood

with herself. They did not grab her, the other girls simply surrounded her.

'They're demanding the penalty from us,' she said sweetly, not at all anxious it seemed. 'We've got to do as they say.'

We were marched by a naked throng to the tables laid out with food. I saw Angela looking smug, told her that I thought all this bloody childish. The young men holding me pushed me face down over one table, arse up and legs on the ground. I saw Bettina bend down over the table next to me without prompting, her fat buttocks thrust up, giggling as settled herself. 'It's just a few strokes of the strap,' she called to me. 'Don't worry.'

I wasn't so much worried as determined not to let these idiots have their way. Trying to rise was not so easy. My unwillingness was recognised and I was held firmly. To help keep me face down a girl sat across my neck, her bush at my nape, kneeling up like a frog over me with her hands pressed to my back. I heard Bettina squeal, more with pleasure than pain, and managed to turn my head to see some boy wielding a short leather strap, applying it to her fat backside with smart cracks. I guessed it was my turn and saw Angela handed the strip of leather. 'I should have known it would be you,' I lifted my head to say as she came up to the table. 'Enjoy your moment of glory for if we ever meet again I'll personally fuck your arse, never mind whip it.'

'Promises, promises,' Angela said sweetly. 'I have this pleasure as the one who reported you. It's the custom. Nothing personal you understand?'

Not much, I thought, and took a thwack across my arse that stung with the venom of her strike. I grimly held on, counted up to six, seven and then on to nine. 'Six of the best only, Angie,' I heard someone call. 'Give the chap a break.'

I had twisted my head as far as I could to watch her

during the strapping, seeing her reaching up to bring down the belt with full force, her tits rising and bobbing with the exertion. When she relented, she stood back to face me as I was released and rose from the table. My prick, which had with every blow been forced to rub against the table top, was hugely erect. No doubt the warming of my backside so thoroughly, the heat of which had penetrated my groin, had helped bring on such a stander.

'See what you've done now?' I chided her. She turned and walked away, dismissive of me, the lovely cheeks of her pert arse working against each other beautifully.

I was considered a jolly good sport, surrounded by members of both sexes, congratulated on taking the beating so well as it was all in fun – really, old man! Before time to fly back to my party I used the pool for a refreshing swim and to dally with some of the female guests, who had taken note of my endowment, fondling it under the water in turn, which it did not mind in the least.

To give it relief, on emerging from the pool I sought out the voluptuous Bettina again. Her huge tits fascinated me. She was sitting naked in a garden chair as I approached, dripping water from the swim and with a pretty good hard-on from the handling it had received. Bettina saw it with cry of delight. I stood directly before her and she leaned forward, encompassing my prick between her deep cleavage. So I titty-fucked her with Bettina pushing them together for me, my cock thrusting up and down between two big pliant udders until my load drenched the cleft of them.

On take-off I circled the pool, waved off by those remaining below. The scene resembled a battlefield: chairs and tables overturned, food strewn everywhere through bunfights, wet towels left trampled in the grass. The guests had dressed. Now a busy dozen or so white-robed house servants were clearing up the debris, no doubt in good time for Bettina's parents' return; all evidence of a wild time would be removed and none of the guests would lift a finger. Well, it sure beat the hell out of working in a factory.

We arrived at Nairobi before sunset, Nizar Ramji on hand to bow and scrape to his society passengers as they disembarked. He hoped they'd had a pleasant flight, a nice party with their young friends, washing his hands with invisible soap like a veritable Uriah Heep as he paid them obeisance and was largely ignored as usual.

The two girls pressed a kiss on my cheek as they thanked me for the flight. The boyfriends shook my hand, one pressing a hundred-shilling note into my palm. 'You seem to have made a great hit with Bettina,' he said. 'Sorry about the other thing, the whacking you took so well. It's just a custom of our parties and I apologise for you getting dragged into our fun and games. It was Angela who insisted. She can be a real bitch. But of course she's a Gore-Blomley. They own half the country, or think they do.'

'I believe I've heard of them,' I said. Now I had made the acquaintance of the whole family. I was soon to meet them all again but it was just as well I didn't know that at the time.

Chapter Ten

My room at the Shalimar Hotel had advantages other than price. My employer and hotelier, the ubiquitous Nizar Ramji, was an entrepreneur with a fat finger in many pies. Apart from Athi Airways, he owned shops and go-downs dealing in curios, gold and silver, ivory, animal skins, plus taxis and buses in all the main towns of Kenya, Tanganyika and Uganda. He resided in a spacious two-storey house in its own grounds in the select Ngong area, had a remarkably beautiful wife of high Hindu caste clad in silk saris with gold rings on her fingers and toes, a barrister son and a daughter at Oxford, and drove a huge Oldsmobile car with flared wings and multiple headlamps. He could buy and sell most of the Europeans he kow-towed to, but then he kept in with everyone, having an eye for future favours.

He reminisced in the bar on his early days in Nairobi, a street-wise urchin from Bombay with ragged-arse trousers. He had chosen a shop, owned by a Gujarat like himself, walked in with a twig broom and swept it out. The owner said nothing. Ramji went back every day several times and did the same, watched carefully by the proprietor. One day the man sent him on an errand. Ramji returned with the parcel and correct change. In time the owner indicated a mattress under the counter. Ramji slept there, still sweeping the floor, filling shelves, serving customers, never paid but now invited into the room at the rear to share the family's rice and curry. The arrangement went on for several years until the shopkeeper opened another general store and made the young Ramji manager. He was getting on his legs, as he said. He certainly had by the time he employed me.

There might be, he hinted some time after I'd been flying his aircraft, his bright black eyes judging my reaction, some small items of cargo to be picked up at different destinations where makeshift airstrips had been made. 'You're a good fellow, I know,' he flattered me. 'Most skilful pilot. You can do that, find a landing field in the bundu? Top dollar for you –' I knew instinctively it could only be something illegal.

The first trip or two I made took me south to Serengeti, where a fairly well tramped-down strip was lit at night with truck headlights and oil drums burning petrol to guide me in. An English, so-called white hunter was in charge of a tribal crew straight out of a Tarzan picture, armed to the teeth, waiting to load the Dragonfly from which the seats had been removed. On arrival back at Nairobi, parked well on the very edge of the airfield, still in pre-dawn darkness, a truck would be waiting. If I arrived back in daylight the old Dragonfly would be left in the hangar.

I didn't wish to know what I flew in. Tusks, skins and the rhino horn so sought after in those days, I guessed. Every curio shop in Nairobi at that time displayed every kind of local artifact, many grotesque and useless except as souvenirs. There were elephant-foot stools and wastepaper baskets; zebra-leg lamp standards and zebra-skin pouffes; ladies' handbags of hippo skin faced with zebra, leopard and lion fur; Masai spears, shields and beads. Ivory was carved into tribal warriors, napkin rings and all the wildlife from warthogs to the tuskers from whence the ivory came. Crocodile skin shoes were popular. Only the rich and famous came to safari in those pre-package-tour days. For the wealthy industrialist whose bag of game had

In The Mood

not been spectacular, there were mounted heads of snarling lion and leopard or buffalo, complete with brass plaque ready to be engraved with the purchaser's name.

What quotas to hunt for ivory or hides were allowed I never knew. Ramji with his curio shops obviously needed more than the allotted amount. Whatever it was, his man in the bush with his gang of warrior hunters, one Ed Spilsby, a cashiered army officer who was in training to be an alcoholic, boasted there was little to worry about when I sounded him out. Ramji covered himself with forged permits, bribes and still took few chances with his operation; Spilsby and his tribe moving to new areas to hunt throughout East Africa before the district authorities could catch up with them. Airstrips were camouflaged with scrub and bush during daylight, often returned to look naturally part of the landscape when abandoned. No customs officers ever searched the aircraft on my return. I flew with flight plans for Mombasa or some other legit destination made out on each covert flight.

I was now the proud possessor of a Morris Minor Traveller, bought from Ramji, of course, a previous write-off on the pot-holed Kenyan roads which had been resurrected by his Sikh mechanics. On arrival at the hotel I was ready for a shower and bed. There would always be, courtesy of Ramji again, two items on my bed. One was an envelope with a sheaf of banknotes, the other a pretty African girl, usually one of the Somali maidens, picked for their straight noses and thin lips as the elite prostitutes in town. Such a gesture could not be refused. We would fuck and then I'd sleep with her nubile naked body beside me, awakening for a second bout, shower again and go down for a hearty breakfast which could be ordered twenty-four hours a day if required.

Life does have its moments. I savoured experiences. The first kiss as a schoolboy, flying through heavy flak

In The Mood

over Hamburg, landing on a bush strip to be surrounded by wild faces with tribal marks scarring their cheeks and white eyes and teeth reflected in the light of burning wood torches. The women who'd made love with me. Now I was being waited on hand and foot, making good money, doing what I liked as a job. Every morning a *dhobi wallah* took away my used clothes, leaving fresh and perfectly ironed shirts, shorts and underwear. For a few East African cents a barber shaved me and even trimmed my hair while I sat up in bed, often with a naked girl sleeping beside me. Something told me it was all too good to last.

On one of those lovely evenings typical of Kenya, the night air scented with bloom, comfortably cool after the heat of the day, I was joined at a pavement cafe table by Spilsby. He had spotted me coming out of the bar and plonked himself down in an empty chair, pretty well oiled. In a pressed linen safari suit it was a moment before I recognised the armed unshaven tough I'd only met in the bush. He was shaven and shorn, looked years younger if as usual red-eyed, grabbing a passing waiter to order drinks. 'You'll be flying me out tomorrow night,' he informed me. 'Back for another couple of months' exile.'

'I thought you types preferred living in the wild, shooting at everything that moves – '

My sarcasm was wasted on him. 'Not me. This is my natural habitat, the wilds of Nairobi. Nightlife. Where's that fucking waiter? I need a drink – '

'Have mine,' I said, pushing it across. 'That's a wild bunch you run with.'

'Yeah. Masai, some Nandi, even Karamajong and Jie from north Uganda. They do the hunting and trapping, like they always did, only Ramji pays 'em now like he does you and I, hindi bastard. They scare the shit out of me. Were you in the war?'

'Bombers.'

In The Mood

'Long Range Desert Group,' he said. 'Then Kenya Regiment.'

'Ramji always refers to you as Captain Spilsby. DSO, MC.'

'Don't mean a fucking thing. I still got thrown out, you know. Height of the Mau Mau campaign. It's tailing off now; independence will come here and it won't be the same. Bloody white farmers will find a difference. You got a car?'

'Parked by the pavement.'

'Ramji is giving a party tonight and the bastard never invited me. I'm going just the same. He's buttering up some useful people as usual. Future politicians, bankers, influential bigwigs. He shovels his wife off to India and lays it on, and anything goes. There'll be a girl there tonight I'd love to throw a little fuck at. Bloody Angela Gore-Blomley; you should see her. I'd shuffle behind her on my knees kissing her bum.'

'Last time I saw her she thrashed my arse with a leather strap,' I said. 'While bollock naked. I know the young lady.'

Spilsby stared at me, trying to steady his eyes. 'Dirty, rotten, lecherous, lucky bastard,' he called me. 'Let us by all means head for the Ramji residence then.' But it seemed Spilsby could not go far without stopping at a watering hole, at the last of several bars returning to the car with a bottle of whisky tilted to his lips. By the time I'd driven to Ngong and prolonged the ride by circling several times in the area, he was blotto, sunk dead to the wide in his seat as I'd intended. Ramji was greeting guests before his door.

He looked in horror both at the Morris Traveller and at Spilsby slumped beside my driving seat. I was in a line of vehicles ranging from Rolls to Mercedes. Explaining that Spilsby was out for the night, that I'd saved the embarrassment of his unwanted arrival by getting him drunk and driving him around, Ramji clapped my shoulder. If I parked the Morris well

In The Mood

behind the bamboo grove, anywhere but the gravelled driveway before his house, to show his appreciation I could come in for one drink in the kitchen. There were very important people present, he told me.

While he remained to ooze over arriving guests, I went in and followed a couple upstairs to a large room. Some dozen people were already gathered, being served drinks by a host of servants in long white kanzu robes, red fezzes and cummerbunds. I saw Angela had arrived, dressed in a white linen trouser suit, the buttons at the front of her jacket bulging with her full breasts and the trousers tight, showing the curve of hip and arse, the mound of her cunt.

I took a passing glass off a tray and surveyed the scene. The room was carpeted by the biggest Persian rug imaginable. Couches and armchairs were ranged around the walls. Wide French windows led out to a verandah. The most unusual feature was a raised padded platform in the centre of the room, about three foot high and exactly resembling a boxing ring without the corner posts and ropes. Angela spotted me and to my surprise walked across to join me, glass in hand, cigarette in a long ivory holder, nails painted gold on both fingers and toes, every male eye in the room on the jiggling of her tight arse as she moved. 'You are very beautiful,' I told her. 'Pity about being such a spoiled bitch.'

'Oh, we're not back to that, are we?' she said. 'I've been meaning to look you up. I'm still keen on flying. Ramji says you could give me some preliminary lessons, take me with you on some of your flights. I'll be staying in Nairobi for a while. You'd be paid for your trouble, of course.'

'If Ramji says so, yes. I take anybody's money.'

'That's settled then. I'm surprised to see you here.'

'I gatecrashed, wanting to see how the other half lives.'

'You'll see something different here. Ramji arranges

quite a show. Exhibitions, you know. Sexual entertainments. You may want to join in, guests often do. You're very well qualified, as I recall – '

'Do you join in?'

'I've never yet been persuaded, or drunk enough. There are plenty of volunteers, however. It would surprise you who do.'

'Christ, do you Kenyans never fuck without an audience, or somebody wanting to watch?' I said, remembering her mother's great interest in voyeurism. 'Maybe they can't get it up any other way –?'

'I can assure you they can,' Angela smiled sweetly. 'I'm here because it pleases old Ramji to have what he thinks are the best people as his guests. It amuses me to see his shows. Those of us who are present wouldn't normally give him the time of day. He does lay on a good party, however.'

'Bloody snob,' I said. 'Ramji has worked for all he's got, not like some I could mention. You need a first-class fucking to bring you into line, knock some of those high and mighty ideas you have about your exalted position. I just happen to be the right one to do it.'

'Pigs will fly first,' Angela observed coolly, dropping her cigarette into the glass I held. 'You do let your lust show – '

Our attention was diverted by the entrance of a huge negro and a trio of shapely native girls. They mounted the platform to applause from the guests, anticipating a sexual display by handsome and athletic performers. The man was indeed a magnificent specimen, nude, with an oiled rippling torso, his flaccid prick hanging thick and full nine inches over massive shaved bollocks.

'Ramji's star performer,' Angela informed me. 'He has the edge on you, I'd say. And wait until those girls bring it up to full stretch. You'll be jealous – ' She glanced sideways to see how I'd taken her jibe.

In The Mood

'Wouldn't you like to earn a living doing what he does?'

I could have informed her that for a while I had, with the very lovely Moira and a few others Manny had laid on for his photographic sessions. At that moment all the lights except two chandeliers above the raised platform went out, leaving the stage brightly illuminated. The man posed, hands on hips, great trunks of legs braced apart. The three girls got on their knees before him, the middle one lifting the great black penis for herself and the other two to kiss and suck, making exaggerated sounds and gestures of pleasure. The girls smiled around at the darkened audience, wobbling their shapely pointed tits, rubbing their little plump shaven cunts. The cock they toyed with arose and grew thickly until they could hardly take the bulbous purple plum head in their mouths. Now I glanced at Angela, seeing her eyes wide and bright in the reflected light. I laid the palm of my hand on her rounded arse, cupping one cheek, giving it a suggestive squeeze. She let it remain.

The girls on stage then took up set positions, two lying head to toe, the one below with her face under the cunt of the girl above. The man held his big prick between the posed arse of the top girl, sliding up her cunt to his full length, making her cry out, before withdrawing and forcing his rigid tool down for the girl below to suck at the crest. He continued so, fucking one, getting sucked by the other, his buttocks working with his thrusts. The remaining girl, miming she had been left out, appealed to the audience, offering her breasts, fingering herself. She was joined by an Amazon of a woman, ebony black and naked, shining with oiled skin, who wore a large pigskin dildo strapped about her thighs. The women fucked in a variety of positions, joined the man and his two girls, and the stage became a mass of writhing, humping bodies.

In The Mood

Amid the cheers and cries of encouragement from the watchers I saw two men helping a tipsy middle-aged white woman on to the stage, joining her, all helping to get her clothes off. My hand by then was nicely fondling Angela's bum, both cheeks getting my attention. She took my hand away quite gently, almost reluctantly.

'I want some fresh air,' she said, her voice hoarse. 'I'm going out on the balcony for a while –' I took that as an invitation and followed her through the wide french window.

She went to the farthest corner of the balcony, leaning face out into the night with her elbows on the flat concrete surface of the balustrade. Endless night seemed to stretch before us, velvet dark with a million bright stars unmoving above. In the distance I heard the trumpeting of elephant. 'God, I do love Africa,' she said. I agreed, going directly behind her. 'That's why I want to fly so much. To soar over it, see its vastnesses from the sky. It's all so beautiful –'

'Big sky, big country,' I said. 'I already feel the same way about it. You'll make a pilot yet.'

'I intend to,' she said forcefully. 'Do you wish to go back inside now?'

'No. Stay where you are,' I ordered her. I reached around her with both hands, fumbling at the buttons of her tailored suit jacket. She neither helped me or stopped me. I went down from the neck to the waist, seeing it fall open. I put a hand up, held a breast, the hanging of it, the weight, the soft underside. She wore nothing underneath the jacket. My hand roved, cupping both globes, each nipple rolled between my fingers, growing thick.

'You have lovely skin,' I praised her. I felt her tremble. 'Arch your back. Push your bottom into me.' What seemed so stiff it was like a permanent hard-on bulged my trousers. I pressed it against her rear. 'Arch your back,' I repeated.

'Yes,' she whispered. 'But talk to me. Tell me what you are going to do to me –'

'Fuck you. Fuck your cunt like I've been aching to do since I first saw you. First your cunt and then your tight little arse. Like I said I would, remember? Have you had it in your bottom?'

'No. I don't know whether I would like that. I think you are too big. I think you are a beast to do that. I won't let you do that –'

We were, of course, further arousing already aroused feelings with our deliberate talk. 'I shall do it whether you like it or not. And you will like it. Undo those trousers, I want in there. Get them down to your knees.'

I could sense her loosening her belt, unbuttoning the waist-band. 'You do it then,' she said. 'You seem to be doing whatever you want with me.' Her hand came behind, searching, finding a prick which I had already freed from its confines. She grasped it, stroked and squeezed the stalk. I had the trousers tugged over the curve of her buttocks, down to the backs of her knees. Her legs came apart enough for my purpose. She leaned further forward over the balustrade. 'There,' she said. 'Is that what you want?' I touched her with my hand, the soft warm crevice of her nest, the springy flesh. She had surprisingly full lips, thickly parted with arousal, and a large clitoris. When I touched it she quivered, her bottom shook, she groaned as if unable to survive my rubbing.

'Is it nice, Angela? Do you like that?' I teased. 'Ask me nicely and I'll fuck you.'

'Put the thing in,' she demanded. 'You want it as much as I.'

'You have a superb arse,' I told her, stroking it. She was right, of course, I wanted it as urgently as she. Without my say-so almost, poised as it were to her cunt, the helmet nudged and broke into her. She pressed back to me and gasped as if in relief, working

In The Mood

her arse frantically. I gave the left cheek a fair smack. 'Steady,' I ordered. 'This isn't a race. I'm in no great hurry – '

'Too late,' she moaned. 'It's there, yes, it's coming. Push it right in!' There was no stopping her, her backside seemed to lift and her cunt tilted to me. Her undulations slowed but she continued thrusting herself back into me, slowing down but still enjoying the full penetration she was receiving. 'Don't stop,' she said quietly, 'I want it again. Haven't you come?'

'I've been saving the best for last,' I said into her neck. I withdrew and repositioned my stander, clearing her outer lips and sliding it up the inch or so required. The shaft was well lubricated with her juices, slippery in my hand. It met and pressed against her arsehole, its nose forcing an entrance. I left it at that for a long moment, awaiting her reaction.

'No, don't,' she pleaded. 'Not that way – '

'Yes, that way,' I insisted. I gave her another inch or so, hearing her draw a sharp breath, moan softly. She was intrigued, I knew, making no effort to prevent me penetrating her arsehole despite protests. 'Beast,' she called me, but her buttocks were relaxing, even moving gently against my belly. Now I was a 'filthy swine', but said as if to excite her own self. I was tight in her, balls hard to her cushiony rear. She bent over further. It was time for the working. I withdrew some inches and went up again, gripped like a vice, nudging deep, enjoying her groaning. People then appeared on the verandah some yards away, seeking fresh air, silhouetted by the light inside. I stilled my movements, crouched over Angela in our shadow, embedded in her. She began to push back into me furtively, wanting the slide of my prick to continue.

'Go on,' she whispered. I placed an arm around her, seeking her cunt and found her hand already there, frigging herself. The group on the verandah went back inside. Someone threw a cigar butt over the balus-

In The Mood

trade, its red glow turning circles as it fell. 'They've gone, you go on now,' the girl ordered. I recommenced my strokes, could hear the sliding of my prick as the pace increased.

'We're beasts,' she groaned out. 'Aren't we beasts? Doing this. It feels burning hot up my bum. I can feel it fill me, feel its very shape inside me. Push it in more –' My hand clasped over hers, moving it against her cunt. She gave a cry, jerked her bottom, rotating it against me. Sensing her climax I let my own load fly. I lay against her, both supported by the balustrade still inserted, gripped by her tight ring.

'Get off me,' she said at last. 'I suppose you feel one up on me now. I certainly hope you're satisfied. No one has ever done *that* to me before.' She drew up her trousers and briefs, buttoned her jacket. 'I would never have believed it.'

'What?' I asked. 'That pigs can fly –?'

'There is only one flying pig that I know of,' Angela said. 'And that is without question you.'

Chapter Eleven

I was due another flight for a bush pick-up a few days after Ramji's party. The afternoon sun burned down on the roof of the Shalimar and I was stretched out on my bed with the fan in the ceiling working fruitlessly, a Samali girl and myself both naked and tilting bottles of ice-cold Tusker lager to our mouths. It made for a pleasant way to pass the time. Her body glistened with sweat, shining on brown smooth skin, and her free hand dandled my prick idly. Between each mouthful of lager she held the frosted bottle between her pear-shaped tits. I'd never seen such nipples on a girl, an inch or so long at least. She had a trick she asked me to perform, one she loved with the obvious sensitivity of those proud projections on her tits. Each time she visited I was asked to do it, namely tap her nipples with an ordinary pencil.

She would sit up facing me, cupping her tits to hold them out for me, and I'd be instructed to use the pencil to tap each nipple. I mean tap, raising the full-length pencil by the sharpened end, bringing it down smartly so that the other end, the very tip, struck a nipple. That she liked this was evident from the expression on her face, by her repeated pleas to strike harder, and her amazing nipples would stretch and tilt like a prick gaining tumescence. Her thighs would grind together too, until she gasped and gave muscular contractions of her pelvis, obviously brought to orgasm.

She told me how, picked up one evening in a bar by

In The Mood

an American couple, she had been taken to their hotel room and discovered it was for the benefit of the wife. The pair were obviously rich, as were all early tourists to the region. During the romp she showed them how she liked her nipples rapped. She had then used the elongated tips on the woman's clitoris, the woman lying back with her legs splayed and holding her cunt lips open. Amazing what some people will do. The lady had climaxed, her husband had taken pictures of the scene. The generous couple had presented the Samali girl with one hundred dollars American, a fortune to her.

I was thinking seriously about another fuck at the girl before showering when Ramji tapped at my door and entered. She rose, pulled on her dress and left at the merest nod from him. 'I shall send her back up when I leave,' he said. 'You Europeans, do you not have women who let you fuck them in your own countries? Out here it seems you cannot get enough of the local girls, any tribe, any colour.' He shook his head. 'Sometimes I think your brains are in your penises; but then perhaps for you it would have been better to have stuck to Africans. Do you know a District Commissioner Bellinger?'

This made me sit up. 'Not really. It was his daughter I knew. Anything we did was okay with her – '

'I did not know you knew her in Nairobi. You have been a very busy young man.'

'I didn't know her in Nairobi. It was on the ship coming out.'

'She is here now. Left her parents in the Northern District and set up home with another woman, a Miss Marigold Gore-Blomley. A most curious arrangement, I must say.'

'What's that to do with me?'

'The young lady had a terrible row with her parents when she left them, I hear. She unwisely told them a few home truths, as you say. Wanted to shock them in

In The Mood

the heat of the argument, no doubt. Your name was mentioned as a lover, and that you had advised her to leave home, desert her parents – '

'I only told her to stand up to them.'

'It is unwise to interfere in families. No Asian father would tolerate it. District Commissioner Bellinger evidently feels the same way. He has made enquiries about a certain Mr Tyler Wight – '

'Well, fuck him,' I laughed. 'What he thinks don't mean a thing to me. So I screwed his precious daughter. She was all for it. What's he going to do, sue me?'

'Horsewhip you, the word is around Nairobi. An old-fashioned custom carried out by irate English fathers, I believe.'

'Let the old bastard try. That went out with Queen Victoria. I've had irate fathers and husbands after me before now – '

'Do not joke about this,' Ramji said sadly. 'I do not wish to lose my very good pilot. But Mr Bellinger is an old Kenya man, he has many influential friends here among the magistrates and police even. They have had undesirable people sent home before now. For my sake I hope it will not come to that – '

'Fuck your sake, Ramji,' I told him. I was beginning to get slightly apprehensive about losing what is known as a good billet. I was living in a fascinating country with almost permanent sun, never having to lift a finger for the mundane chores of life, the washing, cleaning and cooking one is sometimes forced to do. Even my shoes were polished for me, waiting under my bed when I got up. 'How do you know all this?' I asked. 'It can't be that serious, can it?'

In reply Ramji tapped his nose. 'I hear all that goes on in Nairobi. But even worse may follow. Terrible scandal. The living arrangements of Miss Bellinger and Miss Gore-Blomley is now the subject of much discussion. It is circulated that they were both encouraged in this relationship by the same person who seduced Miss Bellinger and probably Miss Gore-Blomley.'

'Well, fuck my horrible luck,' I considered. 'Bellinger again?'

'Yes,' Ramji agreed. 'And there is the distinct possibility that word of all this will reach the ears of Miss Gore-Blomley's brother. Now there is a man to reckon with, a very powerful person indeed. He is not aware yet of his sister's liaison with Miss Bellinger, but he is bound to find out and want to know all the facts. Then it will be all hell let loose. He can be very angry man. Worse for you than District Commissioner Bellinger even – '

'Thanks a bunch. You really know how to put a guy at ease. So you came here to tell me to lay low?' All of a sudden life had become complicated, and I didn't want it. And if the bubble really burst and the worst came out, that I had fucked Gore-Blomley's wife as well as his daughter, my days in paradise were numbered. 'What do you suggest I do?' I had to say, forcing the words out.

'I have a camp bed placed for you in the hangar. One of the Sikh mechanics already lives there. He can cook for you. I hope you like Madras curry – '

'Fucking marvellous,' I said. 'You're enjoying this, you old hindi con artist. So I live the life of a hermit, tucked away in a bloody old shed that lets in the rain, but handy to fly your aircraft. I suppose you'll be charging me rent?'

'A minimal sum can be deducted from your salary. But it is all for your own good, young friend. Do not set legs in Nairobi while this unfortunate turn of events is afoot. If and when it ends peacefully, I will inform you.'

'I have my doubts about that. You'd like to have me by the balls working for Athi Air. How come I feel you own me?'

'Probably because I do,' smiled the crafty Gujarat.

In The Mood

'Get your case packed and leave as soon as you're ready. I'll sent the Samali *bibi* up for you to have one last poke before you go.'

I was squatting on my camp bed in a corner of the hangar, ruminating on the latest turn of events, when next I saw Ramji. He came hurrying in, not half so cocky, mopping the sweat from his dark brown fat face. 'You will take a passenger tonight,' he informed me worriedly. 'Of all people, a Gore-Blomley. Miss Angela. I could not say no to her.' He wrung his hands. 'Foolish me, I told her she could fly with you sometime, she is keen to get the knowledge. But not tonight! She came here today and the bloody stupid mechanic said you were flying tonight. So now she insists to go with you.'

The idea of seeing Angela again when soon her old man might well be headhunting me was a bit much. For my immediate future's sake I wanted nothing to do with any Gore-Blomley, even the lovely Angela. 'You should have told her no,' I said. 'Simple as that.'

'How could I? They are very important. I have business with the father. He is a banker too.'

'Nothing surprises me about that crowd. So let her come. She won't know what we pick up isn't regular quota stuff.'

Ramji seemed relieved. 'Just be careful what you say to her. You do not know of her Aunt Marigold or this Miss Bellinger — '

I almost wished I'd never heard of them. The Sikh mechanics began pushing the old Dragonfly out onto the apron, she was filled and ready to go, even to a case of whisky for the thirsty Captain Spilsby. Up came Angela in her sporty car, a red convertible that shouted money. She was dressed for what she considered highly suitable for a night flight, leather jacket over a white opened neck shirt, jean trousers. Her hair was tied back in the usual ponytail. She looked scrumptious. We got permission from the tower to take off, flew into a darkening sky. I explained certain routines then settled back on the auto pilot, course southwest.

She handed me a hip-flask as the cabin grew colder. It was excellent brandy and I took several nips before handing it back. 'This is fun,' she said. 'Again I'm impressed.'

'Pretty routine stuff.'

'You're a man of few words tonight,' she observed. 'What is it? Conscience? You usually have too much to say. Is it because of what you did to me, buggered me? It was a new experience at least. I'm none the worse for it.'

'Glad to hear that.'

'Do you like to have women that way? In the bottom – '

'It makes a change.'

'You mean it makes you feel superior,' she laughed. 'Plugging a poor female's rear. Pretty degrading if it wasn't so pleasurable as well, I think.' She obviously wanted to talk sex, arousing herself, tempting me, her perfume heady even when mingled with the cabin's usual smell of engine oil.

I tried to switch the talk to flying, explaining this and that, letting her listen to the crackle of the messages coming in on the radio. I told her in time to watch for landing lights and to her delight I let her be the first to see them ahead. She buckled her seat belt as I ordered, explaining bush airstrips were not always well laid and there'd be some hairy landings. To this she exclaimed her delight, the hairier the better for her. 'I'm more than ever determined to have you teach me to fly – '

It was Spilsby himself who opened up the aircraft cabin door, swaying half drunk, unshaven and in a filthy safari suit. I feared the worst and got it. 'Great,' he enthused seeing Angela beside me. 'You've brought more cunt with you. I've got it all set up in the tent;

In The Mood

three *bibis* from Mwanza came with us this trip. There'll be a whole lot of fucking tonight, Tyler old boy. Hope you brought my whisky –'

'What an awful man,' Angela said, tickled pink.

I got out beside her and it was truly like a scene from hell. Surrounded by a motley crew of warriors armed to the very teeth, the burning fires of the flight path, the darkness stretching out to utter remoteness. Near the aircraft sat a pile of long elephant tusks, a heap of skins. Some of the Africans were using a fire burning in an oil drum to cook large chunks of still bloody meat, held out pierced on the end of their spears. I spoke to the headman, noting Spilsby was already heading back to his tent and his three women, tilting a bottle. 'Get loaded up,' I ordered. To Angela I said we would be on our way back in a short time.

'Oh, not so soon,' she complained. 'This is marvellous, really wild. Besides, I want to see what goes on in that tent. Your ruffian friend expects us to join him.'

One can hardly knock on a tent, so I looked in lifting the canvas flap. Spilsby was on his back lying along a narrow camp bed, still tilting a bottle to his lips while mounted by a sturdy black girl bouncing up and down on his prick, her feet solid on the dirt floor either side of the bed. The two other girls, as plump and naked as their friend, squatted watching and giggling with a bottle apiece. It was pretty obvious they were all well pissed. The sultry air, magnified in the enclosed greasy tent, was ripe with the smell of cunt. I felt Angela's chin on my shoulder as she looked in, her tits pressed into my back. The pair of spare girls then saw her white face and exclaimed in pleasure. They came forward, took a hand apiece and led her into the centre of the tent.

She allowed herself to go, looking back at me and smirking at my disapproval. In the tent, lit by two hurricane lanterns, naked black skins seemed to reflect the yellow glow, highlighting exaggeratedly

In The Mood

pointed breasts, nipples like thimbles and fat little cunt mounds with wiry pubic hair. The girls admired Angela's clothes. They circled the white girl, ivory teeth shining in invitation to be friends. Spilsby had collapsed, I was pleased at least to note, the bottle on his chest and the whisky soaking his shirt. The third girl joined the others, fascinated by the *mzungu* woman, her blonde hair and fair skin. Angela took off the leather jacket, letting them inspect it. One girl began to unbutton Angela's shirt as if in curiosity to see inside it. She helped them by pulling it out of her jeans, revealing pale shoulders and the full breasts hanging weighty in a white lacy bra.

'They've never seen white tits before,' I said. She was enjoying herself greatly. So was I really. There was an atmosphere present that was somehow highly erotic. 'Take off your bra. You've seen theirs –'

She obligingly unhooked the garment, handing it over to be inspected, displaying her own large rounded pair of milk-white tits. The girls chattered, came close, one standing nipple to nipple with the white girl. Angela's were erect, protruding stiff as fingertips. She stood while all three girls had a feel of her globes, pinching them, discussing and giggling at the same time I could only guess, over their roundness and colour. The fondling continued as Angela let them lift her tits, pull on her nipples, standing stock still before them.

'I don't suppose they've seen a white cunt either,' I suggested. 'Try 'em with your pants off –' She complied at once, stepping out of her jeans and then peeling off tiny lacy briefs that matched the brassiere. One of the girls reached out and touched Angela's mound, remarking something in wonder, no doubt intrigued by the luxuriant fair brush of cunt hair. She touched the outer lips, probed with a finger, cried out an 'aah' to find it lubricated. The others wanted to see, to feel. Angela parted her legs slightly, giving access.

In The Mood

'I don't know what there is about you,' she said, turning to me. 'Every time we get together it seems the most disgusting things occur. I feel like a fuck now. We'll show them how it's done, shall we?'

'I didn't start this,' I complained. 'I'm not fucking in this filthy tent either. You've enjoyed your little experiment. Now I've got to get back to Nairobi before dawn. Put on your clothes and say goodbye to your friends, we're late enough.'

'You've got a mighty hard-on,' she said sweetly. 'I can see it bulge your trousers. What a pity to waste it.'

'It will keep,' I told her. 'You really are the most horny bitch I've ever come across. Is that what you learned in your posh finishing school?'

'I was expelled from three of them actually.'

That didn't surprise me. She sat teasing me for the whole journey back, not knowing my wary attitude was entirely because I felt in deep enough trouble with her clan. When we had landed she asked me where I lived.

'I couldn't take you there,' I said. Actually we were but yards from my living quarters in the old hangar.

'Then come home with me. I've a flat in Ngong. It really belongs to an aunt of mine, but would you believe she has gone off to live with another woman? Quite a young girl too, I believe. Whatever turns you on, as they say.'

'Maybe they are just sharing,' I said hopefully.

'Not a bit of it. I saw them when Aunt Marigold gave me the keys to her flat to use. They're in love, or whatever it is. Only eyes for each other and all that. Are you coming home with me? We can shower while the housegirl makes breakfast, and then off to bed. You must be tired,' she laughed.

I was never that tired and if I was in the shit I decided I might as well be in it up to my neck so I said she was on. We used her car, the morning breeze in

In The Mood

our faces. Once in her aunt's flat she ordered orange juice, bacon and eggs to be cooked, then led me through to a bedroom. She shed her her clothes quickly, kicking them aside for her servant to collect off the floor later. Her lush body was made to fuck, ripe for it. I threw off my own clothes to join her, my prick as ever ready.

'Lord, what a tool,' she said. 'To think that went up my bum.'

'It will again,' I promised her.

'No, not now. Later.' She fell back on the bed and showed me her cunt, legs widespread and lips parted by her fingers. 'Don't you want to? Yes, I know you do. I can see it in your face. Lick me out – '

'After you've showered.' I looked at the pink wet flesh. 'It's been a long hot sticky night – '

'All the better for it.'

I was tempted. 'Say please, then. Ask nicely,' I teased her.

'Your mouth, damn you. I want your mouth. You can do what you like to me after.' She reached up, pulling my face down between her thighs. I was poised to tongue her when I had a sudden thought.

'What would your father say if he knew I was doing this to you?'

'Shoot you probably. He thinks I'm his darling little girl still. Never mind about that. Lick me clean – '

'You make it sound very appetising,' I said moodily as I bent to my allotted task.

Chapter Twelve

For more than a week there was a lull it seemed in the saga of the Gore-Blomleys. Even Ramji with his ear constantly to the ground could report no further action on the scene, only that Marigold Gore-Blomley and Anne Bellinger still shared a love-nest and seemed from all accounts to be set for life. Servants love to exchange gossip about their employers, none more so than the African houseboy or housegirl. That Marigold and Anne were noticed holding hands, exchanging kisses and slept together in a house with three other bedrooms was a source of some puzzlement to their strapping Kikuyu maid. She, of course, told other servants, who in turn took delight in passing on the info to their white mistresses. This system worked as well as any news service.

So the affair was discussed at coffee mornings, at the club, and it became pretty general knowledge in the Kenyan capital that the two ladies were as camp as a field full of tents, as queer as a three-dollar bill, and didn't all Nairobi love that bit of scandal. A Gore-Blomley, sister of the high and mighty Reggie, and with the young daughter of the old puritanical District Commissioner of all people!

All this did nothing to prevent the sense of unease I had about my future tenure in East Africa. I stuck to my corner of the hangar when not flying. Ramji arranged that I made overnight stops in Mombasa. To console myself I met Inga, wife of a Swedish industrialist. She was on the East African part of a round-the-world junket with an all-Scandinavian party of women, no doubt while their husbands worked away at having heart attacks.

I saw her on the beach at Kilindini, blonde and buxom, in a two-piece bathing outfit that showed off fine big freckled tits and a beautiful rounded arse. My kind of woman, obviously. I swam near her, struck up a conversation and was invited back to her hotel for drinks, where she proudly showed off her find to a gaggle of fellow travellers. We spent the afternoon in her hotel room, where I discovered her freckles went all over a most curvaceous soft body. We fucked and sucked at each other until next morning, which took my mind off my troubles no end.

She was a kinky lass, too. She it was who suggested I tie her to the bed ends and whup her arse with my belt before doing what I liked with her. The being-helpless feeling heightened her arousal to fever pitch, causing her to cry out mock protests so loudly that someone banged on our door for quiet. For good measure I took her in the arse while trussed up, and a nice cushiony bum it was to thrust against. I was back in Mombasa that evening with more passengers, looked up Inga and so impressed had she been with my performance that she'd invited her best friend along, a handsome Dane of about fifty who fucked like fury. I spent the night as pig-in-the-middle between two well-fed naked Viking women. Next day they sailed for Bombay and other exotic eastern places.

I was back in my corner, eating a plateful of curry and rice, my staple diet it seemed, when Dalip Singh the Athi Air chief mechanic informed me I was wanted on the telephone in the office. I knew Ramji had fielded any calls from outside for me, including several from Angela Gore-Blomley enquiring about further flights and the promised flying lessons. At that moment my threshhold of boredom had reached its peak. I went to

In The Mood

the office and answered the phone. Angela's voice came through loud and clear, obviously delighted to have contacted me.

'Where have you been?' she enquired. 'You seem to have disappeared off the face of the earth. I've been trying to contact you all week. You've been lying low, haven't you?' Her voice tinkled with merriment, highly amused.

'What makes you say that?'

'Oh, just something that my father has been raging about. That someone I won't need to mention had his sister and another woman romping about a ship's cabin, and the two females evidently preferred each other to the man. Shame on you, Tyler Wight. I thought no lady could resist that big tool of yours – '

'Extremely funny,' I told her. 'I don't think.'

'Did you manage to fuck Aunt Marigold? Please tell me.'

I could have told her it was her own mother that had set it up, causing all the present hassle. I remained silent for want of something to say. It would seem the game was up, anyway.

'And what about Anne Bellinger? Did you fuck her too? I must know. I went to school with her here in Nairobi. I thought then she'd turn out to be an out and out lesbo, always soppy over other girls – '

'More to the point,' I said, 'what does your old man intend to do about all this? I hear he can be slightly vindictive – '

She burst out laughing. 'His wrath is terrible to behold. And that no doubt is why you've gone undercover. Ramji professed to know nothing about you except for your flying. He's kept you at Mombasa, hasn't he?'

'Why so keen to contact me?' I asked. 'Are you doing this for your father, has he asked you to find me?'

'My father has no idea you and I know each other. Do you really think I'd shop you? But he is in Nairobi

In The Mood

with mother this weekend, and District Commissioner Bellinger too. They intend to prise the lovers apart, Aunt Marigold and Anne, and take them off to their respective homes. But finding you is on their agenda too, I know. They say old Bellinger is armed with a kiboko – '

'What the fuck is a kiboko?'

'A whip made of rhinoceros hide.'

'Great. What about your old man?'

There were more giggles. 'Probably his elephant gun.'

I remained silent, mulling this prospect over. She came back on the line. 'They know you work at the airport and are bound to seek you out there. I have a way out. Fly me to Kakamega today, the estate. We'd be alone all weekend, then when they return with Aunt Marigold all this will fizzle out – '

I thought that would be the last straw, putting my head in the very lion's den. But I had to leave Nairobi, and a weekend with Angela was more than tempting. 'Why do this for me?'

'Like attracts like. I find you an incorrigible rogue. It would be rather fun to thwart my father's avowed intention, and there's a chance for me to fly. Knowing you, we'll more than likely fuck all weekend too. So no argument, I'm on my way to the airfield now.'

We were in the air within the hour, flying over the Nairobi escarpment, Kikuyu villages with their straw-roofed mud huts, Lake Naivasha and on over herds of elephant and buffalo until the great expanse of Lake Victoria glinted ahead. Low storm clouds threatened, the first drops of a tropical downpour splashed on the cabin windscreen, the airspeed dropped as a headwind grew strong. Lightning flashes struck the plain ahead from a black sky. Angela was delighted as the turbulence buffeted the old Dragonfly. I was glad to land safely, taxi-ing close to a large mansion-style house with its pillars and verandah, swimming pool and stab-

In The Mood

les. As we got out with our weekend bags, four servants came out to assist us carry them indoors.

On the polished stone verandah, a large gin in hand and well into getting drunk it would seem, Vee Gore-Blomley sat in a bamboo chair regarding our approach. I turned to return to the aircraft, getting out, making it seem I had flown Angela home as a paying passenger. She held my arm and said, 'Oh no you don't.'

'I thought you were in Nairobi for the weekend,' she said to her mother. 'I'd better introduce you two –'

'I know who he is,' said Vee. 'We met on the ship.' She put a hand to her mouth to cover a hiccup. 'I wasn't going to spend a whole weekend talking Marigold out of living with another woman. She can live with who the hell she likes. It's a lot better here without her. How is it that you know this person?'

So now I was a person. I had to acknowledge Vee looked very attractive in a kaftan gown, if slightly inebriated, an older version of her beautiful daughter. The gown was unbuttoned and revealed the cleavage and swell of her big breasts. As if to know that, she held the neck of the gown together.

'He's here to give my flying lessons,' Angela explained.

'Then he can stay in the annexe. Get Ignatius to show him.'

The tall Nandi servant understood every word, raising an umbrella and picking up my travelling hold-all to lead me off to a large bungalow a short distance from the main house, built to accommodate an overflow of guests. I found myself the sole occupier of several bedrooms and bathrooms. The rain lashed down and thunder rolled. I showered, lay on a bed thinking of how things might have been had Vee gone to Nairobi; uneasy too in case she telephoned her husband to say the culprit he sought was in his very house. A footstep in the passageway had me sitting up to see Ignatius with a covered tray, my dinner. He silently handed me a note he'd been slipped. It was from Angela and said 'Sorry. I didn't know the old lady would be here – ' and a row of X's meant no doubt as kisses.

I couldn't blame her for playing safe. Outside the tropical storm ravaged as wild as ever. But for that I would have gone to the aircraft and taken off. I slept a while, wakened by a hand on my shoulder. The bedside lamp was turned on and I blinked up to see Vee bending over me, nightdress sodden. The wet cloth clung to her luscious body, showing her tits and nipples as clearly as if they were bare, the contours moulded.

'I had to talk to you,' she said. 'This business with Reggie's sister. They want you too. If my husband catches up with you, do you intend to tell all? That I was involved in it?'

'That wouldn't do me any good, would it?' I said. 'No. Whatever happens I won't say a word. Marigold might.'

'I don't think so. I telephoned to warn her that Reggie was on his way to Nairobi, to get out while he's there. She's promised to say nothing.'

'Then you are safe enough.'

She nodded. 'God, I'm soaked.' As she stood beside the bed she peeled off the drenched nightdress, standing before me most gloriously damp and naked. From my position on the bed I was at eye level with her prominent cunt mound, jutting fatly with the covering of hair flattened by the wet. Looking upwards I saw the underside of a magnificent pair of rounded tits, the nipples thick. 'I was half pissed when you arrived,' she said.

'You seem okay now – '

'I went to bed, slept it off. Then woke up thinking if you told your story, all hell would be let loose. So I came here. I'm going to dry myself.'

She left the room, returning with a large towel and a bottle, two glasses held between her fingers. 'For the

In The Mood

use of guests,' she said. 'Help yourself. I could use one too.'

I poured out two stiff whiskies, watching her dry herself, her tits bobbing, rubbing her pubic hair back into curls. 'I feel cold, move over,' she told me, slipping her nakedness in beside mine. 'You know Angela, it seems. Have you fucked her? It would be the only Gore-Blomley female you haven't, unless you have –'

I didn't answer, taking her glass and putting it on the beside table. She came to my arms, pressing her whole body to mine, pliant tits flattened to my chest, her cunt mound hard to my rigid erection. I fingered her clitoris, sucked hard at her nipples, she sinking down in the bed and pulling me to her. She suddenly, in the midst of her arousal, gave a short laugh even as I penetrated her cunt to the hilt. 'Reggie is looking for you in Nairobi, and you are here up his wife! Come on then, fuck me harder, I'm dying for a good come again. Shove that thing right in my cunt, balls and all if you can. Oh God, oh heaven. I can feel it touching my stomach. Did you ever fuck Angela like this?'

She wanted to know in the middle of a fuck because it aroused her, horny cow. Know that her daughter had taken the big cock now making her writhe and cry out. I fucked harder, humping over her like a demented hound, feeling her mounting convulsions. Again she shouted, 'Tell me, tell me! Did you fuck Angela?'

'Yes he did,' came a voice from the doorway, and I looked over my shoulder to see Angela there. 'You bastards,' she said, giggling at the sight. 'You horny pair of fuckers. I might have known. I'll bet you fucked mother on that ship, too.' Her mother in the throes of an orgasm, carried on thrusting to me, grunting and gasping. The cover had slipped off, revealing our bodies.

'Is this a private party or can anyone join in?' Angela said. I rolled sideways off Vee, my prick glistening with cunt lubrication but still mightily erect, me hold-

In The Mood

ing off so I could give Vee some multiples. I loved having a woman go berserk under me, it was the best part of a fuck, and I could always let it go in the end.

'Angela!' Vee said, recovering somewhat and looking up. 'You shouldn't be here – '

'You're damn right,' her daughter said. She drew off her dressing gown to stand as bare as the rest of us. 'But now that I am, I'm getting in on the act. Did you ask if Tyler had ever fucked me? Several times, so far. Not as many times as he's screwed you, perhaps, but he's had it up my bottom even. Have you ever had that, mummy? Has father ever corked your bottom? It's quite an experience to have a prick up your arse. You wouldn't think that tight little hole would stretch for it, would you, especially Tyler's monster? But it did and I loved it – '

'Why are you saying these things to me?' Vee pleaded.

'Because you and daddy have been down on me since I first grew tits. Watched like a hawk, while you fucked like a rabbit.'

Vee, stretched out naked and steaming from our fuck, gave up the contest. 'So all right. I fuck! I fucked with this young man all the way out on the ship. Your father's no use to me. I have feelings like anyone else.'

'Good,' said Angela. 'So fuck her again, Tyler. I want to see it. Fuck her in the arse if you like. That would be even better. Then you can fuck me, and she can watch – '

For all this most fascinating talk flying between the mother and daughter, I was still aware of hearing a motor driving up outside. There was light shining from my window, of course, giving our position away. I pushed the frame open, seeing Reginald Gore-Blomley himself leaping from a mud-splattered Land Rover with another man I took to be Anne Bellinger's father. Not for the first time in my life I began to dress in double-quick time, Vee and Angela looking startled.

In The Mood

As well they might too. Even as I pulled up my trousers and tried to step into my shoes at the same time, the furious pair burst into the bedroom, followed by Ignatius and several other servants carrying wooden staves. I don't know what would have been said had Gore-Blomley found me alone. To see his wife and daughter naked as fish in the same room as me was no doubt a shock, for want of a better word. He uttered a 'My God!' and I did not wait to hear any more, grabbing my hold-all and leaping out of the window, giving thanks that the place was a ranch-style bungalow. It was still pre-dawn, about four in the morning, I guessed, though my wristwatch, the very one Vee had given me for services rendered on the ship, had been laid on my bedside table after my shower earlier.

I got in the aircraft, reaching for the ignition, praying for a first-time start. Even as I twisted the key, a report sounded, followed by a second, both barrels of a shotgun peppering the fuselage of the aircraft. Mad bastard, I thought, saw him raise his gun again on the run and ducked as the cabin door window shattered. What I thought was blood on my hand was oil, leaking from Christ knows where but serious enough in a flying machine. I hopped out of the far side of the cabin, head down, running like an Olympic sprinter into the night. When I stopped running my heart was pounding like a trip-hammer, a stitch in my side utter agony. I limped on gasping, wanting to put as much distance between myself and the Gore-Blomley entourage as possible. One thing was in my favour, I considered, what Reggie was having to say to his wife and daughter was probably enough for him to be getting on with.

It was then I realised my predicament. I heard what was to me a definite roar of a lion in the night. I walked on cautiously. There were movements around me, shapes even in the utter dark. I saw buffalo so

In The Mood

near I could touch, lying down in a large group I circled as if walking on eggs. Then more lion calls, or was it hyena? Those bastards were vicious too. I passed stunted trees, typical of the African plain, where leopard liked to spend the night. 'Well, fuck me rigid,' I thought, after all I'd been through in life to end up eaten by some wild animal, some mangy carnivore! Oh endless night!

Dawn came, even more welcome than the first light revealing the patchwork fields of South-East England on my return from bombing raids over Germany. At least now I could see any animal who fancied me for breakfast. The only weapon I carried was my zipped-up weekend hold-all bag, which even in my haste I had grabbed. Before leaving on the flight with Angela I had put all my valuables in it: passport, pilot's licence, all the money I'd drawn out of the bank in case of a quick departure. Between a group of trees I met a small herd of elephants, the old bad-tempered tusker in charge trumpeting at me, throwing up dust with his trunk, making me retreat slowly and backwards before him. Then with sun-up I saw a hutted village, walking by to the great curiosity of its inhabitants. They pointed me in the direction of a road, which I found a mile or so on, a rutted dirt track but still a sign of civilization. In the African heat the downpour of the previous night had already dried out, but I saw tyre tracks.

I sat, glad to rest, and thinking back on the previous night's escapades could not but shake with laughter, roaring-type laughter, my sides aching. 'Never a dull moment, Tyler old boy,' I told myself. I was still wiping my eyes when a Vauxhall car drew up beside me. The man who got out was tall, ebony black, quite a magnificent specimen. He wore a grey suit, collar and tie, polished shoes. 'You should not be here,' he said in excellent English. 'Has your vehicle broken down somewhere? Can I give you a lift?'

In The Mood

'Yes,' I said. 'Anywhere you are going except near the Gore-Blomley estate.'

'I don't know of them,' he said. 'I am from Uganda and I'm driving back there now.'

'Well, you know I always fancied seeing Uganda,' I said. 'If you can take me there I'll be glad to pay for your trouble.'

'That won't be necessary,' said the man. 'Hop in.'

Chapter Thirteen

I discovered my new acquaintance was called Edoku, just that, he said. Later as we drove and talked it came out he was a newly commissioned lieutenant in the Ugandan battalion of the then King's African Rifles. Sandhurst trained, too. After service in Kenya in the Mau Mau campaign as a platoon leader he had been selected as officer material, preparing for the day the protectorate became independent. When I explained my appearance, a lone *mzungu* lost in wild country after fleeing an irate father, his broad black face creased in a grin, showing great tombstones of perfect white teeth with the central tooth of the lower jaw missing. This I knew was a tribal custom, a defence against lockjaw, which is not uncommon in the villages. Water and soup can be poured in a mouth through the gap to feed an afflicted person. I don't know if that works!

I had been lucky. His reason for being in the Kakamega district of Kenya was that the company had been granted leave. He had been taking a fellow soldier back to his village. Now Edoku was driving to his father's wedding. The old warrior was chief of the encampment of Ilok, which was beside Lake Kyoga in Central Uganda. Their tribe was the Iteso and they were Nilotic people, not Bantu like most of Uganda, hence he was so black and not brown. His words not mine. The Iteso were cattle people and cows were their wealth. Lake Kyoga was actually part of the great

263

In The Mood

Nile river which came out of Lake Victoria and curled north-west into the shallow Kyoga before resuming its course north to Sudan and Egypt.

He talked of his father, Emok. It appeared the old chap had four wives already, one of them Lieutenant Edoku's mother. They were getting old, however, and too respected as a chief's wives to cook, fetch food and water. Then of course there was Emok's late brother's wives, four more. It was a brother's duty to take them on. I understood. In a land with no old age or widows pensions they could not be left to starve. If they were attractive enough, young enough, they could be of use in the chief's bed too, Edoku said. Otherwise they were built separate huts and Emok sent them food and water.

This was one reason, I knew, why African girls were so keen to have children, especially boys who would care for them in old age in case no one else would. Whenever I'd taken one to bed they wanted to be made pregnant. 'Put water there,' they would say, taking my hand down to the plump little cunts, meaning shoot a bellyful of liquid into me and give me a son. In or out of wedlock, as soon as little pointy tits or their periods showed up, they were eager to breed as insurance for a hard old age. Not that they didn't like fucking for its own sake. Girls were raised to please men in every way, be their chattels. Driving through villages one saw men squatting, debating serious subjects under the shade of a tree like when Nambosa killed a lion with one spear thrust. All round them women would be carrying wood, water, tending fires, breast-feeding babies, cheerful souls who cackled with laughter as they cut up meat or pounded grain. Africa and its people certainly gets to you. Never leaves you.

So I wanted to know more of the old chief's wedding. His intended bride was from the next village, an Iteso virgin of all of sixteen. Of course he would have to pay a heavy bride price for her to her parents, a hefty

In The Mood

dowry. I said I would like to be there for that and even help with the dowry, having several thousand East African shillings in my hold-all. Edoku glanced at me, asking if I was certain. His home was just a bush village with no modern amenities, little hygiene, prowled by wild animals, infested by snakes and *dudus* which I knew was Swahili for any kind of creepy-crawly. Well, even living in the Athi Airway hanger I'd encountered spiders big as your fist and cockroaches big as mice. 'It could even kill you to drink our water,' Edoku warned. People, I told him, had been trying to kill me for some years. Over Berlin, for instance, where if the flak didn't get you the night fighters did. What the hell, I was bowling along in bright sunshine through great country. 'Of course I want an invite to this wedding,' I said. After all, any old chap of seventy about to take a wife of sixteen deserved all the support he could get.

At the Uganda border I showed my British passport and thus entered a country where more was to happen to me than would fill a hundred lifetimes. I filled the car with petrol there, a gesture appreciated by Edoku, who explained his father's wedding had put him in debt for the rest of the year. The first town we encountered in Uganda was Tororo, where Edoku informed me we would be picking up another wedding guest, a sergeant serving in his company. Someone who knew his father.

We stopped in the carpark of the Crested Crane Hotel, a new construction for the tourist trade. Waiting there in tropical army khaki was the biggest hulk of a man I'd ever seen, towering over six feet, broad and black as night, war medal ribbons above his breast pocket, sergeant's stripes on each arm, a holstered revolver on his webbing belt.

'This is Sergeant Idi Amin,' Edoku introduced. 'Flight Lieutenant Wight.' My hand disappeared in a huge grip. The broad face before me grinned, then

In The Mood

Amin drew himself stiffly to attention and threw up a magnificent salute. Scrub round that, I told him, as I was strictly a civilian. The hotel looked tempting to me. I badly needed a shave and shower, a meal too. I suggested we all go in and have a beer. The two soldiers hesitated. It was for rich white visitors, Edoku explained. Sergeant Idi Amin was less impressed. It was obvious he was not the backward kind. He laughed and slapped his holster, speaking in Swahili. I got the gist of it, my Swahili now coming along. He'd said, 'If they don't let us in, we will shoot some of them.' Well, nothing like starting the way you intend to continue, as I was to discover.

So refreshed we took the Soroti road, Amin in the back of the Vauxhall, which I'd learned belonged to the English colonel of the Edoku's battalion and had been loaned to Edoku for the wedding trip. He must have been a decent sort. The road petered out to a dirt track as we headed for Ilok. In places elephant grass grew high as the car either side of the track, some of it on fire and sending up flames some thirty feet or more. Under a burning sun, with the heat of the fires just yards away, I feared the petrol tank might explode. It was like driving through an inferno. Both Edoku and Idi Amin did not seem perturbed. I asked if we were in a bush fire. Both men laughed. Amin joked that the *mzungu* did not know of our habits. It was all perfectly natural, and he took delight at my ignorance.

'Look,' said Edoku, pointing over the wheel to a group of men on the track, several dozen spaced out over two hundred yards or so. They wore blankets draped about them and carried spears, pangas and shields. 'They have set fire to the grass to drive out the animals. It is for my father's wedding feast.'

Sure enough, terrified antelope or gazelle bounded out onto the track to be pursued by the whooping men, hurling spears. There was the sudden crack of a pistol shot in my ear and I leapt in shock. Amin was leaning over my shoulder, firing out my side window at the animals with his service revolver. He emptied the cylinder and I saw a fleeing Thompson's gazelle fall kicking wildly. He reloaded and continued firing past my head as we drove along.

'Fuck me, Jesus Christ,' I shouted. 'A bloody wild man from way back!' Amin roared with laughter again. 'You've got a real nutter here,' I told Edoku. 'A fucking maniac –' and Amin clapped me on the back as if I'd praised him.

'His English is not all that good,' Edoku said, 'but I would be careful what you say about him. He is not of our tribe, but is a Kakwa from the north. Wild people, very cruel.'

I settled back, glad to pass out of the burning area. Soon we saw the lake and drove over foot-high grassland with men and boys guarding cattle. Edoku waved to many of them. Then we were at a hutted village beside the lake shore. We drove in through a space in a high thorn bush barricade that surrounded the village. 'It is closed at night and the cattle are brought in,' Edoku explained. 'They are many who come to raid our beasts and our women even. The Langi and Acholi, even the Suk and the Jie from Karamoja. But then we raid them, too, and take their cattle. It is expected.'

The car was an object of curiosity with small boys, as I appeared to be with the women and girls. I had never seen such a fine display of bare titties. Sprouting ones on the young girls and fully heavy ones on the women. All went bare breasted in the village, wearing coloured cloth around their waists that draped to the ankles. Some handsome buxom girls too, who looked at me giggling behind their hands, tits jiggling.

Edoku's dad was too high in the order of things to come to meet us. We had to go to him, a wizened old skinny man sitting in a chair draped with leopard skins. He was rheumaticky, I reckoned, hauling him-

In The Mood

self up to meet us, using his long spear as an aid. For all that he was magnificent, straightening himself up to well over six foot, proud and fierce looking. More, he was dressed for the part. He actually wore a topper, a once shiny operagoer's top hat now a dull grey. Over his shoulder was a lion's skin, the tail trailing the dust. Pinned to this on his breast were British First World War medals, no doubt for fighting the askaris of Imperial Germany's former East African colony of Tanganyika. I was proud to shake his hand and bow my head to him. Edoku knelt at his feet. Idi Amin shook his hand and clapped his back heartily. The old man was not amused, staggering under the pounding. I wondered how the hell he'd get on with a sixteen-year-old bride.

We were shown a hut, which I discovered I would have to share with Sergeant Amin, not my favourite person even then. I left my hold-all, being assured that it was safe there, even though it contained everything I had in the world. Then we were introduced to Edoku's wives. We found him sitting outside a nearby hut with three pretty girls attending him. One was combing his hair, another cutting his fingernails, the third kneeling before her husband's chair washing his feet. He had changed into a long white cool kanzu robe, the Sandhurst graduate at home and at ease. His wives smiled up to me with their young faces beaming and beautiful white teeth, smooth ebony skins, firm breasts sticking out proud and solidly fat. I knew why the crew of HMS Bounty had mutinied at Tahiti. The sun, the verdant foliage around, the easygoing style of life, and most of all bare-breasted pretty brown things. It was not Captain Bligh, take it from me. The wives chattered.

'They want to know how old you are, and how many wives you keep,' said Edoku.

'Twenty-nine, and no wife.' When he translated they gave great cries of surprise to my answer.

In The Mood

'They say they will find you a wife. For tonight at least.' His wives giggled like schoolgirls. They were not much older.

'It would be ill-mannered to refuse,' I said. 'Lieutenant Edoku, you've got it made. Tell me,' with my European mind I could not resist the question, 'do you ever get all three of 'em in bed together, have a good romp?'

'No,' he said surprised. 'It is not easy. I must take it in turn to sleep beside them. When they are in married quarters at the barracks at Jinja, I must buy them dresses; all of them want the same money spent on them. I will have trouble if I don't use them in turn. Why should a man want three women in his bed?'

'Good question,' I said, 'I can't imagine why. Would you?'

'One woman is enough at a time,' he said seriously. 'They like it too much. We are going fishing now. To get fish for the feast. Would you like to watch us?'

'I'll join in. Maybe I'd catch something.'

He translated this to his wives and they pealed with laughter. As the state of dress around was almost nudist-colony style, I went to my hut to change into bathing trunks, which I'd packed for use in Angela Gore-Blomley's pool, if necessary! In the dark corner of the mud-sided and grass-roofed hut, I made out a huge shining black arse bouncing up and down, with grunts and squeals from a girl being pounded under the bare naked bulk of Idi Amin. While I undressed and got into my trunks his backside went at it like a fiddler's elbow. The girl continued to shriek, her legs hugging his broad back. He had wasted no time. Outside in the evening sun men and women were gathering, all carrying cone-shaped baskets made of wicker. The baskets were about four foot long, for all the world like upside-down ice-cream cones. They headed for the lake so I followed.

There the approach to the water was easy walking, made up of flat volcanic rocks like paving stones.

In The Mood

Beside the lake a line of huge Nile crocodiles sat unmoving, still as stone statues, great jaws wide open to catch the air. Teeth like small daggers filled top and bottom jaws, in which coloured birds pecked at titbits of food between the teeth and butterflies settled and sipped moisture. The crocs ignored them. Small boys, running on ahead, took leaps over the crocodiles' backs, their version of a daring game, I supposed. It was the reptiles' sluggish time it seemed. One or two snapped with their jaws as the boys darted away, none slid into the lake. I was glad to note this. People were entering the water with their basket cones only some hundred yards away from the crocs. They began to line up shoulder to shoulder, up to their waists in the water.

Watching all this with interest, I felt a tug at my elbow, turning to see a most handsome girl grinning at me and offering one of the two fishing baskets she held. She was fully grown, rounded in arms, hips, thighs and legs, with a pair of tits thrusting out that one could have balanced a tray of drinks on quite safely. Her jutting buttocks matched her bosom. She wore a string of beads around her waist, her sole adornment. A fat little cunt mound was sparsely covered in short wiry hair. What could I do but accept the basket and enter the water with her? We stood shoulder to shoulder, the line of men and women straightening out like soldiers on parade, more than a hundred of us.

A cry went up from the appointed leader, 'AY-YUP-HO!' This was echoed in perfect unison by the line, at each HO! the wide ends of the cones dipped into the lake. To my great surprise at my third dip I found an ugly looking mudfish with whiskers in my basket. The girl smiled, pulled it out for me and threw it to the bank. We proceeded like this for half an hour or so until the spot on the bank was a mass of flapping, gasping fish.

In The Mood

On my way back to the village, the girl holding my hand tightly, she led me into a clump of bushes, smiling, lying down and offering the obvious. When I took off my trunks, played with her tits and cunt, she nodded her approval of my prick, erect and in her grasp. She shrieked too as we fucked, it seemed expected of the girls. To her dismay when I came, I leapt off her, shooting the sperm over her breasts. She was quite annoyed, showing it by deep frowns and Iteso words I could not understand but guessed. I just never did give babies that I wouldn't know about or what kind of life they'd lead.

She slept beside me that night in the hut. It was hardly the Hilton. For a start we lay on a hippopotamus hide that stank even more than the rest of the hut, whose walls had been plastered over the mud with cow dung, the traditional method of sealing the place against rain. Across the hut Amin fucked noisily for most of the night, occasionally a new girl arriving to take over from the previous lucky girl. Up above me in the dried grass and banana leaf roof enough insects and bats busied about to satisfy even Sir David Attenborough. Things fell down at times and scuttled away. The girl I was with, cuddlesome creature that she was, wanted to be played with or fucked all the time. I had spent the previous night in a hairy trek across a wild animals' domain and was frankly bushed. Doing my best, I rose to the occasion enough to satisfy her. Our bodies clung with sweat, greasy with perspiring. I thought back with some nostalgia to the spotless tiled bathroom I had used to shower in the Gore-Blomley guest house, another world away.

Come morning the cry was that a hippo had been seen in a pool nearby. I was standing naked, sluicing myself with water brought to me by my new Girl Friday, making several journeys with the pot on her head, breasts tilted and back straight as a guardsman as she walked. I arrived at the pool to see the hippo speared by a dozen barbs, the pool red with blood. It was dragged on shore, its belly cut open, and two very small boys crawled inside with knives, handing out the heart and liver. They emerged absolutely red and slippery with blood from hair to toe. The meat was triumphantly carried back, where we found the delegation from the next village had arrived with the bride and it was dowry time.

This I had to see. In a hut were bales of cloth, cooking pots, two plastic buckets and a bicycle, all of which were closely inspected and scrutinised by the bride's near relatives. There was also a sum of money, a couple of hundred shillings of which I'd thrown in myself. So it was then to the village square, red earth baked and the size of a tennis court. Edoku stood there with his father and both sets of wives, the young army officer now dressed in a leopard-skin cloak and carrying a spear.

The bride was brought forth, a little girl with no more than pimples for breasts, her body hardly filled out in any way, her cunt hairless and with a tight lipless split. The wives of the old chief, harsh in the inspection of their junior wife-to-be, felt in her mouth, inspected her teeth, fingered her vagina, nodding and talking seriously among themselves. Any satisfaction they may have felt was expressed in grunts, while the girl stood frightened and rooted to the spot.

'Her family are getting a good deal on the young bride,' I said to Edoku. 'I've just had a look at the display of dowry laid out in that hut. It's like a general store.'

'It is nothing,' said Edoku. 'They are greedy people. There will be cattle and goats too. Many, as you will see. First the girl will show herself to the village. There is the fertility ceremony. To make sure she has strong sons – '

I looked from the adolescent girl to the old chief in his top hat, moth-eaten lion skin and war medals, deciding they would need one hell of a fertility rite to accomplish anything there. Silence fell as the local witchdoctor came shuffling up into the circle, an ancient old lady so old and bent her black skin was grey with age. She was weighed down in a buffalo hide with painted stripes, circles and triangles over it, so heavy on her back she could hardly move under the thing.

I've never carried a camera, couldn't be bothered, preferring to remember pictures in my mind. That was one time I regretted it. Her wrists were thin skin and bone, in a claw hand she carried an antelope's horn with coloured feathers attached. This she waved in all the most important people's faces, including mine. Her old face was a mass of wrinkles and lines, but her black eyes were button bright. She was then handed a pot by one of the wives, dipped her hand in and smeared the bride with yellow grease on her tiny breasts. The other women joined in until the girl was dripping from head to foot, attracting a million flies.

'Ghee,' Edoku explained to me. 'It is liquid butter. Now she will walk through the village and the unmarried girls will do the same. It is to make them fertile for future husbands.'

I followed the procession, watching the village maids join behind the bride, spreading the oily mess on their breasts and between their thighs, all giggling and waving to their friends. I saw Ndegi, the girl I had slept with among them, and she put out a bright red tongue at me, a universal sign of contempt, I imagine, because I'd leapt off her at crucial moments. The bride, on arriving back at the baked mud square again, stood in the centre of it alone, the rest of us standing around the edge. Cattle and goats were then driven around the girl by herders I knew were Edoku's half-brothers. She became surrounded in a sea of hooves and horns, milling about. Her relatives then began jumping up

In The Mood

high, getting down on their knees, as if to catch a sight of the girl.

'It was decided at the meeting of families to discuss the bride price,' Edoku told me, 'that the dowry would be enough cattle and goats to hide the girl. You can see her people jumping and bending to see if they can still see her. When she is hidden, it will be enough. This is the usual for a virgin girl.'

It took some time to decide, both sides arguing whether she was hidden or not. During the evening we drank and ate I know not what, hoping my insides were up to it, the native beer thick with residue and heady stuff. I did not fancy another night in the hut of horrors, more especially with Sergeant Amin noisily fucking across from me. I got a loaned blanket from Edoku and found a grassy spot within the compound. I was joined by Ndegi with the magnificent tits, who insisted on mounting me hoping to get me to come off in her. So I faked an orgasm for the three times we coupled, then slept like a log to awaken to a great commotion in the village.

The bride had fled. During the night, with the old chief out blotto with food and drink, she had taken off. The morning was spent with her grudging relatives returning the dowry. Edoku and I then got in the car for our return journey, Sergeant Amin appearing with three girls in tow before slumping along the back seat of the car to snore loudly, sleeping off the effects of making merry at the wedding.

I shook hands with the old chief, who seemed to accept that his bride had bunked with a solemn dignity. He offered me back the two hundred shillings I had added to the dowry money, which I refused to take and he refused to accept. Ndegi was standing by to see me off, so as a parting gesture I tucked the grimy banknotes between the tight cleavage of her fine tits, where they were held firm in place.

On the road back Edoku told me I would have to

In The Mood

be dropped at Jinja, regimental depot of his battalion where he would return the car to his colonel. 'But there will be a bus to Kampala and on to Entebbe,' he informed me. 'The airport is there and you will find work as a pilot.' He looked at me smiling. 'My father said to thank you for honouring him at his wedding.'

'It was entirely my pleasure,' I assured him. 'Wouldn't have missed it for the world. Pity about the bride making off.'

'I do not blame her. She would be the young wife and have to cook and make fire, chop wood and carry water for the old ones. Now her own family will beat her for cheating them out of the bride price.'

'He enjoyed himself,' I said, referring to Amin, curled up along the rear seat.

'I did not want him there,' Edoku said, glancing carefully over his shoulder. 'He invited himself. He is a dangerous man. In the campaign in Kenya he killed many people –'

'That was war.'

'You have killed people in war?' he asked.

'Helped to kill thousands, no doubt, over German cities.'

'The sergeant liked what he did too much.'

I remembered when our bombs had been dropped, turning away and leaving the formation, always preferring to fly home low over country areas. Over rail lines and rivers. We would fly down the centre of sleepy village streets and the rear gunner would machine-gun the roofs and upper windows. We would whoop in triumph, on our way back to base. God knows who were asleep in those rooms, old people and children most likely.

'We do terrible things in war,' I said.

'Amin enjoyed doing such things, and boasted of them. He and our commanding officer, a captain called Spilsby.'

'I know that bastard,' I said. 'He told me they paid

him to shoot people and he gave them their money's worth.'

'He and Amin were great *rafikis*, great friends.'

'They are two of a kind,' I said, glancing back at the sleeping giant. When we arrived at the township of Jinja and I was dropped at the bus stop, Amin was still slumbering like a baby. The bus arrived, even as I was saying my farewells to the tall handsome lieutenant. It was packed with humanity, crates of chickens on knees, babies at the breast, me the only white face in the whole crowd bumping along in the old single-decker on my way to pastures new as they say and, as ever, anticipating the change.

So began what was to be a long sojourn in Uganda, and all that was to happen to me there. To meet Moira once more, a State Registered Nurse and midwife working as a missionary. Flying mercenaries into the old Congo where Captain Spilsby hunted people again instead of ivory for Nizar Ramji. Coups and counter-coups, murder and mayhem in Uganda, where I was to renew my acquaintance with Lieutenant Edoku and his sergeant Idi Amin, elevated in time to Field Marshal and President Idi Amin Dada. And the women I was to meet, of course, in my continuation of a rude, lewd life. All that is another story I have to tell.

More Erotic Fiction from Headline:

A LADY OF QUALITY

A romance of lust

ANONYMOUS

Even on the boat to France, Madeleine experiences a taste of the pleasures that await her in the city of Paris. Seduced first by Mona, the luscious Italian opera singer, and then, more conventionally, by the ship's gallant British captain, Madeleine is more sure than ever of her ambition to become a lady of pleasure.

Once in Paris, Madeleine revels in a feast of forbidden delights, each course sweeter than the last. Fires are kindled in her blood by the attentions of worldly Frenchmen as, burning with passion, she embarks on a journey of erotic discovery . . .

**Don't miss VENUS IN PARIS
also from Headline**

FICTION/EROTICA   0 7472 3184 2

More Erotic Fiction from Headline:

Sweet Fanny

The erotic education of a Regency maid

Faye Rossignol

'From the time I was sixteen until the age of thirty-two I "spread the gentlemen's relish" as the saying goes. In short, I was a Lady of Pleasure.'

Fanny, now the Comtesse de C---, looks back on a lifetime of pleasure, of experiment in the myriad Arts of Love. In letters to her granddaughter and namesake, she recounts the erotic education of a young girl at the hands of a mysterious Comte – whose philosophy of life carries hedonism to voluptuous extremes – and his partners in every kind of sin. There is little the young Fanny does not experience – and relate in exquisite detail to the recipient of her remarkably revealing memoirs.

Coming soon from Headline
SWEET FANNY'S DIARIES

FICTION/EROTICA   0 7472 3275 X

More Erotica from Headline:

MAID'S NIGHT IN

A novel of smouldering eroticism

ANONYMOUS

The darkly arousing story of Beatrice, a nubile Victorian newly-wed, lately estranged from her husband and left to the charge of her mysterious aunt and uncle. Ushered into a shadowy Gothic world of champagne and sensuality, the young ingenue finds herself transformed into the prime player in exotic games of lust and power. *Maid's Night In* is a disturbingly erotic revelation of Victorian sexual desire.

More titillating erotica available from Headline

Eros in the Country	A Lady of Quality
Eros in Town	Sweet Fanny
Eros on the Grand Tour	The Love Pagoda
Venus in Paris	The Education of a Maiden

FICTION/EROTICA   0 7472 3333 0

More Erotica from Headline:

Lena's Story

Anonymous

**The Adventures of
a Parisian
Queen of the Night**

Irene was once a dutiful wife. Until, forsaking the protection of her husband, she embarked on a career as a sensuous woman: Lena, the most sought-after mistress in *fin de siècle* Paris. Yet despite the luxury, the champagne and the lavish attentions of her lovers, Lena feels her life is incomplete. She still longs for the one love that can satisfy her, the erotic pinnacle of a life of unbridled pleasure . . .

More titilating erotica available from Headline

Eros in the Country
Eros in Town
Eros on the Grand Tour
Venus in Paris
A Lady of Quality

Sweet Fanny
The Love Pagoda
The Education of a Maiden
Maid's Night In

FICTION/EROTICA   0 7472 3334 9

More Erotic Fiction from Headline:

CREMORNE GARDENS

ANONYMOUS

An erotic romp from the
libidinous age of the Victorians

UPSTAIRS, DOWNSTAIRS...
IN MY LADY'S CHAMBER

Cast into confusion by the wholesale defection of their
domestic staff, the nubile daughters of Sir Paul Arkley are
forced to throw themselves on the mercy of the handsome
young gardener Bob Goggin. And Bob, in turn, is only
too happy to throw himself on the luscious and oh-so-
grateful form of the delicious Penny.

Meanwhile, in the Mayfair mansion of Count Gewirtz of
Galicia, the former Arkley employees prepare a feast
intended to further the Count's erotic education of the
voluptuous singer Vazelina Volpe – and destined to
degenerate into the kind of wild and secret orgy for which
the denizens of Cremorne Gardens are justly famous...

*Here are forbidden extracts drawn from the notorious
chronicles of the Cremorne – a society of hedonists and
debauchees, united in their common aim to glorify the
pleasures of the flesh!*

Further titillating entertainment available from Headline:
**LORD HORNINGTON'S ACADEMY OF LOVE
THE LUSTS OF THE BORGIAS
EROS IN THE NEW WORLD**

FICTION/EROTICA   0 7472 3433 7

A selection of Erotica from Headline

FONDLE ALL OVER	Nadia Adamant	£4.99 ☐
LUST ON THE LOOSE	Noel Amos	£4.99 ☐
GROUPIES	Johnny Angelo	£4.99 ☐
PASSION IN PARADISE	Anonymous	£4.99 ☐
THE ULTIMATE EROS COLLECTION	Anonymous	£6.99 ☐
EXPOSED	Felice Ash	£4.99 ☐
SIN AND MRS SAXON	Lesley Asquith	£4.99 ☐
HIGH JINKS HALL	Erica Boleyn	£4.99 ☐
TWO WEEKS IN MAY	Maria Caprio	£4.99 ☐
THE PHALLUS OF OSIRIS	Valentina Cilescu	£4.99 ☐
NUDE RISING	Faye Rossignol	£4.99 ☐
AMOUR AMOUR	Marie-Claire Villefranche	£4.99 ☐

All Headline books are available at your local bookshop or newsagent, or can be ordered direct from the publisher. Just tick the titles you want and fill in the form below. Prices and availability subject to change without notice.

Headline Book Publishing PLC, Cash Sales Department, Bookpoint, 39 Milton Park, Abingdon, OXON, OX14 4TD, UK. If you have a credit card you may order by telephone – 0235 831700.

Please enclose a cheque or postal order made payable to Bookpoint Ltd to the value of the cover price and allow the following for postage and packing:
UK & BFPO: £1.00 for the first book, 50p for the second book and 30p for each additional book ordered up to a maximum charge of £3.00.
OVERSEAS & EIRE: £2.00 for the first book, £1.00 for the second book and 50p for each additional book.

Name ....

Address ....

....

....

If you would prefer to pay by credit card, please complete:
Please debit my Visa/Access/Diner's Card/American Express (delete as applicable) card no:

Signature .... Expiry Date ....